To Mum,

Happy Birthday

+

Happy Anniversary

(+ Happy Reading)

lots of love

(one + only!)

from Nelly

D1331768

Young Lacey Vernon was being more or less forced to marry the Greek tycoon Troy Andreakis to save her father from ruin—but as time went on she began to realise, unwillingly, that perhaps she wasn't dreading him as much as she had imagined she was. But that was before she learned what kind of a man Troy really was . . .

Another book you will enjoy
by SARA CRAVEN

THE GARDEN OF DREAMS

Lissa wasn't quite sure whether she wanted to marry the attractive Frenchman Paul de Gue or not, so she was glad to accept his invitation to visit the family chateàu in France and meet his relatives. Unfortunately, this also involved meeting the austere Comte Raoul de Gue—who made it clear that he did *not* want Lissa marrying into the family!

STRANGE ADVENTURE

BY

SARA CRAVEN

MILLS & BOON LIMITED
17–19 FOLEY STREET
LONDON W1A 1DR

First published 1977
This edition 1977

© Sara Craven 1977

ISBN 0 263 72390 4

*Made and printed in Great Britain by
Richard Clay (The Chaucer Press), Ltd., Bungay, Suffolk*

CHAPTER ONE

THE last triumphant chords of the sonata died a lingering death, as Lacey stayed her fingers on the piano keys, savouring their harmony.

For a moment she sat motionless as silence surged back into the small room set aside for music practice at the convent of Our Lady of Grace, then with an impatient movement she thrust back under her Alice band the long lock of silver-gilt hair which had come loose while she gave herself to her music. She was thankful that Sister Thérèse had not been within earshot of this particular performance. Too much passion, too much feeling and too little technique would have been her verdict.

She got up from the piano stool and walked across to the square-paned window that overlooked a small corner of the convent garden and the high wall that surrounded it.

She thought, as she had begun to think so often in those long months since her seventeenth birthday, 'I could be safe here always.' And, as before, she noted ironically that she had said 'safe' and not 'happy'.

To the other girls at this convent boarding school, it would have seemed incredible that Lacey Vernon, cherished only daughter of an English merchant banker, could possibly lack any kind of security. Lacey could see a dim reflection of herself in the wintry panes. The dark blue dress with its decorously fashionable length and neat white collar. The dark band holding the smooth, shining fall of hair hanging below her shoulders.

Alice in nowhere land, since . . . Since when?

Since that terrible day at the Conservatoire when the so-eminent professor had dismissed kindly but quite finally her hardly expressed hope to become a concert pianist?

'A charming talent—but not the steel, the fire that takes one to the top. For that one requires a special genius which few possess. Which you, *ma soeur*,' he threw a darkling

5

look at Sister Thérèse, quietly self-contained in her dark habit, 'might have possessed, had it not been for this—calling of yours.

'But for you, my child.' He laid a hand for an instant on the bowed fair head. 'I must speak the truth. Look at that little hand. It can span an octave at the most. For many of the great works, more facility would be needed. Content yourself that you will always play better than most of those you will meet, and leave the concert platform for those with the strength to bear its demands.'

She had not cried. The nuns would have deplored such an unseemly display of emotion. Even Sister Thérèse had not shown a flicker of reaction to this crushing of the hopes of her star pupil—or even regret for the career that might have been hers, Lacey recalled wryly. All she had said on the long drive back to the convent had been, 'It is God's will, my child.'

Lacey had often wished since that she could achieve that kind of acceptance. It had been hard not to rebel when she had written to ask her father if she could opt for the commercial training offered to the older pupils instead of the more usual course in the higher flights of home economics designed to prepare the majority of the girls for the day when they became wives and hostesses. But the reply from home had been as unexpected as it was unwelcome. There were no plans, ran her father's letter, for her to be employed in a secretarial capacity in his firm, or any other, for that matter, and any such training would be a complete waste of time. She would please him far better if she concentrated on the domestic side of the course in her last months at the convent as Michelle would no doubt be glad of some help with the entertaining.

When some of the hurt had died down from this rejection of her attempt to carve out a career for herself, Lacey was able to smile a little at the thought of her glamorous French stepmother permitting her to meddle in any of the domestic details in London or at their country home. Michelle ruled a small but efficient staff with absolute sway and she would not welcome any interference from anyone.

Lacey had often begged to be allowed to help even in a menial capacity when guests were expected, but all her offers had been met with a fairly brusque refusal until her father had intervened before one minor dinner party and suggested that she should be allowed to do the flowers for the centrepiece. She had spent time and thought on her arrangement, floating a mass of full-blown roses around the bases of delicately tapering candles in a shallow but exquisitely shaped dish. Just before the guests had arrived she had peeped into the dining room to see the table in all its finished glory. Her flowers had disappeared and a bowl of long-stemmed hothouse beauties stood in their place. Lacey had looked and bitten her lip, and later, when her father congratulated her boisterously on her efforts, she had given a little noncommittal smile.

She had been twelve years old when her father married again and she had soon learned that to fight Michelle was to lose. But there had been battles in the early days. Lacey, used to being first in her father's affections since her mother's death, could not reconcile herself to the fact that this slender, dark stranger with her beautiful face and incredible chic had simply taken over. And when her initial hostility had given way to genuine admiration for all that glamour and she was prepared to become a worshipper at her stepmother's shrine, she had discovered with bewilderment that her adoration was unwanted. That in fact her own small person was the one flaw in Michelle's vast contentment at having married a man as wealthy and easygoing as James Vernon.

Which, of course, was why she was here at the convent where Michelle herself had been educated. Her friend Vanessa, both of whose parents had embarked on other marriages, had explained it succinctly.

'It's "being got out of the way". If I'd been a baby or a three-year-old my stepmother could have dressed up for photographs with bows in my hair, it might have been O.K. At our age, we're just a pain in the neck. Della said it made her feel old just to look at me.'

As it was, Lacey had grown accustomed to being 'out of the way'. She had learned that it was not always convenient for her to go home for her vacations, but as the alternatives had included carefully selected parties for skiing, sailing and sightseeing, she could not feel too hard done by.

But now she had to face the fact that her schooldays were strictly numbered, and that her future was by no means clear cut. Her father was being over-optimistic, she thought, in envisaging any role-sharing between Michelle and herself, and yet what else was there, if she was not to be allowed to work for her living?

Lacey sighed and leaned her forehead against the cold glass for a moment. There was an alternative which she had come to consider with increasing seriousness as the weeks had passed. She could ask Reverend Mother to allow her to enter the novitiate of the order. It was not an ideal solution, and there were immediate snags. Lacey was not yet eighteen or indeed a Roman Catholic, but none of these obstacles seemed as insuperable as the prospect of being an unwanted third in her stepmother's home. She knew too that the nuns considered a sense of vocation as essential for the religious life, but she also knew from books she had read in the convent library that in bygone times many girls had become nuns because they were unwanted by their families and had become excellent religious. Lacey supposed, rather dubiously, that this could happen to her in time.

She looked again at the high wall, which as Sister Thérèse had often commented, was not to keep the nuns from the world but the world from the nuns.

Lacey sometimes wondered what this 'world' was like that had to be kept at bay, but she had never shared with the other boarders any burning desire to come to terms with it as soon as possible. She knew that many of the other girls were already sexually experienced, although she was rarely invited to join the little groups that gathered secretly late at night to discuss boy-friends and sex, and she realised wryly that she would have had little to contribute if she had been.

Lacey had never had a boy-friend, unless she counted Alan Trevor, the son of neighbours of theirs in the country, whom she had known since her early childhood. Lacey rode with him sometimes in the holidays and found him attractive with a sense of humour, but he had never attempted even to kiss her, and Lacey was secretly relieved that he had not. But it did not prevent her from speculating on how she would cope if and when that momentous occasion ever came about.

The worldly-wise Vanessa had told her that it was rarely the kiss that counted—more what men expected to follow it, but Lacey had never been able to apply any of this information to herself. Her body was something that she bathed and clothed and which obeyed the demands she put upon it without effort. The realisation that there were demands that others might make of it was utterly alien to her. At the convent her studies and her music filled her life. At home, usually in the country, she enjoyed the open air, often in Alan's relaxed company or that of his sister Fran.

Convent life, she supposed vaguely, would go on in much the same way, except that Alan would not be there, and if she was honest that would be no great deprivation although she was fond of him.

She wandered back to the piano and perching on the stool began to pick out a melody with one finger. What, she wondered, was it like to be in love? Her cheeks flushed as she recalled some of the more lurid discussions she had heard from the others, but what had that to do with love?

And this was where one province where even her usual mentor, Sister Thérèse, would not be able to help her, she thought, then started guiltily as Sister herself suddenly spoke from the doorway.

'So you are here, Lacey. Reverend Mother has asked to see you, and I guessed where you might be.'

Lacey closed the piano and rose bewilderedly, shaking out her skirt.

'Reverend Mother? But why? I haven't done anything wrong, have I?'

Sister Thérèse gave a slight smile. 'Now why should you all imagine that Reverend Mother only sends for you when you have been in some kind of mischief?' she asked chidingly. Then, after a slight hesitation, 'You have a visitor, Lacey.'

9

'A visitor?' Lacey stared at the older woman with sudden joyous disbelief. 'It's Father. It must be,' she blurted out, and regardless of Sister Thérèse's restraining 'Lacey!', she ran out of the room and along the spacious panelled corridor to the main staircase.

The door of Reverend Mother's study was slightly ajar, but Lacey still knocked and waited for the word to enter in spite of her inner excitement. Then she slid through the door and dropped a slight curtsey to Reverend Mother, her eyes turning eagerly to see who else was in the room.

Her hands clasped involuntarily in front of her and she stood quite still with all the joy and laughter fading from her piquant little face as Michelle rose from a high-backed chair, a formal smile barely curving her exquisitely made up mouth.

Questions were beating and tearing at Lacey's brain as she forced herself to reply to Michelle's polite greeting and pecked obediently at one scented cheek. One that had to be answered forced its way into speech. 'Father—he is all right?'

Michelle's brows rose. 'Perfectly, but very busy, as he no doubt explained in his last letter. That is why he asked me to perform this errand for him.' She glanced at her wrist-watch, then turned to Reverend Mother who was standing, her usually calm face a little troubled. 'If the child's things could be packed, *ma très révérende mère*.'

'*Mais oui, ma chère enfant*. I will give the necessary instructions and leave you to talk.'

She moved past Lacey as she spoke and the girl with great daring touched her sleeve.

'But why must my things be packed, Reverend Mother?'

The nun hesitated, sending a swift glance towards Michelle.

'Because the time has come for you to leave us, my child,' she replied. 'Your stepmother will explain all to you now, *sans doute*.' She looked down into Lacey's stricken face and her own softened perceptibly. 'It is not the end of the world, *ma petite*,' she said gently, and moved to the door.

'But it is!' Lacey cried, almost hysterically. 'I—I don't want to leave, Reverend Mother. I was going to see you

10

and ask if I could stay here always——'

'How would that be possible, my child?' Reverend Mother stared at her. 'Unless you obtained some teaching qualification, and even then . . .'

Lacey shook her head, almost pleadingly. 'I didn't mean that, Reverend Mother. I intended to ask you to accept me as a novice—to permit me to become a nun.'

There was a stunned silence for a moment, then Michelle exclaimed furiously *'Quelle bêtise!'* only to be halted by Reverend Mother's upraised hand. Her calm eyes bored into Lacey's flushed, unhappy face.

'So you think you are called to the religious life, my child. Sit down and we will discuss the matter.'

'Reverend Mother,' Michelle protested, and the nun gave her a faint smile.

'If you would be good enough to wait in the parlour, *ma chère*. Sister Monique will bring you some coffee and cakes.'

Michelle hesitated, but Reverend Mother's authority was still absolute and after a moment she left the room with obvious ill grace. Reverend Mother gave an almost imperceptible sigh, then moved briskly back to her large desk and sat down.

'Now, Lacey,' she said gently. 'Why do you think you have a vocation?'

There was a long silence. Lacey's hands twisted together in her lap as she tried desperately to marshall her whirling thoughts into reasoned arguments that would convince Reverend Mother of her sincerity, but no words would come and the only sound in the hushed room was the steady tick of the small clock that stood on Reverend Mother's desk.

At last, it was Reverend Mother who spoke. 'Many people have a mistaken idea of what it is to be a nun. They see it as a refuge—an escape from the pressure that life in the world imposes. But they are wrong, Lacey, and you too will be wrong if you are looking for a sanctuary, as I suspect.'

Lacey looked at her tormentedly. 'Oh, Reverend Mother, everything is such a mess!'

'But running away will solve nothing, my dear child. Even

11

if I believed you had a genuine vocation, I would be very reluctant to accept you at present. One thing that we do require of our novices is peace of mind, and you are too confused at the moment to know what it is you truly want. I feel you should do as your stepmother asks and go home with her.'

'But she doesn't really want me,' Lacey burst out.

'How can you know that? Would she have come if that was the case? Besides, there is your father to consider.' Reverend Mother seemed oddly to hesitate for a moment. 'Perhaps he may need you, *ma chère*. Have you considered that?'

Lacey was unhappily silent. Reverend Mother rose, tall in her dark robes, and came round the desk, laying a hand almost in blessing on the girl's head.

'Go home, my child,' she advised quietly. 'Find out what life may have in store for you, and if you still feel it is not enough after a year or two, and that your place is here, then you can write to me.'

Lacey looked at her steadily. 'But you don't believe I will, do you, Reverend Mother?'

'No, my dear. I have an instinct in these things and it tells me that your future lies outside these walls. Now I must see about your packing before your stepmother loses her patience entirely. Shall I ask Vanessa to help you?'

'Please, Reverend Mother.' Lacey's voice was subdued. 'I didn't know whether I would be able to say goodbye to her.'

'But why not? You are not leaving the convent under a cloud, my dear, and we shall all miss you and pray for you. Now come along.'

Lacey had already emptied her clothes cupboard on to the bed by the time Vanessa arrived.

'So it's true,' she observed, as she bounced into the room. 'Cheer up, flower. You look shattered. I'd be turning cartwheels if my people sent for me!'

'I'll be all right.' Lacey summoned up a wan smile. 'It's all been rather a shock, that's all.'

Vanessa's shrewd eyes went over her friend as she began folding the clothes and packing them neatly and economically into the open cases.

'I don't want to interfere, Lacey, but is everything—
quite all right at home?'

'Yes, of course.' Lacey smoothing sweaters into a poly-
thene bag looked at her in surprise. 'Why do you ask?'

'Oh,' Vanessa shrugged rather vaguely, 'there've been
odd rumours in the newspaper lately, that's all.'

Lacey rarely bothered to glance at the supply of English
papers delivered daily to the convent for the pupils, but
she knew Vanessa was an avid reader.

'What sort of rumours?'

'Just hints that all might not be well with Vernon–
Carey—among others, of course.'

Lacey gave a little perplexed frown. 'Well, Daddy hasn't
mentioned anything in his letters, and he seemed quite
cheerful when I was home at Christmas. What did the
papers say?'

Vanessa folded some tissue paper around a dress with
rather exaggerated care.

'I can't really remember. Nothing specific, of course. Just
an impression, really.'

'Just vile innuendoes, you mean,' Lacey said heatedly.
'Some of these financial journalists are the limit! They're
quite capable of starting trouble for a company just to get
a story.'

'This wasn't the gutter press,' Vanessa said slowly, 'or
I might have agreed with you. But I daresay it is just a
rumour. Things are tough for everyone these days.'

They worked for a few moments in silence and Lacey
thought over what had just been said with a growing feeling of unease. She recalled the strangeness in Reverend
Mother's voice when she had said that her father might
need her. Was there trouble brewing for Vernon–Carey of
which she was the only one in ignorance? She made up her
mind to ask Michelle about it at the earliest convenient
opportunity.

After a pause, Vanessa began to chat of everyday things—
of the senior pupils' concert that Lacey would now miss,
of whether she would continue her musical studies at Kings
Winston and how she would otherwise fill her day.

'Perhaps they'll have a change of heart when you get

13

home and let you train for something,' she suggested cheerfully. 'Or you could help Fran Trevor with the stables, perhaps. You've always got on well with her, haven't you?'

'Oh yes,' Lacey agreed abstractedly. It occurred to her that if she was living at home for good, she would probably be thrust more into the limited social life around Kings Winston and would be seeing more of Alan as well, but the thought didn't generate any enthusiasm.

'And you will write, won't you, Lacey?' Vanessa persisted. There was a glint of tears in her blue eyes as she stared at her friend. 'I—I shall miss you, you know.'

Lacey shook off her brooding mood and smiled warmly at her.

'Of course I will, Van. And better than that, I'll ask Michelle if you can come and stay at Kings Winston for Easter.'

She could see no real reason for Michelle to refuse and the thought gave her a touch of optimism as she carried her cases downstairs to the entrance hall where Michelle waited, her foot tapping impatiently on the parquet floor.

The driver of the hired limousine stowed the baggage away in the boot while Lacey made her round of goodbyes to the Sisters and girls. Reverend Mother was last, accompanying them out on to the steps, ignoring the chill of the wind that made Michelle pull up the collar on her fur coat.

'Goodbye, *ma petite*.' Reverend Mother traced a firm sign of the cross on Lacey's forehead. 'Think of us sometimes, and never be afraid of the richness of life.'

Lacey's eyes were hot and blurred with tears as she walked down the shallow flight of steps and got into the back of the big car where Michelle was already waiting. She looked back once as the car turned slowly down the winding drive between the bare branches of the trees, registering like someone in a dream the tall, solid building and the tiny group of black-clad figures waving from the doorway, then the car rounded a bend and they were gone.

She sank back into the soft upholstery feeling utterly bereft. Beside her Michelle was fishing in her handbag for the inevitable cigarette and clicking her lighter irritably.

14

'What an age you made me wait!' she exclaimed. 'We will have to abandon any notion of an afternoon plane and fly back tomorrow instead. It will not be such a bad thing anyway. Perhaps we will do some shopping in Paris,' she added with a disparaging sideways look at Lacey's neat grey flannel coat and plain dark shoes.

'But I've got plenty of clothes,' Lacey protested.

'For a schoolgirl, yes,' Michelle gestured dismissively. 'But now you are a woman, *ma chère*, and you must learn to dress yourself accordingly. Your hair must be styled too.'

'Oh, no.' Lacey clutched protectively at a strand of her rain-straight silvery fair hair and Michelle looked grudging.

'Well, perhaps not,' she conceded. 'It has a certain— charm, I suppose, *comme ça*. And you can always wear it up when you wish to look older.'

'Why should I wish to do that?' Lacey stared at her.

Michelle gave a negligent shrug and looked at her sideways, her glance oddly speculative. 'If you do not, *ma chère*, then you will be the first girl not to wish to be so. Besides, your father will not wish you to appear at parties looking like a child.'

'I'll be going to parties, then?' Lacey said questioningly, and her stepmother raised her eyebrows.

'*Mais certainement*,' she replied sharply. 'What else did you expect?'

'Oh, I don't know.' Lacey wriggled her fingers out of the gloves that every convent-trained girl wore as a matter of course when she went out. She had never cared for the feel of gloves on her hands even in the coldest weather, and it occurred to her that she no longer had to trouble about this little bit of discipline. She stole a glance at her stepmother, who was smoking rather jerkily and staring out of the window at the rather drab landscape with a slight frown. 'Michelle, is everything—all right? At home—with Father, I mean?'

'Naturally.' Michelle gave her a long look. 'Why should it not be?'

'Oh, nothing.' It was Lacey's turn to shrug. 'One—just hears things and I wondered . . .'

'You have heard what?' Her stepmother's tone sharpened.

15

'Who has been talking to you? What has been said?'

'Well, nothing really,' Lacey hastened to assure her, feeling oddly perturbed. 'But Reverend Mother said something odd—about me being needed, and Vanessa said there had been hints in the papers about the bank—that something might be wrong.' She paused, but Michelle made no immediate reply. Her frown, however, had deepened. 'If there is something wrong, I wish you'd tell me. You've just said I'm not a child any longer, so please don't treat me like one if there's something I should know.'

There was silence for a moment, then Michelle gave a harsh little laugh and muttered, '*Touchée*,' as she stubbed her cigarette out in the ashtray beside her. Then she faced the girl sitting tensely beside her.

'To begin with,' she said, 'your father has not been well. He saw a specialist last week and has been told he has a bad heart and must take care. I did not intend to tell you until we reached England, but you wished me to be honest, and I do not agree with your father that you must any longer be protected and sheltered from life. There are realities that very soon you must face, and this is one of them.'

Lacey sat stunned. She moistened her lips. 'Is—Father isn't going to die?' It was a heartrending little cry.

Michelle moved irritably. '*Mon dieu, non*. At least, we must all hope—and pray too, as the good Sisters have promised to do at the convent, that he will live for many years. But he must avoid shocks and any sort of worry, so this—trouble at the bank could not have happened at a worse time for him.'

'What sort of trouble?'

'Lack of foreign investment—some unwise investments of his own. The world of finance is full of these ups and down and always your father has been able to weather any storms that came. People had confidence in him—in his name. But now it is whispered that he is a sick man, confidence is failing. There have been one or two resignations from the board, allegedly for other reasons, it is true, but it causes talk, and then the rumours appear in the newspapers.' She lit another cigarette. 'So—you will come home, and we will give a dance for you and on the surface all will be well. This is the façade that we must present to the world, and you must help.'

Lacey lifted haunted eyes to meet her stepmother's. 'What's going to happen, Michelle?'

Michelle blew a reflective smoke ring and looked at the girl through narrowed eyes. 'We shall—overcome this crisis, or we shall be ruined,' she said almost idly. 'It is as simple as that, *ma chère.*'

'I must get a job,' Lacey said half to herself. 'I—I don't want a dance or any of that nonsense. I want to earn money—and help Father . . .'

She bit back a cry as Michelle's fingers gripped her slender arms.

'And what money could you earn? A drop in the ocean compared to what is needed,' Michelle said contemptuously. 'Be content, Lacey, and do as you are asked. Do not further complicate matters, I beg you.'

Lacey flushed painfully. 'I'll do anything, of course,' she managed.

'Will you?' That reflective note had returned to Michelle's voice and it puzzled Lacey. 'Perhaps I will remind you of that—one day, *ma chère.*'

The remainder of the journey into Paris was accomplished in silence. Lacey was glad to be left in peace with her churning thoughts. In the space of a few hours her entire world had been turned upside down, she thought confusedly. Even the security of her background which she had always taken for granted was no longer certain. Was it conceivable that her father could be ruined? He had always seemed so confident of his ability to keep ahead of the game even in difficult times that it did not seem possible that he could now be facing disaster. But other banks had collapsed, she knew. It was a chilling thought. Michelle had spoken calmly, but Lacey found herself wondering what private thoughts her stepmother might be harbouring. She had relished being the wife of a wealthy and successful man. How would she react to being married to a failure? Lacey shook herself mentally. Poor Father! She was condemning him unheard, treating him as if ruin was staring them in the face already.

But it was the news about his bad heart that had really disturbed her. He had always been so proud of his health and energy, as if it were some private lodestar. Now he was sick and his business too was ailing. It was like some ill omen.

When they arrived at the hotel, Lacey allowed herself to be shepherded up to the palatial suite reserved for them while Michelle went to the reception desk to arrange for an extension of the reservation. They lunched together in the suite on clear soup, followed by grilled trout, but Lacey was too disturbed and upset to eat very much. She was not keen either on the suggested shopping expedition, but Michelle was adamant that she should accompany her, so she gave in with a little sigh.

In the end it was rather fun, she discovered. She would never be wholly at her ease with Michelle, but she had to admit that her stepmother had an unerring eye for colour and line and as the elegantly wrapped boxes began to mount up, Lacey experienced all the genuine pleasures that the possession of new and elegant clothes could give any young woman. She could not feel any real regret when her grey coat was replaced by smooth cream suede trimmed with fur, with high-heeled matching boots.

'Aren't you going to buy anything for yourself?' she asked curiously when they were back in the loaded car and returning to the hotel.

'Hmm.' Michelle consulted her wristwatch, then leaned forward and tapped on the glass partition separating the driver from the passengers. 'Driver!' Briefly she directed him to take them instead to Jean Louis, the fashion house where, Lacey knew, she acquired most of her clothes.

Lacey had always considered it was an odd way to buy clothes, to go into a showroom where there were no racks to pore over but just a few gilt chairs where you sat and watched incredibly slender mannequins parade in the latest creations until you saw something that took your eye.

Today it seemed that Michelle was in the market for evening dresses. Lacey admired the models being paraded with pure objectivity. There was nothing that would have suited her anyway. The models being shown were far too old and sophisticated, and Michelle and the *vendeuse* had their heads together in close consultation.

Then, as the next model appeared on the catwalk, she sat up and gave a little gasp, wondering which of Jean Louis' wealthy clients would have the daring—or the figure —to wear such a gown. It was plain stark black with a long floating skirt that clung revealingly to the girl's hips. But it was the bodice that was the really eye-catching feature, consisting as it did of hardly more than two broad straps of the softly swathed material which barely covered the girl's breasts.

Michelle sat up, her face animated, talking rapidly in French and gesturing to the *vendeuse* who hovered attentively at her side.

Lacey's first shock gave way to disbelief. Surely—surely Michelle could not be thinking of buying such a dress? Whatever would Daddy say when he saw her in it? It was true she had an almost perfect figure, but still ... It would be almost too much for one of their sophisticated London gatherings, while for the quiet dinner parties that entertaining usually amounted to at Kings Winston it would be totally outrageous.

The black gown disappeared and was replaced by a mass of floating panels in printed chiffon without half the impact. It was obvious Michelle thought so too, for she was picking up her handbag and preparing to leave. Lacey would have liked to have asked which dress she had ordered, but her stepmother had a distinctly preoccupied air as they re-emerged on to the pavement, and Lacey decided to remain silent.

Back at the hotel, Michelle asked if Lacey would care to dine with her downstairs in the hotel restaurant, but she refused politely, saying that she preferred to have an early bath and watch television in her dressing gown. She was not altogether surprised when Michelle changed into a dinner gown and disappeared on a cloud of expensive perfume, leaving her alone and not entirely sorry either. Certainly her stepmother would find the busy dining room and the passing crowds of far more interest than a quiet evening's television in the seclusion of her room.

19

Lacey decided she would try on some of her new clothes after her bath. The bathroom to the suite was warm and luxurious and she revelled in it unashamedly. Bathing at the convent had been a hurried business of necessity, for there was always someone waiting more or less patiently to take your place. It was fun too to sample the various bath oils and soaps set out on the glass shelves. Such luxuries had been scorned as worldly vanities by the nuns, who had not encouraged their use by the boarders.

When she had soaked for long enough, feeling some of her worries and tensions dissolve away under the soothing influence of the warm water, she climbed out, reaching for the white fluffy towel awaiting her on the heated rail. But as her wet foot encountered the bathroom carpet she felt something hard and sharp press into her sole and gave a little cry, hobbling sideways to escape the pressure. Wrapping herself in the towel, she felt about on the floor until she discovered what it was. It was part of a man's cuff link, an expensive trinket in gold and enamel in an elegant chequered pattern. Lacey pursed her lips as she stared at it lying in the palm of her hand. It must have belonged to the previous tenant of the suite, she thought disapprovingly, and it did not say much for the standard of cleanliness at one of Paris's top hotels that it had not been discovered during the changeover.

She decided that rather than mention it to Michelle, who would probably make a fuss out of all proportion to the incident, she would simply ring for a chambermaid and hand it over. The owner would probably want it back anyway. It was a distinctive design and it was only one of the links that had given away. It could probably be easily repaired.

Still wrapped in the towel, she went into the sitting room of the suite and was just about to press the bell when the telephone on a table near the door rang with a suddenness that made her gasp. Without a doubt the call was not for her, and she picked up the receiver rather hesitantly. She was about to say, 'Madame Vernon's suite', when a deep, imperious masculine voice said, 'Michelle'?

'Er—*non*.' Lacey transferred the receiver to her other

20

hand and made an ineffectual grab at her slipping towel.

There was a sound suspiciously like a muttered curse from the other end of the telephone, and then the voice said, '*Mé sinhorite*' and a click and the dialling tone told her that the anonymous caller had hung up.

Lacey replaced her own receiver with a little slam. He had had no need to be quite so abrupt, she thought. After all, she was perfectly capable of taking a message for her stepmother, and in French—only his parting shot hadn't sounded at all French but some other far less familiar language. She shrugged and trailed into her bedroom to get her pyjamas and dressing gown before tackling the chambermaid, who was more than inclined to take offence at the suggestion that the bathroom had not been properly cleaned. Had she not vacuumed the carpet with her own hands? she demanded of the room at large, and Lacey in particular. Lacey, who was beginning to long for her bed after a long and wearying day, was glad to hand over the broken cuff link and close the door on the woman's virtuous and slightly aggrieved insistence that it should be handed over to the manager on that instant.

'I hope she wasn't expecting a tip,' she muttered to herself as she went into her bedroom and closed the door. She had left a note for Michelle beside the telephone. 'Someone rang. Wouldn't leave his name.'

She did not find it easy to rest the first night in a strange bed, but this time she was asleep almost as soon as her head touched the pillow. It was a long time later when she opened bewildered and sleepy eyes, wondering what had woken her. Then she heard the sound again. It was Michelle laughing, that uncharacteristic full-throated, sexy laugh that belied her chic, rather cool appearance. For a moment she wondered drowsily who her stepmother could be talking to at this time of night, then she heard the sound of a telephone receiver being replaced. So Michelle had got the message and probably identified the mystery man. All well and good, Lacey thought briefly before sleep claimed her once again.

CHAPTER TWO

'DEAR Vanessa,' wrote Lacey, 'It's hard to believe that I've only been at home for two weeks. It seems much longer. I was so happy to get your letter and know that you really are coming here for Easter. Kings Winston should be at its best by then.'

She laid down her fountain pen and stared reflectively out of the window at the smooth rolling lawn below the terrace. She was finding this letter unexpectedly difficult to write. It was very different from the carefree correspondence that she and Vanessa had enjoyed so far during their school-days, because there was so much she was forced to leave unsaid.

She couldn't tell Vanessa how shocked she had been by the change in her father when she had arrived home a fortnight before. Michelle had warned her that he had been ordered to lose weight by his doctors, but this had not prepared her for the stoop in his shoulders and the way his clothes seemed to hang on his tall, once-burly frame. His face too was lined and almost haggard. But it was the subtle alteration in his personality which had most disturbed her. Where he had been bluff and good-humoured, now his temper was uncertain and inclined to be querulous. Michelle handled him with kid-gloves, and Lacey, rather subdued, followed her lead.

She had had little private conversation with her step-mother since the revelations in the car on the way to Paris, but if Michelle was worried about the immediate prospects facing the family, she kept it well concealed. Occasionally her manner seemed slightly abstracted, but that was all. Again, this was something that she could not confide in Vanessa, nor her increasing feeling of uneasiness that there were still things that were being kept from her.

She sighed and put the unfinished letter back inside her writing case. It was a pretty lame effort so far, but they

22

were giving a dinner party that evening and perhaps something would happen there that she could turn into an amusing story for Vanessa.

She was a little surprised as she went up to her room to find Mrs Osborne the housekeeper and one of the women who came in from the village to help with the cleaning engaged in turning out one of the guest bedrooms, and making up the bed. As far as she knew, tonight's guests were all local people, and she hesitated in the doorway, watching them curiously.

'Who's coming to stay, Mrs Osborne?' she asked at last.

'Madame didn't tell me the gentleman's name, Miss Lacey.'

So it's a man, Lacey thought as she went on her way. That explained it. It must be one of the bank's directors, all of whom had been frequent guests in the past. Only the room was obviously being got ready for a single occupant —and all the directors were married men who usually brought their wives with them.

She had hoped the preparations for the dinner would have added a touch of excitement to an existence which had so far proved boring to the point of monotony. But nothing had changed. Her tentative offers of help were waved irritably away by Michelle, who seemed unusually on edge for such an experienced and accomplished hostess.

Lacey, rather huffily, decided she would take herself off to the village. At least Fran Trevor would welcome her help at the stables, she thought defiantly.

But even in this she was thwarted, for when she arrived at the stables, the place was deserted except for the girl who came in a couple of days a week to do the accounts and the bookwork, and she informed Lacey that Miss Trevor had taken out a group of people staying at the Bull who had welcomed the chance of an afternoon's hacking round lanes and fields. So there was nothing for it but to trudge back to the house again and try to keep out of everyone's way.

The guest bedroom looked very nice, she thought, poking her head round the door for a critical peep, but Mrs

Osborne hadn't put any flowers in there. It was too early in the year for the gardens to yield very much, but Lacey knew there were some early daffodils in a sheltered corner and she decided to pick some as a welcoming gesture of her own.

But just as she was going into the garden she was stopped by Mrs Osborne with a request to help clean some silver, and it was late in the afternoon by the time she could decently escape and find her flowers. It was pleasant in the garden. The day's cold wind had dropped at the onset of dusk, and, wrapped warmly in an ancient duffel coat, Lacey enjoyed quite a leisurely stroll before she headed back to the house with her armful of flowers.

She collected a suitable container from the china cupboard, and went upstairs to the bathroom adjoining the guest room where she filled the vase and arranged her blooms. She had overfilled the vase a little and she picked it up with great care, holding it steadily as she opened the door that communicated with the bedroom and stepped forward.

But the room was no longer in its pristinely unoccupied state. There was an expensive leather suitcase open on the bed, clothes spilling out of it carelessly, and beside it a man was standing, stripped to the waist, as Lacey's stunned eyes immediately registered. She started violently and some of the water in the vase splashed down her faded denim skirt and on to the bedroom carpet.

She was aware of a pair of intensely dark eyes taking her in, from the tangle of pale hair on her shoulders to her drenched skirt and flat shoes. She felt she was being assessed and dismissed, and the colour surged up into her pale skin.

When he spoke, his voice was deep with an intonation that puzzled her. It seemed to hold a faint transatlantic drawl overlaid by a trace of something more foreign, and she wrinkled her brow trying to recognise it until he repeated his remark with a kind of weary patience, that arrested her attention instantly.

'I said, hadn't you better get a cloth and mop up that mess?'

24

Lacey stared at him, dimly aware that she was most certainly not accustomed to being spoken to in that way. It was on the tip of her tongue to tell him so, but he was her father's guest and it was her duty to be courteous however lacking in that respect he himself might be.

She walked over to the chest of drawers, intending to leave her flowers before she went to look for a cloth, but he halted her in her tracks.

'Are you proposing to put a wet vase down on polished wood? You haven't a great deal of idea about how to look after antique furniture.'

Lacey's blood boiled. Of course she knew better than that, but the shock of finding this—creature already installed and half naked had driven her usual common sense from her mind.

He had a shirt in his hand. Why didn't he put it on and and cover himself up? she thought angrily, looking with dislike at his broad brown chest with the black mat of hair, but that was obviously the last thing on his mind, because just then he rolled the shirt into a ball and tossed it back into the case.

'I'll—I'll just put them on the floor for a moment,' she said hastily, averting her gaze.

'Better still, why not take them back where they came from?' He stood watching her, his hands on his hips. 'I don't need flowers in my room, or anywhere around me. I prefer to see them in their natural state.'

Lacey's eyes held an obvious glint. She said, 'Then I think I'll take them to my own room. I don't happen to share your prejudice.'

He looked at her, his piercing dark eyes narrowed, raking her from head to foot.

'Does Lady Vernon usually allow her employees your sort of latitude?' he drawled.

Lacey stood very still, her thoughts whirling. 'Heavens,' she thought, a giggle bubbling up inside her which she instantly suppressed, 'he thinks I'm the upstairs maid or something!'

As if he had read her thoughts, his voice broke in on them with swift abruptness. 'Just who are you?'

25

She shrugged, deliberately vague. 'Oh, I help in the house.'

'Do you?' he said, rather grimly. 'Well, perhaps you'll go and—help somewhere else. I'm waiting to take a bath—unless you include washing guests' backs among your duties.'

He began lazily to unbuckle the belt on the dark, close-fitting trousers, and Lacey observed the manoeuvre with alarm, her cheeks already flushed at what his words had implied.

'I'm sorry to have disturbed your privacy,' she said rather haughtily, turning abruptly towards the bedroom door to make her escape.

His mocking laugh followed her as she closed the door carefully behind her, and she bit her lip angrily as she walked down the corridor to get to her own room. The encounter had totally disconcerted her. No man had ever spoken to her or looked at her like that before, and she was aware that her pulses had quickened and that her mouth felt oddly dry.

She felt almost vindictively glad to picture his embarrassment when they met again later at her father's dinner table. It would teach him to jump to conclusions, she told herself. But at the same time she was uncomfortably aware that the arrogant set of those muscular brown shoulders and the assurance of his heavy-lidded eyes had not suggested a man who would embarrass easily, or respond in any of the conventional ways. Lacey had to admit that she would have been happier if he had remained a totally unknown quantity to her—if, in fact, they had never met at all, and the prospect of the dinner party ahead, not to mention the entire weekend that faced her, filled her with a strange sense of dread.

When Lacey emerged from her bath that evening, she was surprised to find her stepmother's maid waiting for her in her room.

'Madame's asked me to put your hair up for you, Miss Lacey,' Barbara announced, setting a china bowl full of hairpins down on the dressing table.

'Oh.' Lacey digested this, a slight frown wrinkling her

26

forehead. She usually wore her hair very simply, either hanging loose on her shoulders or in two bunches, as she had planned to wear it that night, the fastenings masked by small bunches of artificial daisies. The style was intended to complement the simplicity of the deep blue Empire line dress laid across the bed, and she wondered doubtfully whether a more sophisticated style would suit either her or the dress.

But Barbara was certainly skilful, she decided, as she watched the girl's fingers transform her swathe of hair into a smooth coronet on top of her head, softening the severity of the style with two softly curling strands allowed to rest against her ears. It was the first time she had ever been offered Barbara's services, which were usually Michelle's exclusive prerogative and jealously guarded as such, and she wondered curiously why an exception had been made on this particular evening. Nor did Barbara's ministrations stop at her hair. She gave Lacey a light but effective make-up as well, moisturising her skin and shadowing her eyelids, as well as applying lip gloss to the soft curve of her mouth.

When she had finished, Lacey gazed at herself in astonishment. She hardly recognised herself in this cool, aloof young woman with the mysterious eyes and shining crown of fair hair.

'There, Miss Lacey.' Barbara's tone was plainly self-congratulatory. 'Now if you'll just get into your undies, I'll fetch your dress.' She handed Lacey a pair of briefs and some filmy tights.

'Er—thank you, Barbara.' Lacey flushed a little awkwardly, telling herself that she was perfectly able to dress herself unaided. 'Where's the rest of it?'

Barbara stared at her. 'That's all, miss. You couldn't wear anything else with this dress.'

'But that's ridiculous. I always have in the past,' Lacey swung round vexedly on the dressing stool and gasped as she saw the mass of clinging black fabric Barbara was holding carefully over her arm. 'What's that?'

'Your dress, miss.' Barbara sounded surprised. 'Didn't you think it would arrive in time?'

Lacey's lips parted helplessly as she recognised that

27

Barbara was holding out the daring gown with the minimal bodice that she had seen modelled at Jean Louis.

'There's been some mistake,' she said eventually. 'That dress is for Madame. I—I couldn't wear anything like that.'

'It's definitely your dress, Miss Lacey. Madame said so when I unpacked the box, and besides, this isn't her fitting. It must be a little surprise for you,' she added encouragingly.

Lacey's lips tightened. 'Well, I still don't intend to wear it,' she declared. 'Please take it away and bring me my blue dress instead.'

'But, Miss Lacey,' Barbara's voice was anxious, 'Madame said you had to wear it tonight. I don't know what she'll say if . . .'

'That isn't your problem, Barbara,' Lacey said gently. 'I'll see my stepmother before I go down and explain. I'm sure there's been a mistake of some kind.'

'Mistake? What mistake?' Michelle's cool voice spoke from the doorway. She came gliding across the carpet, elegant in a silver gown, a cigarette held tensely in her fingers, and carrying a glass filled with some pale liquid in her other hand.

'Miss Lacey doesn't want to wear the Jean Louis model, madame.' Barbara sounded subdued, as if she felt she would be blamed for Lacey's rebellion.

Michelle's eyebrows rose. '*Eh bien?* You may go, Barbara. I will deal with this.'

When the door had closed behind the girl, she set the glass down on the dressing table near the bowl of daffodils and stood, looking grimly down at her stepdaughter.

'Were my instructions not clear?' she asked.

'Michelle!' Lacey was totally appalled. 'You surely can't expect me to go downstairs wearing—that.'

'*Pourquoi pas?*' Michelle gave her a hard look. 'It is an an expensive dress, and black will set off your hair and skin admirably.'

Slow colour crept up Lacey's face. 'You know why not,' she protested.

Michelle gave a brief, metallic laugh. 'A prude, *ma chère?* You are no longer at the convent, *tu sais.* Most girls of your

28

age would give much to wear such a dress. What have you to be ashamed of? Your body is young, and your breasts are firm. You have the perfect figure for the gown, which is why I bought it for you. Now please dress yourself in it without further arguments. It is getting late.'

'But, Michelle, what will people think—what will my father say?'

Michelle shrugged. 'What should they think? That you look—charming. And your father will say nothing. He not only approves of the gown but he particularly wishes you to wear it tonight.'

'But why?'

Michelle sighed elaborately. 'It is his wish that you should make a favourable impression on one of his guests.'

'By appearing half naked?' Lacey's mouth twisted in a sudden cynicism that belied her youth. 'And who is this very important person—or am I not allowed to ask?'

But as soon as the words were uttered, she knew. There was only one person it could be—the strange man into whose room she had blundered with her unwanted welcome offering of flowers. She felt suddenly cold and sick, remembering how his eyes had assessed her earlier with all the assurance of a man for whom the female body held few secrets. To have to appear in front of him wearing the black dress would be a total humiliation.

'You asked to be treated as a woman, but you persist in behaving like a child.' Her stepmother's tone was icy. 'His name is Troy Andreakis.'

Lacey had been staring at the bowl of daffodils, trying to fight back her tears, but at the name her head came up sharply and she stared at Michelle disbelievingly.

'The oil and shipping magnate? But what is he doing here? He has no interest in Vernon–Carey.'

'Not yet.' Michelle picked up a hairbrush and studied it with over-absorbed interest. 'Yet—who knows? By the time the weekend is at an end ...' She shrugged again, leaving the sentence unfinished.

Lacey stared at her bewildered. 'I don't understand.'

'Oh, it's quite simple, *ma chère*. A large-scale investment by a man of Andreakis' status would restore confidence in

29

Vernon—Carey. Without it, there could well be a catastrophe —quite soon.'

Lacey gripped the edge of the dressing table. 'Things are that bad?' she managed, her green eyes enormous in her pale face.

'They are that bad,' Michelle corroborated tautly. 'And, believe me, there are no lengths to which I will not go to ensure that your father gets that investment from Andreakis. That is why, *ma chère*, you are going to wear that dress tonight, because you are going to help me—you are going to be an asset to your father for the first time in your life instead of a liability.'

Lacey flinched a little, but her stepmother went on unheeding. 'This is why you are being dressed as an attractive woman, instead of a child. A man like Andreakis does not want to dine in the company of a gawky schoolgirl. You once hoped to occupy a concert platform, and for that you would have needed an ability to act, to project your personality as well as your music. Tonight your father needs that performance from you. He wants you to relax Andreakis, to charm him if you can.'

Lacey closed her eyes for a moment. Now was not the time to confess that she and Troy Andreakis had already encountered and failed to charm each other. Would the transformation from gawky schoolgirl to sophisticate be sufficiently complete to render her unrecognisable? She doubted it, and knew that she was going to need every scrap of social grace that had been imparted to her at the convent to get through the evening without disaster.

'If it's what Daddy wants,' she said wearily, at last.

'Oh, I wouldn't say precisely that.' Michelle's voice was ironic. 'But he appreciates the necessity at least, and he is depending on you.' Her eyes skimmed Lacey's wilting figure appraisingly. 'Barbara has done her work well. Make sure you do the same. Now please hurry. The others will be arriving soon.'

As she turned to go, she indicated the glass on the dressing table. '*Pour toi*. For you—a dry Martini,' she said.

'But I only drink fruit juice,' Lacey protested.

Michelle smiled a little. 'Call it Dutch courage. You may

need it.' And she was gone on a cloud of Balmain perfume.

Lacey tasted the drink gingerly, grimacing slightly at the taste, but it had a warming effect which served to chase away some of the unpleasant butterflies which appeared to have taken up residence in her abdomen.

When she was finally ready, she stood and stared at herself in the full-length mirror, resisting an impulse to cover the upper part of her body with her hands. It was true, she thought detachedly—she did not have to be ashamed of her figure. The stark black of the material made her white skin look almost translucent and gave her slender curves a frank enticement. She just prayed that her untried poise would be able to cope with the promise of almost total revelation that the gown exuded.

But in spite of its provocation, and the sophistication of her shadowed eyes, glowing mouth and softly piled hair, Lacey felt desperately inadequate. Unwillingly she forced her mind back to that earlier encounter, visualising the ruthlessness of his dark face. Not a man who would suffer fools gladly, she surmised, and one for whom a woman would need more than a glossy façade to arouse his interest. What could she find to say that would engage the attention of a man like Andreakis?

With a little groan, she tried to think of what little she knew about him—mostly gleaned from rare newspaper stories, and generally illustrating his loathing of personal publicity. But there had been a story recently—something to do with litigation over a trusteeship involving his young sister— which he had won, she recalled with a slight curl of her lip. She could remember there had been pictures of his beautiful villa on the Ionian island of Theros, taken presumably with a long-range lens out of respect for his dislike of the Press. She could recall gossipy items, too, about beautiful women who had been his guests on Theros for varying periods of time.

A little shiver ran through her body. She felt like a novice swimmer who suddenly finds the water too deep, and too cold.

She gave a shaky little sigh and turned reluctantly towards the door. Better to make her entrance downstairs as inconspicuous as possible than linger, and have Michelle coming in search of her.

As she came slowly down the wide, polished staircase to the hall, Mrs Osborne was just admitting a latecomer. As he shugged off his overcoat and handed it to the housekeeper, Lacey realised it was Alan Trevor and in spite of herself she felt a wave of self-conscious colour rising in her face and had to crush an impulse to turn and run back to her room.

When she spoke, she was amazed to hear how normal, even prim, she sounded. Good evening, Alan.'

He swung round. 'Er—hello, Lacey. Am I the last? I had to stay behind because the vet was coming to look at Domino. She's due to foal any time, but he doesn't think there'll be anything doing tonight.'

'Well, I'm glad you were able to make it.' She moved forward from the foot of the stairs, aware that his eyes were taking in the transformation in her appearance with evident puzzlement. 'Is something the matter?' She looked up at him innocently.

'No—oh, no. It's just . . .' He stared down at her, frowning a little. 'Hell, Lacey, what have you done to yourself?'

'Don't you approve?'

'No—yes. I don't know.' He pushed his hair back impatiently. 'What's more important, will your parents approve? I mean, have they seen that dress?'

'Of course.' Lacey twirled round slowly, letting the filmy skirt float out and settle back against her slender legs. 'What's wrong with it?'

'Oh, it's fine—what there is of it,' he said, heavily sarcastic. 'And black. I've never seen you in black before.'

'And you don't like it?'

'I wouldn't say that. It just takes a bit of getting used to.' His eyes went over her again. They held censure and something less easy to define. 'You just look so—different.'

'Well, I can't always wear jeans and gymslips,' she said defensively. 'I have to grow up some time.'

'We all have to do that,' he muttered. 'Come on. We'd better go in.' He offered her his arm with a strange formality.

'Oh, Alan!' She ignored the gesture, slipping her hand into his with all the confidence of long familiarity. 'I haven't changed that much, believe me. I'm the same person I always was.'

'Are you, Lacey?' He gave her fingers a quick squeeze. 'I guess I'll just have to take your word for it.'

She was glad she did not have to enter the drawing room by herself. Even though her appearance did not cause the sensation she had feared, she was conscious of a number of curious glances, particularly from guests who had known her since childhood. There was admiration mixed with the curiosity too from most of the men, and after a moment or two Lacey felt some of the tension begin to leave her body. Alan released her hand, murmuring that he would fetch her a drink, and she stood alone, looking round the room and returning smiling nods and greetings.

Then she saw him. He was standing by the ornate marble mantelpiece, his arm casually resting along the shelf. He seemed to be paying minute attention to the glowing butt of his cheroot, but as if aware of her scrutiny he raised his head, and their eyes met across the room. Lacey felt the polite smile fading on her lips as she encountered his look. It held recognition bordering on disbelief, and a frankly sensual assessment that brought the colour flaring to her face and an angry light to her eyes. For a moment she stood motionless, then, as she saw him fling the remains of his cheroot on to the blazing logs in the hearth and move away from the fireplace in one swift impatient movement, she realised he was coming towards her and panicked, turning towards the door, regardless of the curious glances she was attracting from the group of people nearest to her.

But the way was blocked by Mrs Osborne's comfortable figure, telling Michelle that dinner was served, and escape was impossible. She gave a swift glance around, searching vainly for Alan, as her father reached her side.

'So there you are, Lacey.' She knew she was not imagining the impatient, anxious note in his voice and turned towards him reluctantly. 'Mr Andreakis has been waiting to meet you, my dear.'

Her hand was encompassed by lean, brown fingers. It was the most conventional of salutes, so it was nonsense to

33

imagine that she could still feel the pressure of his hand, long after he had released her. Dry-throated, she acknowledged his greeting in a small husky voice, registering that he was treating her as a complete stranger although there was no doubt that he had recognised her from that brief encounter in his room earlier. She supposed she should be grateful to him for saving them both from awkward explanations, but whereas she had hoped to be able to make him feel foolish, she now felt at a disadvantage. Resentment kept her silent as he took her arm and escorted her into the dining room, holding her chair as she sat down with a courtesy that she was certain masked—what? Something as simple as mockery? She could not be sure and it irked her as she unfolded the exquisite damask napkin, and picked up her soup spoon.

To her relief, Michael Fairclough, a leading member of the local hunt, was her other neighbour at the table and she was able to start a conversation with him about the forthcoming point-to-point, even pretend for a while that the dark, sardonic figure at her other side did not exist, but a glacial look from Michelle at the end of the table brought her up with a jerk, reminding her of her duties. She turned towards him to find, disconcertingly, that he was watching her. Her colour rose, and the trite remark she had been planning on the weather prospects for the weekend died on her lips.

Wonderingly her eyes searched his face, marking the strongly arched eyebrows above those impenetrably dark eyes, and the hard lines of his mouth and jaw. In spite of the formal elegance of dinner jacket and befrilled white shirt, she was aware of the muscular strength of the chest and shoulders they concealed, and the air of restless, barely controlled energy that suggested these civilised trappings were merely a veneer.

'Do you read characters from faces, Miss Vernon?'

Her nerves jumped both at the appositeness of his question, and at the realisation that she had been guilty of staring at him.

She shook her head, transferring her gaze swiftly back to her plate.

'You must think me very rude,' she said, trying to keep her voice steady.

'You're no thought-reader either.' He picked up his glass and drank some of the wine it contained. 'You've barely touched yours,' he commented. 'It's hardly a compliment to such a fine vintage.'

'I—I don't know a great deal about wine,' she confessed, and his brows rose.

'No? I would have thought such occasions as this would have been second nature to you.'

Was that an edge to his voice or was it her imagination running riot again? she wondered desperately. His remark proved one thing at least—Michelle's outward grooming of her had been impeccable. He obviously thought she was much older than she was. Now all she had to do was to live up to that belief—provide him with the light-hearted flirtation that he would expect from a female companion at dinner.

'Perhaps I find wine of less interest than people,' she ventured, making herself smile at him.

'And some people of more interest than others,' he said, and this time there was no mistaking the satirical note in his voice. 'It's a pity, for example, that I don't share Mr—er —Fairclough's interest in hunting matters. Perhaps that might make me more acceptable to you as a companion.'

Oh God, what a mess she was making of it all! Lacey put down her knife and fork, feeling she would choke if she took another mouthful. She realised her father was watching them, a slight anxious frown wrinkling his forehead, and she felt a pang of self-recrimination as she realised the stress he was undergoing and the importance that the success of this weekend had assumed his mind. Somehow she must make an effort to do and be what he wanted, and to win over this unsmiling man who was totally outside her admittedly limited experience.

Frantically she searched her memory for some of the scraps of worldly wisdom that the girls at the convent had let drop when they were recounting the details of their latest conquests. Hadn't someone said it was sexy to look straight into a man's eyes as you smiled at him? Deliberately she caught and held his gaze, allowing her eyes to widen endlessly while her mouth curved slowly into warmth and charm.

'Horses aren't my sole preoccupation,' she protested with a little shrug.

For a moment as he returned her look unwaveringly, she thought painfully that she had failed, then he smiled too—a cynical twist of her lips, but a smile—and lifted his glass to her in a toast to which she was forced to respond.

'My last doubt is removed,' he said musingly.

'Doubt?' Lacey looked at him from under her lashes, a favourite trick of Vanessa's.

'That you and I will eventually find a topic that will arouse the—interest of us both.'

A little quiver of uncertainty jangled the nerve-endings along her spine and curled around the nape of her neck. Almost involuntarily she lifted her hand to rub her neck, and remembered too late the revealing nature of her dress. She hurriedly folded her hands in her lap again, stealing a glance at Troy Andreakis, but his attention seemed to be centred on his wine glass.

'Is this your first visit to Kings Winston, Mr Andreakis?' Surely that was a safe subject.

'No, I was here last autumn, but only for a day or two. I am glad to have a chance of a longer visit so that I can see something of the surrounding countryside.'

Lacey's heart sank. It seemed that his visit might not be confined to simply a weekend after all.

'I'm surprised at your interest. I didn't picture you as a nature-lover,' she said more tartly than she had intended.

His mouth curled slightly again. 'Because I rejected your flowers? On the contrary, I can appreciate beauty as well as any man. However'—the dark eyes swept over her again— 'as I said, I prefer it in its natural state.' Her eyes met his, frankly indignant, and he laughed softly. 'What a creature of contrasts you are, *pethi mou*—from *gamine* to *femme fatale* in the course of an hour or so. What is real about you, I wonder, and what is an illusion?'

She was thankful that the arrival of the sweet course diverted his attention momentarily and gave her a chance to regain her equilibrium. So much for Michelle's efforts to transform her, she thought wretchedly. The scheme had been doomed to failure from the start. She simply did not have the poise and confidence to hoodwink a man like Troy Andreakis. She was staring miserably at the untouched portion of Crême Chantilly on her plate when she realised he was speaking to her again.

'I think you owe me something for spilling water all over my bedroom and then running away,' he said. 'I'm willing to settle for a tour of the local beauty spots in your company tomorrow—unless you object and prefer to buy my silence in some other way.'

'I don't object,' she said rather woodenly. 'It—it will be delightful.'

There was a disturbing pause while he looked at her again with that faint, cynical amusement.

'You know,' he said softly, 'you have almost convinced me that it will be.'

She was thankful that her family still adhered to the old custom of leaving the men to enjoy brandy and cigars while the women drank coffee in the drawing room. She was kept busy handing round cups and when everyone was served found herself a seat beside Fran Trevor, who was looking like a vivacious robin in her long cherry-coloured dress.

'Hello, love,' she exclaimed as Lacey sat down. 'What a gorgeous dress! Is that what comes of having a French stepmother? I envy you, if so. Mother took one look at me in this and started muttering direly about modesty vests— whatever they are.'

Lacey sighed. 'I think my sympathies are with your mother,' she said uncomfortably. 'I feel an absolute fool.'

Fran looked at her shrewdly. 'Well, I assure you, you don't look one. And that terrifying Mr Andreakis obviously didn't think so. I'm glad he's your guest, and not ours. I wouldn't have a clue what to say to him. Does he ride, by the way?'

'I don't think so. He—he said he wasn't interested in hunting, at any rate.'

Fran shrugged. 'Ah well, you can't have everything. Are

37

you going to come and exercise Starlight for me tomorrow? I'm going to be tied up with these people from the Bull.'

Lacey gave a little groan. 'Oh Fran, I wish I could, but I'm committed to going for a drive with Mr Andreakis.'

Fran whistled humorously. 'I should be so committed! Honestly, love, you are the limit. Pursued by millionaires and still you look glum!'

Lacey wanted to tell her that the pursuit was actually being conducted from the opposite quarter, but she had to remain silent. She had learned long ago not to chatter indiscreetly about Vernon—Carey matters. Instead she shrugged carelessly.

'I'm his host's daughter. I suppose he feels he has to be polite.'

'Hmm.' Fran eyed her. 'I wonder if he'd be as "polite" if you had a squint and legs like tree-trunks. Besides, people like Andreakis don't have to bother with things like politeness. They deal in power, and that's what matters in their world.'

And in mine, Lacey thought rebelliously.

She walked over to replace a cup on the tray, and encountered a taut glance from Michelle. *'Eh bien?'*

Lacey gave a slight shrug. 'I've done as I was told. I suppose it's too much to hope that I can be given my freedom for the rest of the evening.'

Michelle's eyes snapped. 'Are you quite mad?' she questioned glacially. 'What would our guests think if you were to disappear in the middle of the evening? Besides, I have already been asked if you will play for us later. Everyone will be most disappointed if you refuse.'

Lacey bent her head defeatedly. At least if she was at the piano, it would release her from close attendance on Troy Andreakis.

'Very well,' she agreed listlessly. 'Is it all right if I go to my room for some aspirin? I have a slight headache.'

'Certainement. You are by no means a prisoner. Please do not dramatise the situation.' Michelle gave her a final, inimical look before turning to smile graciously at Mrs Taylor who was approaching them.

Lacey was glad to escape from the stuffiness of the

drawing room. Michelle, who loathed the British climate, invariably had the central heating turned full on in the winter months and tonight was no exception. She was walking rather wearily across the hall when she heard the sound of chairs being moved and a crescendo of voices as the dining room door was opened. Lacey picked up her long skirt and fled up the stairs. She had no wish to be caught loitering in the hall—by anyone, she thought crossly as she safely gained the upper landing.

It was with a real sense of refuge that she reached her bedroom. Her fingers had just closed on the handle of her bedroom door when the voice she least wanted to hear spoke lazily just behind her.

'Running out on the party, Miss Vernon?'

She swung round, her heart thudding in sudden ridiculous panic.

'You followed me,' she accused before she could stop herself, then stood, aghast at what she had said, conscious that his lips were twisting in faint amusement.

'Alas, no,' he murmured. 'I was lured here by my cigarette case, not by your charms, Miss Vernon, potent though they are.'

His eyes went over her with a kind of lingering insolence that made her want to cover her body with her hands.

'I'm sorry,' she managed at last. 'If you would excuse me ...'

His hand closed over hers, preventing her from opening her bedroom door.

'You haven't answered my question yet,' he reminded her.

'Question?' she repeated lamely, then flushed as she remembered. 'No, I'm not "running out". I have a headache, and I've come to get something for it.'

'I am desolated to hear it,' he said with a complete absence of expression. 'May I recommend prevention rather than cure as a policy for the future.'

'Prevention?' she echoed bewilderedly.

'My advice would be to avoid alcohol, to which you are patently not accustomed.' His tone was smooth. 'Also hair styles which rely for their effectiveness on quantities of hairpins.'

Her hand was released, and she recoiled instinctively as she felt his hands moving with detestable assurance among the lacquered coils of her hair.

'What are you doing?' She sounded breathless and very young, and saw his teeth gleam suddenly in a smile.

'Curing your headache,' he replied laconically, and Lacey tensed as the long shining strands, released from their restraint, spilled past her shoulders.

'Oh!' She lifted a helpless hand to check on the complete ruin of Barbara's careful creation. 'Oh, how dare you!'

'Oh, I dare.' Totally ignoring her flushed face and eyes filled with angry tears, he reached out and lifted one gleaming tendril between his finger and thumb. 'You have hair like silk, *pethi mou*, why not take pride in it, instead of torturing it into shapes that only serve to make you look older than the child you are.'

'I'm not a child!' she defended herself hotly, forcing herself to forget all her own misgivings about her appearance that night.

'Aren't you?' he said sardonically. He let the long tress of hair fall back on her shoulder, and his fingers followed it to touch the curve of her throat in a caress that, although fleeting, seemed to burn her flesh. A long tremulous quiver shook her body, and, dazed, she heard him laugh softly as if he was quite aware of her reaction. His hand moved almost inexorably along her shoulder to the wide, soft folds of the shoulder-strap which constituted half of her bodice, and she tensed unbelievingly, her eyes flying to his face in swift, outraged denial, as she felt him begin to slide the material aside.

'No!' she got out, pulling herself away almost wildly from the intimate exploration of his touch.

'Why not?' His voice was quiet but with an underlying sensuous warmth that disturbed her as much as the frank appraisal in his dark eyes. 'Your room is here, and I can guarantee no one would disturb us.'

'You're—insulting.' Her voice shook uncontrollably.

'How have you been insulted? I've merely credited your

intelligence by making my intentions clear, instead of merely seducing you as I might have done.'

'I think you must be mad!' Backed against the door, her shoulders pressed against its panels as if she would draw some reserve of strength from its solidarity, she looked incredibly young and defenceless. 'I think your previous—conquests must have gone to your head, Mr Andreakis.'

He laughed. 'How charmingly old-fashioned! I don't look for conquests, however. Submissiveness is the last quality I look for when I take a woman to my bed.'

'That is no concern of mine,' she said, lifting her chin with a kind of forlorn dignity. 'But I am afraid you will have to look elsewhere for your latest—seduction.'

'*Andithetos, pethi mou,*' he said, almost gently, then, as she tried to slip past him, to return to safety and sanity downstairs, his hands reached for her, bruising her bare arms and dragging her with merciless strength against the hardness of his body. For a long moment he held her, writhing impotently in his grip, while his eyes searched her face as if he was etching her features on some inner consciousness, then his mouth came down on hers, parting her lips with sensual ruthlessness and destroying for ever any innocent illusions she might have had about what a kiss would be.

When he let her go, Lacey stood motionless for a moment, her eyes enormous with shock in her pale face, then she pressed her hand almost convulsively over her swollen mouth and ran from him, only to collide with someone else standing at the head of the stairs.

'Lacey!' Michelle's voice was taut. 'Where have you been for this age?' Her eyes narrowed as they swept over her stepdaughter. '*Mon dieu*, your hair! What have you done ...'

'It was my doing, Lady Vernon.' Troy Andreakis joined them unhurriedly, his dark face cool and imperturbable, leaving Lacey wondering dazedly whether she had merely imagined the last few outrageous moments. 'A sovereign remedy for headaches—passed down in our family for generations.'

His eyes, faint amusement in their depths, seemed to

41

challenge Lacey, daring her to take exception to his behaviour. She turned impulsively to her stepmother and
paused, whatever protest she had planned to make trembling unsaid upon her lips, hardly able to believe the unmistakable look of triumph she had surprised on Michelle's
face. Lacey realised then what Troy Andreakis had meant
when he had told her that they would not be disturbed.
Michelle knew already all that there was to know, and
condoned it, as if she had been an actual witness to that
shattering kiss. Lacey felt cold and sick. And would Michelle
also have condoned the lovemaking which would have been
the most probable aftermath to the kiss, if she had not made
her escape? It seemed only too likely.

Michelle gave a little smile. 'It seems to have been very
successful,' she said smoothly. 'But perhaps you should
tidy yourself a little, *ma petite*, before you join us downstairs. We are all waiting to hear you play.'

Lacey murmured something unintelligible and fled to her
room. Some ten minutes later she stood back and looked at
her reflection. It was as if the clock had been turned back
and the girl who stood there slim and straight in her deep
blue dress, with the long silver-blonde hair brushed straight
and shining over her shoulders, was the only one who had
existed that evening. As she turned away, her foot caught
the crumpled folds of the discarded black dress lying on
the floor. For a moment she hesitated, then, as anger and
humiliation welled up inside her again, she bent and picked
it up, wrenching at the delicate fabric until it tore irretriev-
ably. With a grim smile, she let it drop back to the floor.
She would never be forced into that particular charade
again, she vowed.

From now on, any contest would be played according to
her rules, she told herself defiantly, then shivered as in
spite of herself the dark relentless face of her adversary
forced itself into her mind, and her fingers strayed almost
wonderingly to the softness of her mouth which he had
made so totally his own.

In her little talks on morals to the girls at the convent,
Reverend Mother had always stressed that a girl's best protection was her own innocence, yet hers had proved at best

the shakiest of defences, Lacey thought bitterly. And even Reverend Mother had not visualised a situation where that innocence might be placed on sale to a man like Troy Andreakis.

She gave a little trembling sigh. All she could hope to do was keep out of his way as much as possible and see to it that she was never alone with him again. After all, he would not be staying at Kings Winston for ever, and soon, very soon, she would never have to set eyes on him again.

CHAPTER THREE

LACEY awoke early the next morning, after a restless night. She washed and dressed in an old pair of denim pants, topped by an equally ancient thick sweater, then slipped downstairs and let herself quietly out by the side door, collecting her duffel coat on the way. She felt like a fugitive as she made her way down the drive, but her mind was made up. She intended to spend the day working at the stables with Fran Trevor.

It occurred to her that Troy Andreakis might well have mentioned to her stepmother that he had asked her to spend the day with him, and that her disappearance might well involve her in a major row later, but even that was preferable to being forced to spend hours in close proximity with a man whom she disliked and feared. Yes, she was prepared to admit to herself that Troy Andreakis scared her. She had been right when she had gauged that civilisation could just be a veneer with him. There was a latent savagery about him which disturbed her, and made her feel oddly threatened.

Last night while she had played the piano, she had felt his eyes upon her, brooding and enigmatic, and in some strange way this had drawn from her one of her best performances. Normally she hated being paraded at the piano after a dinner party like a child with a party piece, and barely tolerated the over-popular classics that she was expected to play. But last night she had acceded to her father's request and played his favourite Chopin nocturne, a difficult piece which called for all her technical skill and which she had managed to imbue with a fire and imagination she had not realised she possessed. She had not looked at Troy Andreakis to see if he had joined in the applause which greeted her performance, and not long afterwards people began to make their departures and she was able to go to her room, without exchanging another word with him.

Michelle had given her change of dress a long, glittering look, but she had made no comment, to Lacey's relief, nor, as she had rather feared, had she come to Lacey's room to elicit a more complete account of what had passed between Troy Andreakis and herself. However Lacey might feel, Michelle obviously thought that the evening had gone well.

She wondered miserably how much her father had known about Michelle's plans, and whether he had sanctioned them. It was unbearably hurtful to think that he might have agreed to her becoming part of some sordid sexual bargain in order to save Vernon—Carey from collapse, and she was sure that only utter desperation would have made him contemplate such a course of action.

Her rather despondent thoughts occupied her during the brisk ten-minute walk along the lane to the stables on the edge of Kings Winston village.

By the time a yawning and heavy-eyed Fran had put in an appearance, Lacey had already watered the five horses and three ponies that comprised the stables' complement, and had the coffee going in the small office next to the tack room. Fran's eyes widened in surprise and pleasure when she saw Lacey.

'You must be made of steel,' she commented. 'I thought you would be having breakfast in bed this morning to build up your strength for your day out with your millionaire.'

'He is not my millionaire.' Lacey stirred the brimming mugs of coffee with unnecessary vigour. 'And the day out is cancelled, as of now. I've seen quite enough of him already.'

'Ho-hum.' Fran gave her a wondering look. 'And does he feel the same about you?'

'I wouldn't know.' Lacey shrugged with a negligence she was far from feeling. 'But I'm afraid if he wants a guide, he'll simply have to apply to the British Tourist Board. I'm no longer available.'

'Well, if you're sure,' Fran said. 'Actually I wouldn't mind your help today. I'm going to be busy. Those people from the Bull are coming back at ten, and I have pupils this afternoon as well. Alan was going to try and get down, but it looks as if Domino is going to produce her foal today, so he may be tied up. If you'd like to come out with us this morning I'd be grateful. None of them are beginners, but I'd like to be able to give the children some individual attention, if you'd keep an eye on the adults.'

Lacey acquiesced willingly. When inquiries were made for her, as she had no doubt they would be, she wanted to be as far away as possible, and a morning spent hacking around the fields and lanes seemed an ideal refuge.

The next two hours passed swiftly, as the two girls worked together to prepare the animals for the day ahead of them, grooming the horses, attending to their hooves and feeding them. On top of this, each stall had to be scrupulously cleaned out, and the tack that would be used that day looked over and cleaned and polished.

'It's no good, I'm going to have to look for full time help,' Fran grumbled cheerfully, as they saddled up the horses ready for the first ride of the day. 'I can't rely on my friends and relatives for ever.'

'Have you anyone in mind?' Lacey slipped a bit into Fern's mouth, murmuring encouragingly to the mare as she did so.

'Well, I was talking to John Palmer last week and he was saying that his youngest girl Marian is as miserable as sin on this secretarial course she insisted on doing. He seemed to think she'd be only too glad to come home if there was a job of some kind waiting for her. She's a nice kid, Marian, and a good patient rider.'

'You could certainly do far worse,' Lacey agreed. 'I only wish I could help more . . .' Her voice tailed away a little forlornly.

'Oh, love! You already do more than I have any right to expect. And even if Marian does come here, you'll be more than welcome to pop down for a couple of hours whenever you feel like it. But you have a life of your own to live, and I can't expect to have first call on you all the time.'

'Hm.' Lacey gave minute attention to the buckle she was fastening. 'The life of my own you mention doesn't have any great attraction for me at the moment.'

'My dear girl!' Fran's eyes were warm with amusement. 'What an admission for someone who hasn't had her eighteenth birthday yet!'

Lacey sighed. 'I suppose it does sound rather ridiculous. But I seem to be the only person I know who hasn't any definite purpose in mind. I have no idea what sort of a career I want—or even if I'll be allowed to do it when I do decide,' she finished in a despondent little rush.

'Well, I wouldn't worry too much, if I were you,' Fran said bracingly, after a pause. 'Why not enjoy yourself while you can? You've got plenty of time to find a sense of purpose. I don't believe for a moment that you're just going to spend the rest of your life mouldering away in Kings Winston, if that's what you're afraid of.'

Lacey allowed herself a brief unhappy smile. 'I suppose there could be worse fates,' she said with an attempt at lightness.

'Well, I think so, obviously.' Fran gave an affectionately proprietorial glance around the whitewashed stable block. 'But I don't think it's the life for you, somehow.' She gave a hurried glance at her watch. 'Heavens, we must get on. We've only got about fifteen minutes.'

Lacey was in the office taking a telephone booking for a lesson the following week when she heard Fran call to her. Assuming the party from the Bull had arrived, she made a quick entry in the diary and grabbed a hard hat from one of the pegs before going out into the yard. A car was parked near the archway that led to the road, a low-slung foreign sports model which looked as if it concealed power as well as opulence under its sleek exterior. It looked hardly the sort of conveyance that a family with children staying at the Bull would choose, Lacey thought with faint surprise turning to outright dismay as the driver's door swung noiselessly open and Troy Andreakis climbed out.

Bareheaded, a black leather driving coat slung casually over close-fitting dark pants and a polo-necked sweater, he looked tall and formidable in the pale morning sunlight. The deliberately casual attire accentuated his masculinity and brought Lacey an unwelcome picture of their first, unexpected meeting in his room.

'I think the guided tour is on again,' Fran muttered, ruefully turning down the corners of her mouth as Lacey stood

47

motionless and completely lost for words at her side.

He strolled forward until he was only a few feet from the girls, then he made Fran a slight bow. '*Kalimera, thespoinis.* I regret I have to deprive you of your—er—stable girl's services, but she is already promised to me.'

Lacey gasped at his effrontery. Surely he could not believe she was willing to simply go off with him—like a lamb to the slaughter, after what had passed between them the previous night.

'Oh, it's quite all right,' said Fran, a little uncomfortably, avoiding Lacey's horrified gaze. 'I expect she forgot. She's got a terrible memory, haven't you, love?'

Lacey groaned inwardly. 'What about the party from the Bull?' she began almost frantically, but Fran quickly cut in.

'Oh, I can easily manage alone. They're none of them complete beginners, and as I said earlier, you've got your own life to lead. Run along and enjoy yourself.'

Lacey could have screamed with frustration. How could she get it over to Fran that this was not at all what she had in mind when they had talked earlier on? But any hopes she had of telling Troy Andreakis that she had no intention of going anywhere with him were doomed to disappointment. Just at that moment a large estate car pulled into the yard and drew up. It could only be the family from the Bull, on time for their ride, and Lacey intercepted an openly appealing look from Fran, begging her not to make any kind of scene in front of the new arrivals.

With as much dignity as she could muster, she quietly fetched her coat from the office and walked towards the sports car where Troy Andreakis stood waiting by the open passenger door. She had to overcome an impulse to shake off his hand as he helped her in and shut the door for her, and she sat in mute resentment as he swung himself lithely into the driving seat and turned the key in the ignition. The engine broke into a low throbbing rumble of life and in spite of herself, Lacey could not resist a stir of excitement deep down. Her father had never gone in for

48

sports cars and this was the first time she had ridden in a car as powerful as this.

She was forced to admire his expert handling of the car as they turned smoothly out through the narrow archway into the lane and left towards Kings Winston village, but her resolution to maintain an aloof silence while she was forced to remain in his company died a speedy death.

'Where are we going?'

'I thought we would take a trip to the coast. It's a pity to waste such a fine day,' he returned casually.

'But aren't we going home first—back to the house?'

'No.' He drew in neatly to the side of the lane to allow a large van to pass. 'Why should we?'

Lacey stared at him frustratedly. 'But I want to change,' she protested. 'These are my oldest clothes, for one thing, and I must smell of horses.'

He gave a slight smile as he glanced into his mirror. 'Perhaps so, *pethi mou*, but the choice was yours. If you had wished to smell of—roses, for example, you could have spent your morning in a different way. You had promised me your company, and if your appearance is not to your liking, then you have only yourself to blame.'

She could joyfully have bitten him. Her abortive bid for freedom had done her no good whatsoever, she thought bitterly. All she had achieved was the doubtful privilege of spending the day looking like a scruffy schoolgirl. If he had deliberately schemed to place her at a disadvantage, he could not have been more successful, she thought angrily.

She sat staring rigidly in front of her, as they left the village behind and motored into the open countryside that would take them eventually to the sea. Troy Andreakis made no attempt to push his car along the narrow lanes, but seemed content to drive at a steady pace, commenting on the scenery and various landmarks that took his eye. With another companion, Lacey thought furiously, it could have been such fun. She would have suggested stopping the car and looking round the old Saxon church at Cranham, or exploring the ruined house set back off the road which had been abandoned years ago because people claimed it was haunted and would not live there. As it was, she replied to his remarks in chilly monosyllables, or not at all, and eventually he too relapsed into silence.

They had been driving for over an hour when he slowed down, signalling his intention of pulling off the road into the forecourt of a small country hotel, charmingly gabled in the black and white timbers of the Tudor period.

'I think some coffee would be pleasant,' he said, as he switched off the ignition.

Lacey shrank within herself. She knew the hotel well. She had lunched there with her father often in past years, as a holiday treat, and the proprietor and his wife were like old friends. They would be bound to recognise her, she thought, looking down at her stained and creased jeans and the hairs on her sweater with a sinking heart.

'I'll wait for you here,' she said hurriedly.

'Is the coffee so bad?'

'What?' Then she understood. 'Oh—no, it's excellent. I'm just not very thirsty.'

'You're not very truthful, either.' He came round and opened her door. 'Out you get, *pethi mou.* Unless you want me to make you.'

She gave him a glance of pure fury, then scrambled out, icily ignoring his helping hand.

They were served their coffee beside a log fire in the lounge where comfortable leather sofas and armchairs were grouped around small oak tables. The waiter who served them was a stranger to her, and she decided optimistically that she had a fair chance of drinking her coffee and getting out of the hotel before the Hendersons spotted her. Consequently she gulped down the contents of her cup and had a burned tongue to add to her other indignities.

'You seem in a great hurry.' To her chagrin, Troy Andreakis reached for the pot and poured himself a second cup. 'But we have plenty of time in spite of our delayed start. Tell me, where would you like to have lunch?'

'I don't care,' she snapped childishly.

He raised his eyebrows. 'Haven't you a saying—"Don't care was made to care"? Perhaps you should bear it in mind, *pethi mou.*'

'I'm sorry,' she said sullenly. 'I just don't like being made to feel conspicuous, and I'm—hardly dressed for eating in restaurants.'

'Perhaps not. But maybe I wanted to teach you a lesson.'

'What lesson?' She looked at him defiantly, challenging the mockery in his eyes.

'Not to play games with me unless you are a good loser—which I doubt.'

'I have no desire to play games of any kind with you, Mr Andreakis,' she said as coldly as she could have wished.

'I'm disappointed,' he said calmly. 'For I like to win. I would also like you to call me by my given name.'

'No!' She felt herself recoil as violently as if he had leaned forward and placed his hand on her breast.

'Why not?'

She floundered a little. 'Because I don't consider I'm on terms of sufficient intimacy with you to warrant it,' she replied stiltedly at last, and regretted the words even before she saw the glint of his sardonic smile.

'I'm prepared to become as intimate with you as you wish,' he said almost idly. 'But I confess I'm surprised you wish to go to such lengths merely to justify yourself in calling me Troy.'

'You know perfectly well I didn't mean that,' she said, her cheeks hot.

He laughed. 'Wouldn't it be easier to stop this fencing and do as I ask?'

'Perhaps,' she replied stonily. 'But I don't regard that as a valid reason for obeying you.'

'And what would you regard as a valid reason?' He drew sharply on the cheroot he was smoking.

'Loving you,' she almost and disastrously said, but bit the words back just in time before they could become yet another target for his sardonic amusement.

'I can't think of any,' she said lamely at last, as the lengthening silence showed signs of becoming embarrassing.

'Not even the expressed wishes of your parents?' His voice was deceptively soft and she looked at him in sudden alarm.

'I—I don't know what you mean.'

'No?' His smile was not pleasant. 'Then your efforts

51

to charm me last night—that dress, your perfume, your whole manner—were not part of a campaign to persuade me to prop up your father's ailing bank? My apologies for having totally misread the situation.'

She sat stricken for a moment, then very carefully replaced her coffee cup on the tray while she tried to calm the tumult within her his words had aroused. Her dominant feeling was one of total humiliation—for having allowed herself to be involved in the scheme in the first place, and for having failed. She had done her best for her father's sake, but her best had not been good enough. What fools they had been to imagine even for a moment that they could pull the wool over the eyes of a man like Andreakis! Tears of mortification pricked at her eyelids. She tried to smile, to treat the whole thing as a joke instead of the disaster it was.

'Was I so obvious?' She attempted to speak normally in spite of the appalling dryness of her throat.

The dark eyes bored relentlessly into her. 'Not you alone.'

'I see.' She was silent for a moment. 'I—I've no excuse to make, Mr Andreakis. It was just that my father's—a sick man and I love him very much. I'd do anything for him.' She stopped short, her face flaming, as the man beside her moved, suddenly, restlessly. Far better if she had remained silent than have embarked on a naïve, foolish attempt to gain his sympathy. The fact that it was true would not concern a man like Andreakis, she thought bitterly. There was no point in hoping that he would help her father now. On the contrary, she could visualise the saturnine pleasure that refusal would bring him. Hadn't he already warned her that he liked to win? This victory would cost him little.

'Shall we go?' He drained his cup and set it back on the tray. Lacey stared at him nonplussed.

'Go—where?'

'On to the coast. That was the plan, if you remember.' He stood up, shrugging his broad shoulders into the leather coat.

She looked down at the carpet. 'I think I'd prefer to go home.'

'Oh, I have no doubt of that,' he said coolly. 'But you promised me a day in your company, and I intend to hold you to your word.'

'I wouldn't have thought my company had a great deal of appeal for you.' She hated his tallness, the way he towered over her. It reminded her of the previous night when she had been as helpless as a doll against his strength.

'I think I have yet to learn what your company is.' His dark eyes were brooding as they went over her. 'In the past twenty-four hours I've encountered a hostile chambermaid, a fledgling seductress and a sulky schoolgirl. Which of them is the nearest to reality, I wonder?' He paused, but Lacey did not reply. 'I suspect it was the girl who played the piano for us all and then ran away. You care for your music very much, I think.'

'I wanted to make it my life,' she said desolately, and stopped, horrified at the pain she had let him see.

'You seem to thrive on fantasy, *pethi mou*,' he said bleakly. 'Some time, you should try the real world. It may not be as bad as you think. Permit me.'

She stood awkwardly, trying not to flinch away as he helped her on with her coat.

'Besides,' that note of amusement she so disliked was back in his voice, 'you should not be so eager to escape from me. Hasn't it occurred to you that I might still be persuaded to help your father—if the terms were right? I am sure you have not reached the limits of your persuasiveness.'

She faced him stonily. 'And hasn't it occurred to you, Mr Andreakis, that this is the very reason why I didn't want to be alone with you ever again? Last night I—made a mistake which I shall always regret. But you insult me if you think I might be willing to compound that error today.'

He smiled oddly. 'Everything is different in daylight, *pethi mou*—is it not? If you must know, I too regret last night, but for a very different reason.'

She felt her cheeks grow warm again as she walked ahead of him into the foyer and towards the door. His meaning was obvious, she thought angrily. He regretted that her complete seduction had not been an accomplished fact. But not because she meant anything to him as a woman. Oh no, she did not flatter herself to that extent. Simply because, as he'd said himself, he liked to win.

She had hoped against hope that he would change his mind and take her home in the face of her implacable hostility, but it was the coast road he took again as they left the car park, and she was forced to resign herself to the realisation that he meant what he said. She wondered whether anyone had ever succeeded in defying him, or even merely diverting him from some course of action that he had decided on, and thought it was doubtful in the extreme. She stole a sideways look at him from beneath her lashes, noting the harsh lines of his mouth and the jut of his chin. He was like some dark eagle, brooding and remorseless, she thought, then jeered at herself for allowing her imagination to run away with her. He was just so different from her limited experience of men, she told herself emphatically, comparing him mentally with her bluff good-natured father and Alan's rather tentative approach.

She was thankful that he did not attempt to start any more conversations. He had been right about one thing at least. It was much easier not to fence with him.

It was warm in the car and in spite of herself she found her eyelids beginning to droop. She forced them open and hastily pulled herself into a more upright position on the thickly padded seat. But the comfort of the car allied to her restless night and the strenuous couple of hours she had put in earlier at the stables were all combining to bring about her downfall, and within five minutes that insidious drowsiness had crept over her again. This time, she succumbed.

When she opened her eyes again, the car was motionless, and she was alone. She struggled up to peer through the windscreen, thrusting her hair back off her face. The car was off the road, she realised, and parked on the short stubby grass that led to the dunes. Troy Andreakis was nowhere in sight, and after a slight hesitation, Lacey opened her door and got out.

The air felt icy and invigorating after the stuffy atmosphere of the car and Lacey felt her sleepiness dissolving away as the salt-filled wind buffeted her. She walked briskly up to the top of the dunes, screwing up her eyes against the flying particles of sand borne by the wind and wishing she had brought her dark glasses to protect them, or at least a scarf to control her flying hair. The early promise of the day had given way to greyness and a hint of rain to come. The sea was grey too and tumbling, flecked with white horses to the horizon. Troy Andreakis stood down by the water's edge, his back turned to her and the deserted beach, staring out across the empty tossing sea.

She thought involuntarily, 'He looks so alone,' and lifted her hands to her mouth to call him, closing them dazedly over her lips instead when she realised what she had been going to do. Either she was still half asleep, or else she was a complete fool, she told herself vehemently. Besides— she felt a sudden need for self-justification—even if she had called to him, the wind would have carried her voice away and he would never have heard her.

Almost as if he could read her thoughts, he turned and looked at her and she saw him lift a hand to acknowledge her presence. Slowly and reluctantly Lacey gave a half wave, then as he began to come back across the beach with his long easy stride, she turned abruptly to go back the way she had come, moving unwarily, forgetful of the soft, treacherous sand. The dune began to crumble and though she threw out a wild hand at a tuft of tall grass to save herself, she found herself sliding ignominiously, half covered in sand, to the beach below. Before she could drag herself free, he was beside her, his hands hard as he lifted her bodily out of the sand and set her on her feet.

She had wrenched her ankle as the sand started to slide, and she winced slightly as she tested her foot on the ground.

'You are hurt?'

'It's nothing. I should have taken more care.' She could not tell him that it had been a sudden, illogical need to run from him that had got her into this predicament, but she stood smouldering with resentment as he went down on one knee to examine her ankle with practised fingers.

'No bones broken,' he commented, standing up and brushing the sand from his pants.

'I never thought there would be,' she returned coldly.

He gestured towards the dunes. 'Do you wish me to carry you back to the car?'

'No,' she said sharply, and could have kicked herself when she saw the mockery leap in his eyes.

'It was only a chivalrous offer, *pethi mou*. This is hardly the ideal moment for making love among the sand. I have Greek blood in my veins, but not Spartan. You are quite safe to accept my help, I promise you.'

She had to admit that she was glad of his supporting arm as he assisted her to limp up the slope and across the grass to the car. She was not badly hurt, but her ankle was throbbing sufficiently to make her quite thankful to collapse back on to the car seat.

'Your accident has not spoiled your appetite, I hope,' he remarked, sliding in beside her.

'I wasn't hungry before it happened,' she replied coolly.

He shrugged. 'Then you will have to watch me eat.'

But Lacey's stubborn resolution to do precisely that vanished when they arrived in the small village on the other side of the bay, and he parked outside the small quayside hotel advertising bar lunches. Pride seemed unimportant compared to the bowls of thick home-made broth they were brought, and the wedges of French bread packed with ham, lettuce and chicken and served with a variety of delicious pickles.

Eventually Lacey leaned back against the wooden settle with a sigh of repletion. 'That was wonderful!'

'I am relieved. I could hardly have returned you to your father unfed as well as injured.'

She ignored the satirical note in his voice and drank the rest of her tomato juice. She had almost allowed herself to forget that sooner or later she would have to tell her father and Michelle that their hopes of persuading Troy Andreakis to lend financial aid to Vernon—Carey had sadly misfired. She shivered inwardly as she remembered Michelle's insistence that she was prepared to go to any lengths to save the bank from ruin. She did not relish her stepmother's probable reaction to the news that last night's charade had been a complete fiasco. And she would almost certainly be blamed for the failure, with a certain amount of justice, she supposed unhappily, because she could not pretend that her heart had been in the scheme. She had simply not been capable of sustaining the role Michelle had wanted her to play. Almost any of the girls she had known at the convent would have managed it better, she thought drearily.

'What's the matter?'

Shaken out of her thoughts, she glanced up startled into the dark brilliance of his gaze.

'Er—nothing,' she responded lamely.

He sighed sharply. 'Why do you lie to me? Your face is a mirror to your thoughts and I can tell that you are in trouble. And don't say that it is my presence that bothers you. A moment ago you were almost in charity with me.'

'I've told you—it's nothing,' she repeated stubbornly, and saw the angry compression of his mouth.

'*Poli kalo*,' he said icily, and turned to reach for his wallet from the inside pocket of his driving coat. Lacey turned away too and looked out of the window, lashed by the rain which had begun in earnest while they were eating their meal. It was as if the weather was reflecting her own disquiet, and the storm she knew would be waiting for her when they got back to Kings Winston, she thought miserably.

Lacey stood staring out of the drawing room window into the gathering dusk. She had just spent over an hour at the piano trying to force her oddly lethargic fingers through the limbering exercises of scales and studies, but had eventually given up in disgust.

The inquisition she had dreaded had failed to materialise so far. When she had arrived back at the house with Troy Andreakis after a long drive in almost total silence, it was to find that Michelle had taken the car and gone shopping in Westford, while Sir James was resting in his room according to his specialist's instructions.

Lacey knew that in her stepmother's absence it was up to her to fill the role of hostess and see that their guest was properly entertained, but the thought of having to spend any more time exclusively in his company frankly appalled her. Probably he felt the same, she thought, for he had not shown as much as a flicker of resentment when she had rather defiantly announced her intention of going upstairs to have a bath and change her clothes.

Nor had he joined her later for afternoon tea which Mrs Osborne had served in the drawing room. Her father too had been absent, and when Lacey inquired for him, the housekeeper mentioned that she believed he was in the billiards room with Mr Andreakis. Lacey wondered as she sipped her tea and ate one of the featherlight scones whether it was really billiards or a game for much higher stakes that was being fought out behind the closed door. It sent a little chill of apprehension curling along her spine, but she knew that whatever happened she was powerless to intervene.

She knew that it was anxiety that had come between her and her music. Even as she touched the keys, she found herself wondering whether the piano would be hers for very much longer. If Vernon–Carey was ruined, as now seemed likely, she supposed they would lose everything, including this house where she had been born. It was an agonising thought, but it had to be faced.

She was almost relieved when the shrill of the telephone broke in on her brooding thoughts, and a faint smile touched her mouth when she heard Alan's voice at the other end.

'Lacey? Great news. Domino has foaled—a little filly. How about coming out with me this evening to celebrate? Funds are a bit low, but I can manage a visit to the new Chinese restaurant in Westford if that would appeal to you.'

Lacey was hardly in a mood to celebrate, but she could sympathise with Alan's delight over the new foal, and she had to admit that she would be glad to escape from the uncomfortable atmosphere that reigned over the house—as if it was waiting, hushed, for news of some disaster. It would also mean a further delay in the inevitable inquisition as to why her stepmother's scheme to save the family fortunes had gone wrong.

Alan was obviously delighted at her agreement to go out with him, and arranged to call for her in about an hour's time. Lacey decided that the dark green dress she was wearing with the long tight-fitting sleeves and slightly flared skirt would be ideal, topped with her new coat. She would put on some make-up, and brush her hair out of its neat ponytail, she thought, and turned towards the stairs to go to her room.

'Lacey.' Her father's voice reached her from his open study door. 'Can you spare me a few minutes, my dear? I want to talk to you.'

'Of course, Daddy.' She walked across the hall into the study, shutting the door behind her. 'I hope it won't take too long. Alan's calling for me just after seven, and I have to get ready.'

'Young Trevor?' Her father pursed his lips slightly. 'I didn't know that you were seeing him.'

'Well, he's only just rung up,' Lacey said, a little puzzled. 'There's nothing wrong, is there, Daddy? I've been out with Alan before and you've never objected. After all, I've known him all my life.'

'Yes, of course.' Sir James rubbed his chin in the way that Lacey knew meant that he was upset and worried, and her heart lurched anxiously for him.

'Daddy love, sit down,' she begged. 'I hope you haven't been overdoing things.' As she spoke, her eyes fell on the whisky decanter on his desk and the used glass beside it, and she gave a little cry of distress. 'Whisky in the afternoon—Daddy! You know what the specialist said.'

'Damn the specialist,' Sir James said roundly. 'If I need a whisky I'll have one, and that's all there is to it.'

Lacey sighed inwardly. She knew it was imperative not to argue with him or allow him to become upset, but at times he made this very difficult.

'Anyway, I haven't asked you in here to discuss my daily habits,' he went on, his temper still dangerously near the surface. 'Something has happened this afternoon that it's only right you should know about at once, as you'll be the person most nearly affected.'

'It's all right, Daddy. I know what's happened.' Lacey

felt uncannily calm. 'I'm sorry everything went wrong last night, but I honestly don't think it would ever have worked. He's—he's the wrong sort of man ...'

'What in the world are you talking about?' her father said testily. 'I thought everything went well. I must say, Lacey, I was damnably proud of you. Perhaps that dress was a little extreme—but I dare say you and your stepmother know more about that than I do.'

Lacey stared at him, her lips parted. 'But Daddy, it was a failure—a total disaster! I didn't convince Mr Andreakis for a minute. He knew I disliked him and he went out of his way to humiliate me.' She swallowed nervously. 'He—he even tried to make love to me.'

'A not unnatural reaction under the circumstances,' Sir James said drily, but Lacey realised incredulously that he was smiling. Then he had known after all what Michelle intended, she thought despairingly.

She moved towards him. 'Daddy, what I'm trying to tell you is that he knows that last night was a put-up job, and that I was only trying to get round him for your sake. But it didn't work. Vernon–Carey can sink as far as he's concerned, I know that. You don't have to shield me from the truth ...'

Her voice tailed away in bewilderment in the face of her father's open amusement.

'Oh, my dear Lacey! No wonder Andreakis finds your innocence such a delight.'

'My—innocence?' Her heart was thudding queerly and painfully. 'What do you mean?'

'We've had a long talk this afternoon, Andreakis and I.' He came over and stroked her cheek affectionately. 'A long talk. I don't think you need to worry about Vernon–Carey, my dear. There'll be no shortage of confidence once the word gets around that Troy Andreakis has become a member of the family as well as the board.'

'A member of the family?' she repeated, numb with disbelief at the terrible realisation that was beginning slowly to dawn on her.

'Oh, I know he hasn't spoken to you yet. But he's acted correctly according to the customs prevailing in his own part of the world. Arranged marriages are still very much the thing in Greece, you know.'

'I don't understand.' She was lying, willing the truth away, refusing to accept the unmistakable implication in her father's words.

'Oh, come, my dear.' He smiled at her fondly but with a slight trace of irritation. 'I'm sure I don't have to spell it out for you. Besides, Andreakis himself would prefer to do that, I have no doubt. He has asked for you to become his wife in return for a major investment in Vernon–Carey and a seat on the board.'

The room swam dizzily in front of her, and she had to seize the back of a nearby chair for support. She heard herself cry out 'No!' and her father's face darken angrily.

'No? Are you completely mad, girl? He's offering us all a lifeline and you want to throw it back in his face!'

'I—I can't help it.' Lacey was crying now, the tears spilling endlessly down the pallor of her face. 'You can't make me do this, Daddy—please! Promise him anything else—anything he wants—but not me. Please—not me!'

'He doesn't want anything else,' Sir James thundered, then stopped abruptly, making his way rather unsteadily to the nearest chair and half collapsing into it.

'Daddy, you're ill!' Lacey rushed to his side, her own misery forgotten in anxiety for her father.

'What do you expect?' He closed his eyes, waving her away from him. 'We're offered a solution to all our worries and for purely selfish reasons you decide instead to plunge us all into ruin and chaos.'

Lacey knelt beside his chair, the words beating and reverberating in her brain. 'Ruin and chaos—selfish—a solution.' But at what cost to herself? she thought, a huge sob rising in her throat.

'You don't understand,' she said unsteadily.

'You're damned right, I don't. Good God, you get the sort of offer that most girls only dream about, and you don't want to know about it. What have you got against him?'

She stared unhappily at the carpet. 'He's a stranger. And—he frightens me.'

There was a pause, then her father stirred restlessly.

'Well, naturally, you'll be given time to get to know him. He's not a barbarian. As for frightening you,' he gave her a shrewd glance, 'he's well aware of your youth and—inexperience. He'll make allowances, I'm sure.'

Will he? she thought, remembering with despair the hardness of the mouth that had crushed hers, the cruel strength of his hands and arms.

'But why me?' She stared appealingly up at her father. 'He must know a dozen girls in Greece who would make him a suitable wife—who would understand this—arrangement.'

'Ah, but he isn't wholly Greek,' her father said slowly. 'His mother was an American, and this is one of the reasons ...'

'Yes?' Dry-eyed now, she prompted him.

'He has a young sister, half American like himself. When their mother died, she left a letter asking her sister to bring the little girl up in California. Andreakis' father agreed—reluctantly—but it was not a success. According to Andreakis the girl has been allowed to do as she likes, spoiled beyond reason by this aunt. There was a court case some time ago and Andreakis managed to gain the custody of the the girl, who's about fifteen now. She had tried to run off and join some sort of commune and he was able to prove that the aunt was not exercising proper control. Consequently his sister is now coming to live with him at his villa on Theros.'

'She has my sympathy,' Lacey said bitterly.

Her father snorted impatiently. 'It's not your sympathy he wants, it's your companionship. He feels that someone of your age might be able to bring more influence to bear on the girl than an older woman who might try to be too restrictive and rigid.'

Lacey touched his sleeve eagerly. 'But if that's all he wants, a companion for his sister, couldn't I just be that? I'd willingly be that, until she's old enough to marry the man he no doubt has picked out for her,' she added bitterly. 'Surely I don't need to marry him myself.'

'Don't be a fool.' Sir James looked down at her coldly. 'That isn't the only reason he wants to marry you. You're

62

not blind, Lacey, nor do you suffer from false modesty, I should hope. You're a lovely girl, and you're going to be a beautiful woman. It's perfectly natural that he should want you for himself.'

She controlled an involuntary shiver as the realisation of what being the wife of a man like Troy Andreakis would entail came home to her.

'I need time,' she said dully. 'Time to think.'

'Well, of course.' There was a pause, then he said rather awkwardly, 'I'm sure I don't have to repeat, Lacey, how important this decision is for us all. Not merely your step-mother and myself, but for the bank as well. A great many people are depending on your answer, my dear. I wouldn't suggest any course of action that I didn't think would be for your good as well. After all, you have no career to think of, and you are bound to marry eventually. For my part, I would be thankful to know you were being so amply pro-tected and provided for now that I can no longer guarantee to do so for very much longer.'

She looked at him, startled. He had always been so dis-missive about his ill-health. This was the first indication he had given her that he knew just how precarious his health was. But she knew better than to irritate him by probing further. She got up slowly.

'I'll think about it, Daddy,' she said very quietly. 'But I must have time. And now I'd better go and get ready. Alan will be here soon.'

'Do you still intend to spend the evening with him?' Her father gave a swift frown. 'I hardly think that's wise.'

'Because my prospective bridegroom might object?' Lacey gave a little wintry smile. 'My promise to Alan was made before I knew anything about this, and Mr Andreakis is a great believer in promises being kept, so he should understand.' She bent and gave her father a light kiss, be-fore leaving the room.

Outside the study, she leaned against the closed door for a moment, shutting her eyes. Time, she found herself think-ing. Time to consider, yes—but also time to escape.

CHAPTER FOUR

'But that's barbaric!' Alan declared. 'I've never heard anything like it in this day and age. You're surely not going to go through with it.'

Lacey bit her lip, thankful that the restaurant was only half full and that no one was really within earshot of their small alcove table. She wished she had chosen a less public spot to warn Alan about Troy Andreakis' plans for her future, but he had been so obviously full of schemes of his own for her entertainment that she had felt it was only fair to tell him and not allow him to build up his hopes too much. In any case, she was not altogether sure that she wanted Alan to monopolise her so completely. She could not visualise their relationship ever deepening, on her side at least, into anything other than the pleasant, undemanding companionship they shared now.

She had also the problem of only being able to tell Alan half the story. There were so many facets of the situation that had to remain taboo to outsiders, the Vernon—Carey involvement being the main one.

'I haven't decided yet what I'm going to do,' she said, staring at the patterned weave of the white tablecloth. 'I—I shall have to think it over very carefully, of course ...'

'I don't see there's anything to think over.' Alan gave a short laugh. 'It may be the Greek way of arranging things, but it's not ours. I'm surprised your father even mentioned it to you. He can't want you to marry a complete stranger— someone of a different nationality, a different culture even.'

'He's only half Greek.' Lacey attributed her defensiveness to the implied criticism of her father in Alan's remarks. 'His mother was an American.'

Alan shrugged. 'Maybe so, but that doesn't explain why he thinks you're the person to help keep this sister of his in line. I should have thought a strict Greek sister-in-law would have been a far better bet. I mean, what notice is she going to take of someone your age?'

'Probably none.' Lacey's tone was wry. 'But I suppose he feels I might be more of an influence than a Greek girl who would probably disapprove openly of everything she did and put her back up at once.'

Alan gave her a narrow glance. 'If it wasn't so crazy, I'd say you were seriously considering this. You certainly seem to be weighing up the pros and cons.'

Lacey sighed. 'I promised Daddy I would think it over, but that doesn't mean my attitude has basically altered from what it was when he first mentioned it.'

'Then you're definitely going to turn him down,' he said hopefully.

Lacey bent her head. 'It's not as simple as that, Alan. Please don't ask me to explain, but I should need a very good reason to refuse.'

'I should think you had at least a dozen.' Alan stared at her. 'Heading the list,' he counted off on his fingers. 'You hardly know the man—and what you know, you don't like. I would have thought that was enough. After all, his money can't mean anything to you.'

Not to me, no, Lacey thought bitterly. But it means everything to Vernon—Carey, and that seems to balance out anything else.

She said listlessly, 'Perhaps when he knows me better, he'll change his mind anyway.'

Alan snorted. 'And perhaps he won't. He's not a fool. I—I don't think any man would ever change his mind about wanting you, Lacey.'

'Oh, Alan,' she said helplessly as his hand covered hers.

'I know it's much too soon,' he said, his colour heightened. 'I didn't want to rush you into anything, but when I heard you were coming home for good, I couldn't help thinking ... I've always thought, Lacey, that one day it might be—you and me. And if your father knew that, it might make a difference.'

'That's very sweet of you, Alan,' she said gently. 'But I can't take advantage of you like that. You're only just twenty after all, and you have years before you need think of getting married. Besides, what would your mother and father say?'

'Oh, well,' he said with an assumed nonchalance. 'I'm sure they would soon come round. They're very fond of you, Lacey.'

'Yes, but hardly fond enough to accept me being foisted on them as an unwanted daughter-in-law,' she pointed out, and knew she had not imagined the fleeting expression of relief that came into his eyes.

'I didn't think you'd agree at once,' he said. 'But at least it's an alternative if you get desperate. And if you should change your mind, you only have to tell me. I can't offer you the material advantages that he can, of course, but I'm not trying to buy you either.'

That was true, she thought, but Alan did not know that she was for sale, and bitterness choked her again.

They talked of other things then, as they drank their coffee, and later as they drove home in Alan's Landrover through the dark lanes—a coming party at the Faircloughs' and the point-to-point being organised by the local hunt. Safe, impersonal topics about which she could talk and laugh while her tired brain seemed to circle endlessly on the treadmill of her problems.

There was no oblivion to be gained, even when Alan parked the Landrover on the broad gravel sweep in front of her house and drew her into his arms. Lacey went reluctantly, wishing that he had not insisted on the intimacy of an embrace, and remained passive under his kiss. But Alan did not seem put down by her lack of response.

'Oh, Lacey,' he looked down into her face, 'you're so sweet.' And his lips crushed hers again, more fiercely. 'I think this is what sickens me the most. The thought of a man like that—with you!' He laughed almost savagely. 'I suppose that's the Greek side of his nature—the double standard. One code of behaviour for men, and another for women.'

'Alan, please.' She tried to free herself as gently as she could. 'I—I don't want to talk about it any more, and anyway I must go in. It's getting late.'

'Oh, all right,' he said, a little sulkily. 'I'll phone you tomorrow, then. After all, he doesn't own you yet.'

'No, not yet,' she said.

She stood on the gravel watching the tail light of the Landrover disappear round the curve of the drive, then walked up the wide shallow stone steps that led to the front door and let herself into the house.

It was dark in the hall, and quiet. Distantly she could hear a faint sound of music, and knew that her father and Michelle would be in the sitting room, doubtless watching television with their guest. Her lips tightened. She would not join them, even if she was laying herself open to an accusation of bad manners. She would simply slip quietly up to her room before anyone realised she was home.

But just as she reached the bottom of the stairs, the hall was suddenly flooded with light, dazzling her and making her stumble slightly. She turned in alarm and saw Troy Andreakis standing outside her father's study, his hand still on the light switch.

'You—you startled me!' Even to her own ears, her voice sounded high and unnatural.

'You startled me,' he returned coolly. 'That coat and all that pale hair—you're like a little ghost slipping into the house.'

She flushed slightly. He must know that she was trying to avoid him, and yet he would not allow her to escape a confrontation between them.

He walked unhurriedly across the hall and stood looking at her. In spite of the fact that she was on the bottom step, he could still look down at her, she thought with a flash of irritation. It was not merely the ruthlessness she sensed in his personality that troubled her, it was this physical power that he possessed and the knowledge that he had the strength to force her to his will.

'Well, have you nothing to say to me, Lacey *mou?*' The dark brilliance of his eyes searched her face, pausing with suddenly sharpened intensity on her mouth, its soft rose blurred and smudged, she realised with something like panic, by Alan's ardour.

Almost instinctively, she lifted her hand to hide her lips, embarrassed at the betrayal of smeared lipstick, only to find her wrist seized in a grip that bruised her flesh and forced an involuntary cry from her.

67

'Do they stir your blood—that boy's kisses?' he said almost meditatively, but with a note in his voice that chilled her.

'You have no right to ask that.' She tried unavailingly to pull herself free. 'I don't belong to you.'

'Not yet,' he said softly. 'But you will do—isn't that so, *pethi mou*? That's why I have been waiting for you to return, so that you could tell me so.'

'But I can't answer you now—not yet,' she said almost wildly. 'I must have time . . . I told my father.'

'Oh, I know what you told your father.' His eyes glinted dangerously. 'But I am not impressed by your excuses. You are not a fool and you have a simple choice to make. It's not time you need, but resolution.'

'You're so sure that I'll agree.' She stared angrily at him.

'As I said, *pethi mou*, you're not a fool.'

'But even you must see that we ought to wait—at least get to know each other before . . .'

'I fail to see why. What we need to know of each other can be learned as well after marriage as before.'

'But isn't that how we do things in this country.' She was close to tears of desperation.

'Another argument that fails to impress me.' His voice was ironic. 'Our marriages may be arranged, but they remain stable. The divorce rate in this country is soaring.'

'You think you have an answer for everything, don't you?' she said, dully. 'But nothing you can say changes the fact that I don't love you, and I never will.'

'Never is a long time,' he said slowly. 'How can you be so sure?'

'Because I know myself,' she told him defiantly.

'Do you, Lacey *mou*?' His smile mocked her. 'And if I tell you that you have emotions and feelings you are not even aware of yet, might you not be willing to concede that —ultimately—they might make a difference?'

'No!' she flung at him. 'Besides, I might not be quite as inexperienced as you seem to think.'

His smile deepened. 'Any doubts I might have had on that score were satisfied when I held you in my arms,' he said coolly. 'It was a piquant contrast, believe me, the provocation of your dress and manner compared with the total innocence I found on your lips. If you had not been totally untouched, *pethi mou*, do you imagine I would have asked you to marry me?'

She gasped. 'Are you saying that if I'd ... if I wasn't ...'

'A virgin,' he supplied smoothly, his eyes lazily appreciating the heightened flush on her cheeks. 'Does it disturb you that I am sufficiently Greek to require chastity as a desirable attribute in my bride? When I said that knowing could best be learned after marriage I did not just mean discovering each other's tastes in food and furnishings, you know.'

For a moment she stared at him incredulously, then she bent her head, covering her burning face with her hands.

From what seemed a great distance, she heard his voice again. 'Consider your virginity as your dowry, Lacey *mou*. I ask for nothing more.'

'Good.' She had to force the word from her tightened throat. 'Then you won't also expect my willing submission.'

His eyebrows lifted lazily. 'Oh, that, my fierce angel, I think I can achieve for myself.'

His fingers, warm and caressing, lifted the pale fall of her hair and touched the back of her neck in a long, slow whisper along her skin. And awoke in turn a quiver of response that curled along her spine and ignited every nerve ending in her body before, appalled at her own reaction, she could tear herself from his reach. She heard his laughter follow her up the stairs as she ran from him.

There was a large tree overhanging the end of the drive and Lacey was grateful for its shelter from the slight chilly drizzle that was falling as she stood, waiting for Alan, her body huddled inside the warmth of her sheepskin coat. Her escape had been altogether easier than she had supposed. She had merely pleaded a headache soon after dinner.

Beyond inquiring if she had anything to take for it, and expressing the hope that it would not develop into the 'flu that was currently sweeping through the village, Michelle had taken little interest, and Lacey was sure that her stepmother would not be sufficiently concerned to check on her later in the evening. That meant she was safe at least until breakfast-time.

A slight shiver that had nothing to do with the penetrating cold of the wind ran through her body. She did not want to think about the following morning and what it would bring. More particularly she did not want to consider the night that was to precede it, but she realised reluctantly that it was something that had to be faced.

In the week that had passed since she had fled from Troy Andreakis, she had had plenty of time to think—to plan the act that would place her beyond his reach quite inevitably, but she had not permitted herself to dwell too fully on the other consequences of her scheme.

She wrapped her arms tightly across her breasts, trying to control the tremor of her senses. Alan was late. Oh, why didn't he come, before this introspection that threatened to possess her destroyed her courage, and sent her back to the house and the destiny she was trying so hard to elude?

Surely he couldn't have changed his mind. He had openly expressed his doubts about what they were trying to do, but she thought she had managed to convince him that the urgency of her situation demanded drastic action. And he had said that he loved her, and would do anything for her—even risk the wrath of both their families by this forced elopement. Perhaps he was hurt that she wanted to go away with him principally to avoid marriage with another man, rather than for himself alone. Yet he had said he would take her on any terms—unlike the Andreakis man whose uncompromising attitude was forcing her into the headlong flight. God, how she hated him! She wondered how that sensual arrogance of his would serve him, when he learned she had deliberately given the virginity he prized so highly to another man in order to escape him.

And he would know it. That was why she and Alan had arranged to spend this particular night together, the night before Andreakis arrived to stay for the weekend, and find out her answer to his proposal of marriage, her father had warned her. He would know exactly what she thought of him and his degrading offer—tomorrow.

A drop of water found its way under her collar and ran down her back, and she blamed this for the sudden chill that seemed to grip her. After all, her knowledge of the basic facts of the physical relationship between men and women was adequate. It was her inexperience of the emotions that should accompany such a relationship that frightened her, she realised reluctantly, particularly after the revealing glimpse she had been afforded into the possibilities of her own feelings and desires. And this by a man she despised.

She tried to comfort herself with the reflection that at least it would not be the terrifying Troy Andreakis who would be responsible for her initiation. The taunt he had flung at her on the stairs would never be made reality, she thought with a kind of fierce triumph.

And she was fond of Alan—of course she was. They had been friends since childhood, and he was as familiar to her as a brother in many ways. Yet the role he was about to take in her life was the opposite of brotherly, she realised miserably. She supposed that she was experiencing bridal nerves—except that she was not going to be a bride, or at least, not at once.

Lacey was only concerned with the immediate future, and putting herself once and for all beyond the reach of Troy Andreakis. Up to now she had resolutely ignored the questions in her own mind about what would happen when she and Alan returned to Kings Winston. She tried to still her conscience by insisting that perhaps her father would not be too angry. Alan's parents were not poor, after all, although the kind of wealth and position enjoyed by Andreakis was totally beyond their reach.

Her confidence was bolstered too by the fact that strong hints of the Andreakis involvement in a rescue of Vernon–Carey had appeared in the financial pages of several leading newspapers in the past few days. Obviously he thought their bargain was sealed, and that her consent was simply a matter of form. It was doubtful whether he would back down from his agreement to help her father now, and risk the revelations that consequent publicity might bring. No man in his position would want the world to know that he had been made a fool of by a girl not yet eighteen.

And ultimately, she supposed rather dully, her father would agree to her marriage with Alan, however little it might fit in with his plans. After all, and Lacey felt a sudden surge of heat flooding through her body at the thought, after tonight there might not just be Alan and herself to consider.

As for Alan himself, he would never have cause to regret their relationship, she told herself resolutely. She would make him a good wife, and if there was a baby . . . She bit her lip. She would cross that bridge when she came to it.

It was incredible that only weeks ago she had been secure in the convent with little beyond her music to occupy her mind. Now she was contemplating marriage and motherhood, without any real desire for either of them.

She saw the headlights of an approaching vehicle and shrank further into the concealment of the hedge. But it was the Landrover with Alan at the wheel, and she picked up her small weekend case and stepped out to meet him, forcing a smile to her dry mouth.

He stowed her case in the back of the vehicle and opened the door on the passenger side for her. He looked very sober, and unusually pale, she thought with a pang of real tenderness. Was she being altogether fair to expose him to this unwanted upheaval in his life? Alan, she knew, would have preferred a leisurely engagement with celebratory parties given by their respective families and congratulatory announcements in the papers and at the Hunt Ball to underline how lucky he considered himself to have won the girl he wanted. She was spoiling all those dreams for him.

He climbed into the driving seat and slammed his door, not looking at her. For a moment, he sat quite still and then he said quietly, 'Lacey, are you sure you want to go through with this?'

'Quite sure.' The firmness of the words belied the slight tremor in her voice and, shrugging, he leaned forward to release the handbrake. They were just moving forward when a car, its headlights full on, overtook them on the narrow road. Its horn blared in warning and Alan swore under his breath, pulling the wheel over until the Landrover scraped along the hedge.

'That was close.' Lacey found she was trembling, as the other vehicle's tail lights disappeared into the darkness.

'My fault,' Alan muttered. 'I—I didn't signal I was pulling out. It was a good job that chap had his wits about him.'

'I hope it wasn't anyone we know,' Lacey said, the thought of recognition and discovery big in her mind, but Alan shook his head.

'If it had been one of the neighbours, they would have stopped and given me a blasting,' he said.

More in control of himself now, he re-started the Landrover and drove off. He seemed disinclined to chat as they wove their way through the dark and dripping lanes to the main road and Lacey was glad. As it was the swish of the tyres on the wet road, and the rhythmic click of the windscreen wipers, had an oddly soothing effect and she even began to feel drowsy.

They drove through the village and turned north, heading for the major roads and the eventual motorway. The traffic began to get heavier and Lacey blinked sleepily at the approaching headlights and the dazzle on the road. She felt more relaxed now and the silence between Alan and herself was beginning to be embarrassing.

'Where are we going to stay?' she asked, glad that it was dark and he could not see her instinctive blush.

'I thought we would go up to the motel at the service centre. They'll be less likely to ask questions,' Alan said drily, and Lacey sat back again, feeling guilty at having put him in a situation where he had to use a deceit that was foreign to his nature.

'I—I've brought you a ring,' he went on, after a pause. 'It's only a signet ring, but I think it will fit your finger, and you can turn it round so that the signet part doesn't show before we go in.'

Lacey was silent for a moment, then she said in a small voice, 'That was thoughtful of you, Alan.'

He sighed impatiently. 'I don't suppose it will deceive anyone really. I'm bound to say or do something that will give us away. I'm just not used ...' He broke off abruptly and Lacey guessed he was embarrassed at not being able to assume the mantle of a man of the world for her sake. Dear Alan, she thought. It's so wrong to use him like this, but what else can I do?

They drove in silence again after that and Lacey allowed her drowsiness to conquer her overwrought nerves and slept for a while. She awoke when a sudden swing of the vehicle threw her slightly against Alan and realised they were turning into a large car park.

'Well, we're here,' Alan said gruffly. 'If you like to hang on, I'll go and fix everything up.'

She nodded mutely and after a brief hesitation, he got out of the Landrover and walked away towards the large garishly lit building in front of them. It was everything Lacey most hated, all glass and concrete with neon lights flashing, yet it was somehow right. If Alan had taken her to some quiet country hotel, she would have felt even worse than she was feeling now, she realised.

'I'm doing a sordid thing,' she thought. 'So how can I complain if the setting is sordid too?'

He was a long time away and she was just beginning to get nervous, wondering whether the management were demanding to see their marriage certificate, when his large figure loomed out of the misty drizzle. He dropped a key attached to a large plastic tag into her lap.

'We're on the second floor,' he said. 'The lift's right opposite the entrance so you won't have to face the reception desk. If you'd like to go on up, I'll put the Landrover away and bring up the cases.'

The room was more pleasant than she had any right to expect, she thought, looking critically round at its oyster walls and the gay cherry-coloured carpet and toning patterned curtains. She avoided looking at the two single beds with their neat candlewick fitted bedspreads and went instead to investigate the small but scrupulously clean bathroom that opened off the bedroom.

She took off her coat and hung it in the fitted wardrobe. There was an electric fire on the wall in addition to the central heating and she found a coin for the meter and

74

switched it on. There was a knock on the door and she scrambled off her knees and went to open it. Alan came in carrying their cases and he gave a surprised whistle as he looked around their accommodation.

Then he saw the beds and Lacey knew that he too was embarrassed. He gestured awkwardly.

'Which one do you ...?'

Flushing, she pointed at the nearest and he swung her case on to it, depositing his own on its twin.

He went over and stood by the fire. 'How about something to eat?'

Lacey realised that in spite of her nervousness she was quite hungry and she nodded, then looked at him in sudden alarm. 'But, Alan—the dining room. There might be someone we know down there.'

'That's true.' He bit his lip. 'Perhaps we could eat up here. Would sandwiches and some coffee do?'

'That would be fine.' She moistened her lips, smiling faintly at him. 'I don't think I could manage a big meal, anyway.'

'Nor could I,' he admitted. 'I'll go down and see what I can arrange, shall I?'

She was just about to point out the telephone on the table between the beds when she realised he was deliberately giving himself an excuse to get out of the room and give her some privacy.

'Yes,' she smiled at him again, this time with real warmth. 'That would be wonderful. Thank you, Alan.'

But the words sounded stilted even to her own ears and she knew she would have to do something to put their relationship on a more relaxed and even intimate footing.

Forcing herself to sound natural, she said, 'Before you go, if you could just manage the hook at the back of my dress. It's a bit awkward to reach.'

'Yes, of course.' He came across the room and she turned her back to him, bending her head a little so that he could reach it more easily. She could feel his hands shaking as he touched her and she wondered wryly which of them was the most nervous about the night to follow.

But she knew at once when, the hook dealt with, his

hands gripped her shoulders and turned her towards him. He was going to kiss her and she knew with a sudden deadly certainty that she did not want him to, and because of that certainty and the panic it aroused she made herself respond with an ardour she had never been further from feeling, putting her arms around him and holding him close.

'Gosh, Lacey!' He let her go at last and stepped backwards. He was smiling and there was something in that smile that suddenly transformed him from the Alan she had known for so long into a new and disconcerting stranger. 'I'd better go for that coffee. That is'—he reached for her again—'if you really want it.'

'Yes, please.' She evaded his seeking hands, forcing a smile to her own lips. 'I really am hungry.'

'So am I.' There was a jauntiness in his words she had never heard before as he went to the door. He smiled at her again. 'Don't take too long.'

'No,' she said dry-mouthed.

She was alone with this nightmare of her own creation. She had committed herself to spending the night with a boy whose desire she did not share, and she had to go through with it. Alan's kiss had told her that there was not the least chance he would allow her to sleep alone. She could not even expect it. She had offered herself to him, after all, and he was going to have to have to bear the main burden of the recriminations in the row that would follow their return, so he would feel entitled to the only reward she could give him.

Perhaps everyone felt like this—the first time, she tried unavailingly to bolster her confidence, and a sob caught in her throat. Clenching her nails into the palms of her hands, she turned determinedly towards her case. Whatever she might feel, the fact remained that Alan would be back soon, and she would prefer to get ready in his absence.

She clicked open the locks and took out her simple towelling bathrobes and matching mules, reaching for the new white broderie anglaise nightdress that should have lain underneath with her toilet bag. But it wasn't there. She shook the robe in case the nightdress had got tangled up in its folds, and groaned aloud. In her hurry, she must have left it behind on her bed at home.

How could she have been such a fool? she thought desperately—and then, unbidden, came the realisation that this was the least of her worries, together with the unwelcome thought of Alan's probable reaction. Colouring furiously, she picked up her robe and slippers and went slowly to the bathroom.

She was thankful to find the bedroom still empty when she returned. She looked in the dressing table mirror at the white, strained face of the girl who was supposed to be eagerly awaiting the return of her lover, and turned away with a shiver, vividly conscious of her body's nakedness under the soft towelling.

She walked over to the window and stood looking down at the service station area which was being used by quite a number of vehicles. She had a sudden urge to dress and rush downstairs and beg the driver of one of those vehicles to take her away from here—take her home. But she knew that such an action would merely be taking her out of the frying pan into the fire.

The hand holding the curtain aside froze as she heard the key turn in the lock behind her and the door open. She could not look round, but went on staring down at the cars and toy figures moving round the petrol pumps and the bustle that she could not hear but which could be no louder than the pounding of her own heart.

He was standing behind her. She could feel his breath warm on her neck, then his hands touched her shoulders lightly, his fingers sliding under the neckline of her robe. She continued to cling to the curtain, willing herself to relax, to endure what was going to follow because it was what she wanted—it really was, only she was being stupid and young and frightened, and there was no need to be frightened of Alan who loved her.

And then with a suddenness that was almost more shocking than action itself, his caressing hands slid down inside her robe, cupping her breasts with a sensual urgency that drew from her at last a cry of outrage and a complete rejection of the madness that had brought her to this situation.

'Alan.' She tore herself away from the intimacy of his caress, forcing herself to turn and face him. 'I'm sorry— but I—I can't . . .'

The words died on her trembling lips, as she stared unbelievingly into the dark, unsmiling face of Troy Andreakis.

CHAPTER FIVE

'You!' The word was almost torn from her throat as she faced him, her hands instinctively gathering the folds of the robe protectively about her body.

The harsh lines of his face had a perceptibly sneering expression as he observed her.

'But of course, *pethi mou*. Whom else did you expect?' His voice was heavy with irony. 'After all, your father must have told you that I intended to see you this weekend. You have chosen a strange rendezvous, I admit, but . . .'

'Oh, stop it!' She pressed her fingers against suddenly throbbing temples. 'Where's Alan? What have you done with him?'

His mouth hardened. 'What do you expect me to have done? Murdered him in a fit of jealous rage? You flatter yourself, my sweet one.' His eyes went over her, their glitter chilling her. 'Besides, if I judged your reaction correctly just now, I have little to be jealous of. He is more to be pitied than blamed, I think.'

'Where is Alan?' she demanded again, her voice rising hysterically.

'On his way back to Kings Winston, nursing a split lip,' he said almost laconically.

'You hurt him!'

'Only a little—a mere trifle compared with the injury he would have done me.' There was no escaping the grimness in his tone—no point in trying to evade his anger by denying what must be self-evident.

'How did you find us?' Suddenly she felt deathly cold. She edged past him and went over to the fire, sinking down in front of it on her knees. 'You couldn't have known —couldn't have guessed . . .'

'I came down earlier than I intended.' He came and stood beside her, leaning his powerful shoulders against the wall as he stared down at her. 'I saw the Landrover at your gate—in fact I almost collided with it—and when I realised you were the passenger, I was curious and I followed.'

She remembered too late the blazing headlights of that other car, and the warning blare of its horn. It would have been so easy for him to wait further on and then quietly fall in behind them. Both she and Alan had been too preoccupied to realise they might be followed.

She gave a little groan and buried her face in her hands. The room was very quiet, only the sharp click of his lighter disturbing the silence as he lit the inevitable cheroot. When at last she looked up, she had in some measure regained her self-control and was beginning to think clearly again.

'Does—does my father know?' she asked in a low voice.

He was staring broodingly into space, but at the sound of her voice, he looked down at her and she saw a frown deepening the lines on his face.

'Haven't you left your concern for him a little late?' he said curtly.

'What do you mean?'

He made an impatient gesture. 'I mean it might have been better to have considered the effect this—escapade would have before you embarked on it. But since you ask, no, I have told him nothing. And you?'

'I left a note. They'll find it in the morning,' she said dully.

'I think not. I think it would be better if you found it tonight and destroyed it before more harm is done,' he said.

She shifted uneasily. 'But I'm not going home.'

That much at least she had clear in her mind. She had some money with her, and this would have to support her until she found work of some kind.

'Oh, but you are.' His voice was silky. 'When you have dressed yourself, we will be on our way.'

'You can't make me.' She looked at him defiantly.

'Yes, I can, *pethi mou*,' he said drily. 'But we will not quarrel. If you prefer to remain here for the night, then we will do so.' He looked sardonically down at Lacey, whose lips had parted in alarm at the implication in his words. 'I am not totally heartless, you see. I don't deprive you of one lover without providing you with another in his place. And if your heart is set on anticipating your marriage vows tonight . . .' He flicked his cheroot butt into an ashtray and bent, gripping her arms and lifting her inexorably to her feet. 'Perhaps your father will not be too angry with us when we tell him we were carried away by our feelings.'

'You're mad!' She pushed her hands against his chest, trying vainly to thrust him away from her. 'The only reason I came with Alan was so that I wouldn't have to marry you. You said you wouldn't have wanted me if I'd—been with another man.'

'Perhaps not.' His lips twisted almost self-derisively. 'But all the more reason, my sweet one, to make sure of you myself here and now.'

'But you never will be sure.' Her words were wild, born of the desire to hurt him, to send him from her. 'Even if you marry me, you'll never really know if I belong to you alone. I hate you. Can't you see that? I hate you!'

His laugh was soft, but to Lacey's quivering senses, it seemed to fill the room with menace.

'So you tell me, *pethi mou*, but what will you say in the morning, I wonder? Besides, hatred may add an extra spice to our relationship. Undiluted adoration can become a wearying trait in a woman.'

She struck at him blindly, fear and anger getting the better of her, but he evaded the blow effortlessly, pinioning her wrists behind her in one lean hand and watching, a little cruelly, as she struggled impotently against his superior strength. At last she stood unmoving, her breasts rising and falling unevenly with the stress of her quickened breathing, and her eyes brilliant with furious tears. With almost insolent calculation, he made her wait for his kiss, his other hand caressing her throat and her ears and the clear young line of her jaw. Dry-mouthed, she summoned all her will to fight the feeling of warm languor that in spite of herself was threatening to invade her whole body.

As if he sensed her inner struggle, Troy Andreakis smiled and his mouth came down on hers, not to crush and demand as she had expected, but lightly in the merest whisper of a caress that teased as it aroused.

Her wrists suddenly were free. He was not holding her or coercing her in any way. The only contact between them was this breath of a kiss, coaxing and tantalising, making her forget that all she had to do was step backwards away from him, prompting her instead to move forward, close to him, so close that she could feel his body hardening against her own, making her want to slide her arms around his neck and draw him down to her. Almost unknowingly, her lips parted for him as the wave of longing his slow, expert awakening of her had engendered began to overwhelm her.

His kiss deepened intimately, evoking sensations from her she had never dreamed could exist, and she knew she wanted to feel his arms around her, to know again the strength that only minutes before she had defied so desperately.

'Troy?' she whispered, the ache in her voice echoing that other unfamiliar ache that had taken possession deep in her body.

'Say that you belong to me.' There was a fierce quietness in the words he ground out against her lips. 'Tell me that you're mine, and that you will be my wife.'

'Yes,' she said. Her body was trembling now in reaction, and there was the sharp bitterness of tears in her throat. Tears of shame, she thought, at her own weakness, at the wantonness she had not known she possessed.

'Very well.' He stood away from her with such suddenness that she found herself swaying, her eyes flying to his dark face in swift alarm. 'Now go and dress yourself and we will take the happy news to your father.'

'But ...' The word was uttered before she could stop herself and a wave of hot colour flooded her body. She could not have been more obvious if she had thrown herself at his feet and begged him to take her, she thought furiously, pressing her hands to her burning face. She turned away hurriedly, avoiding his gaze and the mockery she knew it would hold, and walked across to the bathroom where she had left her clothes.

When she returned, he was standing smoking another

cheroot, and he watched in silence as she re-packed the few items she had taken from her case. The task completed, she stood with lowered gaze as he strolled across the room, and lifted the case off the bed.

'In answer to your unfinished question,' he said almost casually, 'it is simply that I think tonight's lesson has gone far enough. But remember this, *pethi mou*. Run away from me again, and you will not find me so forbearing. Now we will go to your father.'

He walked across the room and opened the bedroom door, holding it so that Lacey could walk out ahead of him into the corridor.

Vanessa's train was late, Lacey thought as she glanced at at her watch. After a moment's indecision, she walked slowly back up the platform avoiding the small groups of passengers who were heralding the Easter rush to come, and entered the station buffet. She ordered herself a cup of coffee and took it to a seat by the window.

She had not imagined when she had first asked Vanessa to spend Easter at Kings Winston that it would be to act as her bridesmaid, and she wondered wryly what Vanessa had thought when her letter had arrived. Her reply of acceptance had been circumspect in the extreme, but Lacey had no doubt that she would demand a fuller account of Lacey's whirlwind courtship on her arrival.

Courtship. Lacey suppressed a little sigh almost unconsciously as she sipped her coffee. Was that really the way to describe the series of events leading her so inevitably to a quiet ceremony in the parish church on Easter Monday?

Ever since her return home with Troy that night weeks before, she had realised that she no longer had control over her own destiny. Her life had taken on a strange disturbing momentum of its own, and in spite of herself, she was being swept along with it.

She was thankful that at least she had been able to insist on a quiet wedding, instead of the big, fashionable affair in London that she had dreaded might be forced upon her. Her own inclination notwithstanding, she had been able to use her father's health as a more urgent excuse. He had suffered another slight attack, and been ordered to rest by his doctor.

In consequence there had been frequent business conferences over the future of Vernon—Carey held at Kings Winston. These were invariably attended by Troy Andreakis with advisers and executives from his corporation, but although he was so often at the house, Lacey found she saw little of him. It was true that at first she had made a determined effort to keep out of his way, nevertheless it was disconcerting to find that he made no attempt to seek her out or exhibit any apparent awareness of her behaviour.

Nor when they were together had he shown any overwhelming desire to make love to her. In fact since the night he had found her at the motel, he had only kissed her once, and that was when he had put the large uncut emerald she now wore on her engagement finger. And as her father and Michelle had both been present at the time, it had been less of a kiss than a formality.

Lacey set her cup back in her saucer and gave herself an angry mental shake. She should be glad of it, she told herself vehemently. She had no wish for him to behave as her lover. It was quite bad enough to know that in a few short days she would have to accept him as a husband with all a husband's rights. The few prolonged conversations she had had with him since their engagement had served to drive this point gallingly home.

'Where do you want to spend our honeymoon?' he asked almost idly one evening when he had joined her after dinner in the drawing room where she was quietly playing the piano. 'Apart from the usual place, of course.'

Lacey's cheeks grew warm as she realised the implication in his words.

'I wish you wouldn't,' she exclaimed helplessly.

'Wouldn't what?'

'Say—things like that.'

'Does it disturb you so much to be reminded of what our exact relationship will be?' His eyes assessed her coolly. 'Perhaps I do it because I hope one day I'll get a reaction that will prove there really is a woman under that polite well-behaved schoolgirl exterior you present to me these days. Is there, Lacey *mou?*' His voice sank almost to a whisper. 'Or is it just an exquisite fragile shell that my money is buying for me?'

There was an odd bitterness in his tone, but she chose to disregard it, stung by his taunt.

'There is a saying *"caveat emptor"*—let the buyer beware,' she said, her voice clipped and brittle.

'I have heard it.' His smile was mirthless as he got up. He walked across to her and stood looking down at her for a moment. Then his hand reached out and circled her throat, his thumb brutally forcing up her chin so that she was obliged to meet his gaze. 'But I think it is you that needs to beware. In fact I promise you it is.'

'I'm not afraid of you,' she said a little breathlessly, hoping his grip on her throat would not betray the sudden tumult of her pulses.

'Not now, perhaps, in your father's house with people nearby to run to. But soon, *pethi mou*, there will only be my arms to run to—or run from.'

'I know that.' She pulled herself free, willing herself to withstand him and give him no hint of the treacherous warmth that his touch aroused in her. 'Don't you realise that my every waking hour is sickened by the thought?'

He shrugged, his dark eyes under their heavy lids enigmatic. 'Fire your little barbs,' he said almost casually. 'You'll pay for them all eventually, my dove. Willingly or unwillingly. The choice is yours.'

He had left her then and Lacey had slumped over the piano keys, feeling the release from an almost unbearable tension.

Remembering, now, she felt a swift shiver curl along her spine. There had been no tenderness in his attitude, nothing that could give her anything to hope for in their relationship. Just talk of payment and possession. And there was the other aspect of their bargain—his need for a companion for his young sister. That too was not without complications. Troy had elaborated little on what her father had already told her, except to repeat that Eleni had been thoroughly spoiled by her stay in America, and that he expected Lacey to befriend her when they arrived on Theros.

Lacey wondered wryly whether he meant her to be a friend or a guard to the wayward Eleni, and she felt dubious about the girl's possible reaction when she was presented to a brand-new sister-in-law who was also a complete stranger to her. She had suggested tentatively that Eleni should come to England for the wedding, perhaps even act as her bridesmaid with Vanessa, but Troy had vetoed the suggestion emphatically.

Eleni was not being rewarded for her recent behaviour by a trip to England, he had said coldly, adding that in any case his elderly aunt Sofia, who lived at his villa and was at present, Lacey gathered, giving Eleni some reluctant chaperonage, was a very religious woman and would not care to be away from the island during Holy Week. And that, Lacey felt, was unanswerable.

She was aroused from her unhappy reverie by the noise of the train's arrival. As she emerged from the buffet, it had already halted and she could see Vanessa leaning out of the window of a first class compartment scanning the people on the platform in search of her.

'Van!' she called, breaking into a run, and was rewarded with an answering wave.

'Well,' Vanessa greeted her with a warm hug, and she stood back grinning, 'of all the dark horses! I wonder if there'll be a Greek tycoon waiting for me when I finally leave prison. Honestly, Lacey, your engagement knocked the whole convent sideways. The only one to take it in her stride was Reverend Ma, and she told me to give you her blessing and say she had never had any doubt you would ultimately establish yourself entirely satisfactorily.' Vanessa mimicked the nun's resonant tones with a fair degree of accuracy and threw in a grimace for good measure.

Lacey gave a forced little smile. 'I'm glad she approves.'

Vanessa gave her a considering look. 'Are you?' she said drily. 'Well, lead me to the waiting taxi. I've had quite enough travelling for one morning.'

On their way back to Kings Winston, Vanessa regaled her friend with stories and gossip about the other girls who had been at the convent with them, and Lacey was shocked to find how remote all that part of her life now seemed.

86

Yet it was not so very long ago that she had seriously considered spending the rest of her life in that environment, she thought. She came back with a start to what Vanessa was saying.

'I'm dying to meet your fiancé, Lacey. Is he at Kings Winston now?'

'Er—no. I think he's in London, but I'm not sure,' Lacey said vaguely, and flushed slightly as she met a puzzled look from Vanessa.

'Is this some new casual approach to offset that awful blushing bride image?' Vanessa inquired after a pause.

'No, not really. It's just that he really is very busy, and it's not always easy to keep track of his comings and goings,' Lacey said rather lamely.

'Hm.' Vanessa still sounded sceptical, but she changed the subject. 'What are the dresses like, Lacey? Are they nearly finished?'

'Very nearly. Mrs Burton is coming to give you a fitting this afternoon. I hope you like the colour, Van. Mrs B. was very dubious. She says green is unlucky.'

'Pooh, that's just superstition. What better colour is there for a spring wedding? Is your dress ready?'

'All but the hem.' Lacey wrinkled her nose, smilingly. 'Another of Mrs Burton's superstitions. She always saves a few last stitches for the wedding morning itself. Swears it brings good fortune and that all her brides are happy brides.'

'Well, it's a nice idea,' Vanessa approved. 'I suppose that's the sort of personal touch you get when you employ the local dressmaker rather than one of the couture houses. How did you manage it, by the way? I would have thought Michelle would have insisted on Dior at the very least.'

'Oh, she said it was entirely up to me.' Lacey spoke rather awkwardly. A glass partition divided them from the driver, but this was still not the time or the place to confide in Vanessa how oddly lukewarm Michelle's attitude had been towards the wedding.

Indeed, when she had first learned the news after they had returned from the motel that night, she had appeared almost stunned, although this had been more than coun-

tered by Sir James' blatant relief and boisterous congratulations. He had fetched champagne and insisted on toasts
being drunk to the newly engaged pair, and it was while
this was going on that Lacey had suddenly caught sight of
her stepmother, standing a little apart, a frozen look on her
face and her lower lip caught almost savagely in her teeth.
It was only momentary. Next minute, Michelle was laughing
and adding her own good wishes, but afterwards when
Lacey came to recall that strangely dreamlike evening of
her life, Michelle's icy face had been one of the few realities.

Since, she had wondered whether Michelle had been
offended because Sir James had neglected to tell her of the
bargain that Troy Andreakis had struck with Vernon—Carey,
but she had dismissed this fancy. Michelle herself had said
she would go to any lengths to obtain Andreakis' support
for the bank, and she had been quite prepared to sell her
stepdaughter to him outside marriage. Lacey was surprised
that Michelle was not more pleased that her scheming had
ultimately turned out to be so successful.

Perhaps too she was aggrieved that the wedding was not
to be the fashionable Town affair that she would undoubtedly have chosen herself, but again she was one of the first
to agree that in the circumstances of Sir James' health, a
small country wedding was desirable.

She proceeded with the arrangements with her usual
efficiency, contacting caterers and ordering flowers, but
giving no more of her attention and interest than she would
have devoted to one of her normal dinner parties, Lacey
thought, mystified. She had accepted Lacey's decision to
have her simple gown of wild silk made by Mrs Burton who
had dressed so many Kings Winston brides almost with
indifference and had attended none of the fittings. Her own
outfit had necessitated a further trip to Paris.

Vanessa was speaking again. 'Thanks for asking me to
be bridesmaid, Lacey. Am I the only one? I'd have thought
you would have asked Fran Trevor as well.'

Lacey bit her lip. 'Fran's going to be very busy over the
Easter period. She's taken on Marian Palmer to help her,
but she isn't quite experienced enough yet to be left in
charge.'

'What a shame,' Vanessa said cheerfully. 'And what about that brother of hers? Will he be at the wedding?'

'No.' Lacey felt as if she was treading through quicksand. 'Alan's up in Westmorland for a few months, learning about sheep. His uncle has a farm there.'

She hoped Vanessa would not notice the slight catch in her voice. She felt so guilty about Alan whose departure north had followed so swiftly upon the announcement of her engagement. And there was Fran, too. Things had not been the same with her since it had happened. Lacey did not know how much Alan had confided in his sister, but Fran treated her with an aloof civility which Lacey found more hurtful than downright hostility. When Lacey had tentatively mentioned that the wedding was to be at Easter, Fran had hastened to make it clear she would not be able to be there, probably to save them both the inevitable embarrassment of an outright refusal of an invitation. As it was, only Mr and Mrs Trevor were attending the wedding, and Lacey felt curiously bereft.

Her unhappy musings were cut short by their arrival at the house, and the remainder of the morning was taken up with showing Vanessa the house and helping her to unpack. Shortly after lunch, Mrs Burton arrived to fit the filmy drift of pale green organza that Vanessa was to wear, and when she finally departed, at Vanessa's insistence, Lacey showed her the clothes she had chosen for her honeymoon.

She felt absurdly self-conscious as she displayed the array of dresses and slacks suits, together with the beachwear that would take her to Nassau for the first month of her married life, before they went on to Theros. When they came to the piles of filmy lingerie and nightwear, she half expected some ribald comment from Vanessa, but her friend seemed oddly subdued as if she had realised for the first time the barrier that Lacey's marrige would inevitably erect in their friendship.

Her eyes opened wide as she studied the set of matched luggage that had been Troy's birthday present to Lacey when she had become eighteen only ten days before.

'It's beautifully light,' she breathed as she handled one of the pale honey-coloured cases.

'They have to be, because we shall be doing so much flying,' Lacey explained. 'And his yacht, the *Artemis*, is tied up at Nassau. We'll be taking a short cruise while we're there, I think.'

'Life's going to be incredibly different for you.' Vanessa examined the fittings of the dressing case with a rather sober expression. 'I'm glad it's not me, Lacey. I don't think I could cope.'

Lacey sat down on her dressing stool, her fingers toying idly with the stopper of a scent bottle. 'I'm not sure whether I can either,' she admitted eventually in a low voice.

Vanessa stared at her. 'There's something wrong, isn't there?' she said grimly. 'This isn't just bridal nerves. What is it—Vernon–Carey?'

Lacey looked at her wretchedly. 'I shouldn't be telling you, Van, but those rumours in the papers—they were all true.'

'I was afraid they would be.' Vanessa gave a little sigh. 'So there's been some kind of deal, and you're included?'

Lacey hesitated for a moment, then nodded unhappily. 'You—you don't seem particularly surprised—or shocked.'

'It happens.' Vanessa gave a little shrug. 'But it's you I'm concerned about. Are you going to be able to go through with it?'

Lacey sighed. 'I have no choice. No wedding—no deal, as you put it. And if anything happened to Vernon–Carey, it would kill Daddy.'

'Hm—so you've been cast in the role of virgin sacrifice.'

Lacey gave a visible start and Vanessa's eyes narrowed.

'Now what have I said?' she inquired. 'That was meant to be a joke, but I presume I've touched some sort of nerve.'

'Not really.' Lacey looked down uncomfortably. 'It's just that—that was one of the—conditions for the marriage. Oh, and I'm supposed to become some kind of unofficial guardian for his young sister. She's a bit of a handful, and I'm supposed to exercise a beneficent influence on her somehow,' she ended a little incoherently.

'No wonder you're finding it all a bit of a tall order.' Vanessa gave her a shrewd look. 'But what about Andreakis himself? Do you find him attractive?'

Colour swamped the usual pallor of Lacey's face. 'I don't know.'

Vanessa got up from the ledge of Lacey's bed where she had been sitting and shook some creases out of her skirt. 'A totally dishonest reply if ever I heard one,' she commented. 'I don't doubt you feel resentful, but you shouldn't let it blind you to everything else.'

'Is that what I'm doing?' Lacey's lips twisted wryly. 'Perhaps—but I do feel so utterly confused, Van. You see, I know so little about him. In about three days' time I'm marrying a stranger—and I'm frightened.'

'I must confess I find it odd that you're being rushed into it like this,' Vanessa said slowly. 'I would have thought he would have been content with a long engagement, giving you both a chance to get to know each other—for you to feel at ease with him.'

'I know.' Lacey sighed again, forlornly.

'Well, cheer up.' Vanessa gave her a robust hug. 'It does have a rather fairy-tale side to it, you know. Do you remember when we went to Phil's school to see that end-of-term production of *The Yeomen of the Guard*. Well, you know what happened to Elsie—"Strange adventure, maiden wedded to a groom she's never seen." That's rather you, isn't it, sweetie?'

Lacey smiled in spite of herself. 'Except that I have seen him, of course.'

But later, when she was alone, she found herself wondering whether that was strictly true, or whether she had been shown only what Troy Andreakis wanted her to see. And she asked herself again just what sort of a man she was committed to marry in such a few days' time.

By Easter Saturday, many of the guests who were to attend the wedding had arrived and were installed at Kings Winston. Troy Andreakis was due to arrive himself during the afternoon, Lacey learned from her father, and together with his chief financial advisor Stephanos Lindos, who was also to act as his best man, was to stay at the Bull. Apart from the conventions, Lacey supposed, there simply wasn't room to accommodate them at the house, now that her godparents, with Aunt Mary and her husband and three of her married cousins, were staying there.

After a busy morning unpacking yet more wedding presents and writing notes of thanks, as well as replying to letters of congratulation from friends and well-wishers who would be missing the ceremony, Lacey was quite glad to escape after lunch and go for a walk across the fields with Vanessa. The weather had turned quite mild, in keeping with the season, but it was damp with a fine, wetting drizzle falling.

Lacey lifted her face to it. 'I shall miss this,' she said rather absently.

Vanessa grimaced. 'I wish I could,' she said tartly. 'Just think of all that sunshine!'

'And just how parched and dry everything will be compared to this,' Lacey retorted, nimbly side-stepping a particularly marshy patch of ground. She stared round at the familiar landmarks, from the clump of willows bending to the stream at the bottom of the meadow, to the church tower rising above the clustering roofs of the village in the distance.

'Well, at the moment parched and dry seems a marked improvement on soggy and wet,' Vanessa grumbled good-humouredly. 'Besides, I don't believe Theros will be as arid as you seem to think. After all, both Corfu and Rhodes are lovely.' She gave a hitch to the collar of her raincoat. 'We'd better go back before you catch cold. You can't go up the aisle in that lovely dress with a red nose.'

When they got back to the house, Lacey saw with alarm that the doctor's car was standing on the drive. She gave a little exclamation and ran up the steps and in through the front door, leaving Vanessa to follow more slowly. Lacey made straight for the stairs, oblivious to everything but the need to get to her father's room, and found herself colliding with someone who had just completed the descent and was standing at the foot of the staircase. Strong hands steadied her and she looked up startled into Troy's dark face.

'My father!' she gasped, and his rather harsh expression softened slightly as he noted the worry in her eyes.

'He's had another slight attack. The doctor is talking to your stepmother in the study now.'

Lacey broke free and whirling round, ran into the study.

'How is he?' she demanded breathlessly.

Michelle, who was sitting at the desk, was clearly irritated at the interruption, but Dr Gervase turned to Lacey with a reassuring smile.

'He'll do,' he said succinctly. 'But he must take things very quietly for some time.'

'Should we postpone the wedding?' Lacey was aware of a slight hiss of breath from Troy, who had followed her into the room.

'No—in fact he became very agitated when Lady Vernon suggested this might be possible. A wedding is a time of joy, after all, not stress and upset, which Sir James needs at all costs to avoid just now. But it might be better if someone else gave you away.' He turned back to Michelle. 'I've left a repeat prescription in his room, but please don't hesitate to call me, Lady Vernon, if you are at all worried. Don't look so frightened, Lacey. Your father is determined to see his grandchildren, you know. Goodbye, my dear. I wish you every happiness.'

Michelle accompanied the doctor to his car and Troy and Lacey were left alone.

'So,' he said his voice expressionless. 'Even now you are looking for ways to escape—for any excuse to delay our marriage.'

'You call my father's health an excuse?'

'You really feel it would improve matters to defer the wedding—to provide him with just the sort of stress the doctor has warned he must avoid?' He stared grimly down at her and saw her bowed head give a faint shake.

'He needs the reassurance of our marriage,' he said more gently. 'Perhaps, as the doctor said, even the prospect of a grandchild.'

'Your concern for him is most admirable,' she said tonelessly.

'Don't give me credit for too much unselfishness.' He threw her a sardonic glance. 'I am also concerned for myself. I want my wife.'

93

She thought he was going to take her in his arms and moved hastily to the door. 'I—I'd like you to meet someone —my school friend Vanessa Arnold. She's going to be my bridesmaid.'

'Then that is yet another pleasure that should not be delayed any longer.' His faint smile was derisive, but Lacey could not be sure if he mocked her or himself. 'I can hardly contain myself.'

But when she brought Vanessa into the study and performed the introductions, he was charm itself, all barbed remarks forgotten, ignoring the fact that she was still to all intents and purposes a schoolgirl and treating her very much as if she was one of the young sophisticates from his own world. Vanessa was clearly overwhelmed and Lacey realised with a slight sigh that her disturbing fiancé had made another conquest.

Afterwards they went to look at the presents which had been set out in the drawing room, Vanessa accompanying them at Lacey's insistence. Soon she would be obliged to be alone with him, she told herself defiantly. Until then she could please herself.

Lacey had been anxious in case Troy looked down on some of the more modest offerings of china and linen from people in the village who had known her all her life, but he paid them the same careful attention as he did the Georgian silver candelabra given by Aunt Mary and Uncle David.

'And what about the bridegroom's present to the bride?' Vanessa asked incorrigibly. 'You have bought her something, haven't you, Troy?'

'Oh yes.' He smiled a little. 'But it is not here. It is waiting for Lacey on Theros, and she will have to be patient until then.'

Lacey was crimson and she flashed a furious glance at Vanessa.

'You don't have to give me anything,' she said in a low voice. 'It's not necessary. You've done quite enough already.'

He raised his eyebrows. 'You think so, *pethi mou*? Perhaps when you see what awaits you on Theros, you will be a little better pleased.'

Lacey, realising that embarrassment had made her ungracious, relapsed into silence.

Easter Sunday passed quietly. In the morning, everyone except Sir James attended the service at the parish church and Troy had to run the gauntlet of the village, with the majority of the congregation craning their necks to catch a glimpse of him. For someone who set such a high value on personal privacy, he bore it remarkably well, Lacey was forced to admit.

During the afternoon, a brief rehearsal of the following day's ceremony was held with the vicar, and it was not until he was about to return to the Bull with Stephanos after dinner that evening that Lacey found herself alone with Troy. She had half hoped to be able to say goodnight to him in the drawing room in front of everyone, but she soon realised from the expectant glances that she was obliged to accompany him to the front door and say her farewells in private. The breeze felt fresh on her skin, and the night sky was clear.

'It looks as if we will have a fine day tomorrow,' she said stiltedly.

'The start of many, Lacey *mou*.' There was an odd note in his voice, and she looked up at him, a little startled, and he bent and put his mouth to hers. She stayed rigid in his arms, forcing herself to deny him the response he sought, and heard him laugh softly as he released her.

'If this is how you wish it, then so be it, Lacey,' he said. 'But in twenty-four hours' time, you will not find me so patient.'

He reached out almost casually, cupping her small breast under the soft fabric of her dress in his lean fingers, and smiled mockingly into the sudden outrage in her face.

'Your body wants me, my sweet one. It is only that stubborn mind of yours that denies me, and it is a woman's privilege to change her mind, is it not? I would think about it, if I were you.'

He let her go, and she heard the gravel crunch under his feet as he set off after Stephanos, who had started for the Bull ahead of him.

She went back slowly into the house, her thoughts as

disturbed as the senses he could apparently awaken at will, she realised almost with despair. But by the time she rejoined the party in the drawing room she had calmed herself sufficiently to hold her own in a game of backgammon with her father, and this successfully diverted her attention until it was time to go to bed.

She had finished undressing and was giving her long hair its nightly brushing routine when her bedroom door opened and Michelle came in. For one rather hysterical moment, Lacey wondered if her stepmother had come to give her the traditional advice offered to brides on their wedding eves, but one look at her stepmother's set lips and blazing eyes told her that Michelle had nothing so well-meaning in mind.

For a moment the older woman looked her up and down, taking in the simple nightdress and the loosened hair with a visible curl of her lip.

'It is to be hoped that you have something slightly more alluring for tomorrow night. You will need it,' she said, and Lacey felt a sudden heat through her body at the implication in her words.

She gestured quietly towards the cases which stood packed and ready at the side of the room. 'My trousseau is there. You may examine it if you wish . . .'

'If I wish!' Michelle's laugh sounded strident. 'Since when have my wishes been of the least account?'

'Michelle!' Lacey felt uncomfortable. She was totally unprepared for this open hostility and found it inexplicable. 'I know you're upset about something—I've been aware of it for weeks. I wish you'd tell me what it is. I'd like us to at least part on good terms. Is it the wedding? Are you upset because I wanted to have it here instead of in London, or . . .'

Michelle interrupted and there was real venom in her voice. 'Yes,' she said slowly, 'I am upset, but not for the petty reasons you seem to think. I am angry that it is taking place at all.'

'But surely,' Lacey felt thoroughly confused, 'surely it's what you wanted—the answer to all our problems . . .'

'What I wanted?' Michelle laughed again, a desperate

sound. 'How do you know—how can you tell what I want? What do you know of anything—you, a little convent schoolgirl, frigid like all the English? How can you hope to hold a man like Troy Andreakis?'

Lacey was trembling. 'But it was your idea. You—packaged me and presented me to him. You know that.'

'C'est ça. But for one night only, as one gives a child a toy to amuse him for an hour and then be forgotten. I never dreamed he would offer marriage—not now, not to you.'

'I think you'd better go back to your room.' Lacey was too disturbed by the look on her stepmother's face to pay much attention to what she was saying. 'You're overwrought—all the work you've done for the wedding, and then the worry about Daddy.'

'Thank you for the reminder,' Michelle almost spat at her. 'That is all I will be left with—the worry, and a sick old man to nurse—while you, *petite salude* . . .'

She got no further. A firm tap on the door broke across the torrent of words, and Vanessa appeared in the doorway in her dressing gown.

'I do hope I'm not interrupting,' she said too brightly. 'Have you got any aspirin, Lacey? I've a splitting head. All the excitement, I expect.'

Michelle muttered something under her breath in French and swept out, brushing past Vanessa as she went. As the door closed behind her, Vanessa gave vent to a low whistle.

'What was all that about?' she exclaimed. 'I could hear her from the corridor and thought you might want to be rescued.'

Lacey was still shaking. 'I think she's mad,' she said in a choked voice. 'She doesn't want me to marry him.'

'I don't suppose she does,' Vanessa said calmly. 'After all, she's nearer his age than you are, love, and her prospects aren't exactly lively just at the moment. No islands in the Ionian Sea, or Mediterranean cruises for her. Just a quiet existence here looking after your father, which doesn't seem quite her métier.'

'She talked about Daddy—she called him a sick old man. It was as if she hated him,' Lacey said numbly.

Vanessa spoke gently. 'Now don't imagine things. She was probably so full of jealousy and resentment that she didn't know what she was saying. Besides, you've never had any illusions as to why she married your father. She wanted wealth and position, and he gave them to her. She wasn't to know that the going would suddenly get tough, and for Michelle the unforgivable thing is for someone to do better materially than herself. She's probably been brooding for weeks, comparing lots, and tonight she just couldn't keep quiet any longer. Now don't think about her any more. She's a malicious woman and tomorrow you'll be rid of her. She won't be able to hurt you any more. Now get into bed, and I'll tuck you in. You need your beauty sleep. You don't want to give her the triumph of seeing you look less than radiant tomorrow.'

Lacey obeyed silently. After Vanessa had gone, she lay sleeplessly, staring into the darkness, and going over and over the scene that had just taken place. It seemed to her that there was something else as well, something that she ought to remember, hiding in some corner of her mind, but she couldn't think what it could be, and it was while she was struggling to recall it that she finally drifted off into an uneasy sleep.

CHAPTER SIX

LACEY stood by the window of the hotel suite, staring out into the gathering darkness. There was little but the traffic in the street below to engage her attention, but at least it gave her the semblance of an occupation, and that was what seemed most important just at present.

Behind her she could hear the muted clatter of dishes as the waiter cleared the remains of their dinner on his trolley. Lacey had eaten little. She knew she would be hungry if she did not try, but sheer nervousness made it difficult for her to swallow, and she had only sipped at the vintage champagne which had been delivered to the suite with the management's compliments.

The day had passed in a blur. The last moment of reality had been her father's face smiling up at her as she came down the stairs in her wedding gown, Troy's flowers, the palest of orchids veined delicately in pink and gold, clasped in her hands. Everything else after that had assumed a strangely dream-like quality, Troy waiting for her by the altar banked high with Easter flowers, her own voice, clear and unreal, repeating the vows, the blaze of flash bulbs as they emerged from the church and faced the local and national press who had seized eagerly on a millionaire's wedding to break the monotony of the holiday period.

She could remember standing beside Troy at the reception, smiling until her face ached, and presenting her cheek to be kissed what seemed a thousand times, laughingly agreeing with the voices that told her, 'Happy the bride that the sun shines on.' Then it was time to change, and she was going upstairs with Vanessa obediently taking off the delicate gown, and putting on the grey shantung dress and jacket she was to go away in, brushing her hair free of the elaborate coronet she had worn for the ceremony, and fastening it back instead into a simple French pleat.

Then there had been the emotionalism of the goodbyes.

Aunt Mary's eyes shining with tears, her father's voice gruff with emotion as he held her to him, saying, 'Goodbye, my darling girl,' the chorus of good wishes that had followed them down to the waiting car which was to take them to London for the first night of their marriage before they left for the Bahamas the following day. The only dissident element had been Michelle. She had said nothing, merely stepped forward and laid her cheek for the briefest moment against Lacey's. The contact, though fleeting, had been cold and unpleasant and Lacey shivered as she remembered it.

And now here she was in the suite that Troy usually occupied during his sojourns in London, she had gathered. She was thankful it was not the bridal suite. As it was, everyone in this vast hotel must be aware that they were starting their honeymoon. Everything Troy Andreakis did was news, she thought wryly, understanding a little better why he was apparently prepared to go to such lengths to preserve his privacy when he was on Theros.

From behind her, she heard the waiter's voice, low and deferential. 'Will there be anything else, Mr Andreakis?' Followed by the rustle of money and a delighted, 'Thank *you*, sir.' Presumably a bribe substantial enough to ensure that they would not be disturbed for the rest of the evening, she thought. And the presence of Stephanos on the floor above would ensure that any messages that would normally come direct to the Andreakis suite would be re-routed.

She heard the outside door of the suite close and knew that she and her husband were alone. A sudden tension gripped her. Troy had not displayed any embarrassing ardour in front of any of the hotel staff, but she could not suppose he would hesitate any longer to transfer their relationship to a more intimate footing. Even as she felt panic begin to rise in her at the thought, she heard his voice.

'Come here, Lacey.'

Slowly she turned. He was sitting on the low luxurious sofa, his jacket discarded and his tie loosened, looking completely at his ease.

'I said come here.' He frowned impatiently. 'Don't force me to make you obey me, Lacey *mou*. Let us start off our marriage with a little dignity, if nothing else.'

Her hesitation was only momentary, then she walked stiffly and reluctantly across the room and stood in front of him.

'That's better.' He leaned back against the cushions, staring up at her under lowered lids. 'Don't look so petrified. I am only a man, you know, not a monster.' He waited for a moment, but she made no reply, so he went on, 'You looked very charming today, my sweet one. You made a picture as you came up the aisle to me that I find totally unforgettable.'

'I shall not find it easy to forget today either,' she answered, and his eyes narrowed.

'More little barbs?' he questioned. 'Someone should have taught you to respond more sweetly when you are being wooed, *pethi mou*.'

'Am I supposed to be grateful for your wooing?' She looked at him defiantly. 'We do have a bargain, and I'm quite aware of the price I have to pay.'

As soon as the words were uttered, she wished them unsaid, but they did not provoke the angry outburst she half expected. He just went on looking at her for a long moment, with a frankly sensual appraisal that made her want to cringe away.

'As you wish,' he said evenly. 'My only desire was to try and ease you through the inevitable difficulties of this sort of situation. But if you find it unnecessary . . .'

Before she could move, he had reached for her, gripping her wrist and half dragging her down on top of him. He hurt her and she cried out in protest, but the cry was smothered under the pressure of his lips and the strength of his hands quelled her ineffectual struggles, turning her in his arms as easily as if she was a doll. At last she lay breathless and still in his embrace, her lips parted helplessly beneath his insistence, her whole body alive, in spite of herself, to his utterly sensuous exploration of her slenderness.

'Please—no,' she managed at last, against his mouth.

'Please—yes.' There was a laziness in his voice which matched the insidious languor which threatened to overwhelm her.

'But you're creasing my dress.' Her protest sounded lame even to her own ears. 'It will be ruined.'

She felt a quiver of laughter run through him.

'That is easily remedied,' he murmured, and she felt the long zip fastener at the back of the dress give way under his fingers. 'Take it off,' he said, his mouth moving persuasively against her ear.

'No!' She clutched the loosened bodice against her.

'What's the matter?' He studied her, his dark eyes slumbrous with desire. 'Didn't it occur to you that this might be part of the price you spoke of?'

'No—yes.' She moistened her lips desperately. 'But please —not here, like this.'

There was a long pause, then he sighed softly, and she found herself lifted away from him and set on her feet.

'Your period of modest seclusion will last precisely ten minutes.' His voice was deceptively soft.

Still holding her dress, she looked at him doubtfully.

'You—you won't come in? You promise?'

'I promise—this time,' he said, and smiled faintly. 'But don't keep me waiting. A minute of your ten has gone already.'

Lacey fled into the bedroom, closing the door behind her. She slipped her arms out of the grey dress and let it fall to her feet, stepping out of it on her way to the case where her nightgown—white threaded with silver—and negligée were packed. She just had time for a shower, she thought, discarding her waist slip and tights on the way to the bathroom that adjoined the master bedroom.

'Lacey!'

She turned unbelievingly to see him framed in the bedroom doorway. Her face flamed and she held the nightdress in front of her.

'You promised!' she accused him hotly. 'You said you wouldn't come in.'

But he seemed totally unaware of her state of undress. He walked slowly across the room to her side, and his hands gripped her bare shoulders. But there was no passion in his touch. It seemed instead as if he was trying to impart to her some of his own strength. There was an odd look in his eyes—almost pitying, she thought wonderingly. Then he spoke.

'You must get dressed, *pethi mou*. We have to go on a journey.'

'A journey?' Her eyes searched his face. She was puzzled and a little frightened by this change in him. 'But where?'

'To Kings Winston, Lacey. Take only what you need for tonight. Stephanos will follow with the rest of our luggage.'

'Daddy?' Her face was paper-white, and he bent his head in silent affirmation.

'Oh God!' The cry burst from her. 'Oh, Troy, I must hurry. I must go to him.'

'You shall go to him, *pethi mou*.' For a moment she felt his lips move like a benediction against her hair. 'But I have to tell you there is no longer any need to hurry.'

Someone had kindled a log fire in the wide hearth of the drawing room at Kings Winston. Stretching her hands out to it, Lacey wondered drearily whether she would ever feel warm again. Outside the rain lashed against the windows with a sombre monotony that reflected the melancholy atmosphere prevailing within the house.

Somewhere a door closed and Lacey lifted her head to listen, her slim body filled with sudden tension. Following her father's funeral which had been held that morning, Troy had brought some of the Vernon–Carey board back to the house for a business lunch. It was now midway through the afternoon, and she supposed they would be leaving soon and that she would be called upon to say goodbye to them, as Michelle had shown so clearly that she was either not capable or not prepared to carry out the normal duties of a hostess.

She bit her lip. Perhaps she was being unfair, she told herself. Perhaps the near-collapse that Michelle seemed to have suffered was quite genuine, and she was more devoted to her late husband than Lacey had ever believed.

When they arrived back at the house three nights before, it was to find the household in a weird state of disorganisation. With the exception of Lacey's aunt and uncle, most of the wedding guests had departed during the afternoon, and Mrs Osborne and the hired staff were engaged in clearing up the aftermath when Sir James' collapse had occurred. Dr Gervase had been sent for and arrived within minutes, but before the ambulance he had summoned had come, it was all over.

During the swift drive through the darkness, Lacey had felt almost numb with disbelief. It was the quiet, stunned atmosphere in the house, and Mrs Osborne's reddened eyelids as she came forward to greet them that brought her loss home to her. For a moment she felt a child again, helpless and terrified, and then Troy had stepped forward, taking charge, prompting people to respond with their usual efficiency and creating order out of the prevailing chaos.

Michelle, they learned, was in her room, and Troy asked the doctor whether she had been given any sedation. Dr Gervase shook his head quietly, and Lacey saw him mouth something at Troy. Later when she went herself to Michelle's room to see if her stepmother wanted anything and found her lying fully dressed across her bed, she was immediately conscious of a strong smell of alcohol, and understood why no tranquillisers had been prescribed for the widow. What did it matter? she thought wearily, as she left the room. One form of oblivion was much the same as another.

But even once the initial shock of bereavement had worn off, Michelle had shown no sign of wanting to take over her duties once again. She spent most of her time in her room, and trays of food were sent to her there. While Troy attended to the funeral arrangements, with the help of Stephanos, it was left to Lacey and her aunt to deal with the domestic routine, answer the letters of condolence that poured in, and even fend off the inquiries from the press who scented a story in the fact that a millionaire's bride had been robbed of her honeymoon by a family tragedy. Lacey hated the sentimental headlines that had appeared, but she was thankful that none of the stories revived any of the doubts about the solvency of Vernon—Carey. The Andreakis name had stemmed the flood of those rumours, she realised.

Her eyes fell on the broad gold band on her wedding

finger and she touched it almost questioningly. She still had not fully assimilated the fact that the Andreakis name was now hers. Since they had been back at Kings Winston, Troy had made no attempt to pursue a more intimate relationship. Lacey had occupied her old room, alone, while he slept in a hastily refurbished guest room, but she knew that this state of affairs could not be expected to continue indefinitely.

The sound of men's voices in the hall roused her from her reverie, and she went out to join them, looking slender and fragile in her black dress. The goodbyes said, she stood on the steps watching the last of the cars pull away down the drive, then she turned, and with a faint sigh, walked back into the house.

'I would like to speak to you, Lacey.' Troy was standing holding open the study door.

'But I was just going to my room to lie down. I'm rather tired.'

'Nevertheless, I should still be glad of a few moments of your time. I will not keep you long.'

After a momentary hesitation, she walked past him into the study and stood looking round as he closed the door. He walked over to her and stood looking down at her with a slight frown. His hand came up and lightly touched the shadows beneath her eyes.

'Didn't Dr Gervase give you something to help you sleep?'

'Yes,' she said helplessly. 'But they don't stop me—thinking during the day.'

'Of course not.' He produced his cigar case and lit a cigar with a certain amount of deliberation. 'However, I feel that a change of air and scenery is what you most need now, and I have arranged for Stephanos to escort you to Theros tomorrow.'

She stared up at him, her lips parted in astonishment.

'Theros?' she echoed. 'But I don't understand.'

'Well, you would hardly wish to continue with our trip to the Bahamas under the circumstances.'

'But they won't be expecting us.'

He looked impatiently at her. 'I have already cabled Aunt Sofia and told her to make all the necessary arrangements to receive you. I shall expect you to have lost those hollows in your cheeks when I see you next.'

'Aren't you coming with me?' she asked before she could stop herself. That sounded altogether too much like an appeal for his company.

He shook his head. 'Have I not said that Stephanos will escort you? I shall be tied up here for some time. Certain— complications have arisen which require my attention.'

Lacey supposed dully it was something to do with Vernon–Carey, but she did not inquire further. She was too preoccupied with her imminent journey to Theros, and the subsequent meeting with his family, to worry about anything else.

'Troy.' She put a beseeching hand on his sleeve. 'Please don't make me go to Theros just now. I don't feel like meeting anyone, and I don't think I could cope with Eleni at the moment.'

'That is nonsense,' he said coldly. 'Aunt Sofia will treat you like a mother, and Eleni will at least give you something else to think about than your own grief. If you remain here, *pethi mou,* you will simply brood yourself into illness. That will do no good either to yourself or your father's memory. Now I advise you to go and start your packing.'

'Very well,' she yielded listlessly. 'I suppose I have no choice anyway.'

'Very little,' he said, smiling grimly.

As she prepared for bed that night, Lacey realised that this was probably the last night she would ever spend in this room—perhaps even in this house. She knew that her father's will had left the bulk of his property, including Kings Winston, to Michelle and she could not imagine her stepmother wanting to retain the property. She had never cared for country life after all. Climbing into bed, she gave a long, quivering sigh and buried her face in her pillow. It seemed that all her ties with her old way of life were being irrevocably cut one after another. While her father had lived, she had at least had an element of stability, of comforting sameness to rely on. Now all she had was a husband who was still a relative stranger to her, and a new home in the alien surroundings of a Greek island.

Since her father's death, she had not been able to shed a single tear. She had even remained dry-eyed at his graveside, but now fear and uncertainty about the future, allied to her real sense of loss, overwhelmed her, and with a shuddering sob she abandoned herself to her grief.

'Oh, Daddy, Daddy,' she whispered brokenly, as the tears rained down unchecked.

She was too immersed in her sorrow to hear her door open, and the first indication she had that she was not alone was Troy's voice close beside her, sharply repeating her name. She lifted her head from the pillow and stared up at him, her pale face drenched and stained with tears.

'Wh—what are you doing here?'

'I have come every night to make sure you were sleeping,' he said. 'But eventually this had to happen, I suppose.' He sat down wearily on the edge of the bed and gathered her into his arms. 'Have your cry out, *pethi mou*. It isn't good to be too brave always.'

A long time after her long, quivering sobs had finally died away, she stayed quietly, her wet face pressed against his chest, warm through the thin silk of his dressing gown. At last she felt him stir, as if to move away, and a sudden feeling of alarm, almost desolation, gripped her.

'Troy,' she murmured, a slight catch lingering in her voice. 'Don't go yet—please. Don't leave me.'

'No,' he said, his voice oddly husky. 'I shan't leave you, my sweet one.'

She heard the faint rustle as his dressing gown slid to the floor in the darkness and then he was lying beside her, the warmth of his body igniting a fire in her own. For a moment she was tense, as she realised too late what her need for comfort had invited, then his mouth covered hers and his hands began to move, caressingly, expertly on her body so that fear and doubt, even the sharpness of grief, began to recede under this torrent of strange, new emotion that he could evoke in her. She was bewildered by the fierceness of her own desire, by this wild sweet urgency which transcended everything—even the inevitable pain of her first surrender.

As she lay in his arms afterwards, she heard him whisper, '*Yineka mou.*'

She looked up at him, drowsy-eyed. 'What does that mean?'

'It means—my wife.' He bent and kissed her with a warm possessiveness that once she would have resented.

'I suppose you will want me to learn the Greek for "husband",' she said sleepily.

'Among other things.' He gave a soft laugh. 'I think you will be an apt pupil, my sweet one. Now you must sleep. You have a long journey ahead of you tomorrow.'

At his words, all thoughts of slumber deserted Lacey. She sat up, staring at him in growing indignation.

'You mean—you're still going to send me away?'

'Of course,' he said calmly. 'Why not?'

'I should have thought it would have been obvious why not.' Lacey's cheeks grew warm. 'Doesn't—what happened —tonight mean anything to you?'

'That is a foolish question,' he said flatly. 'Do you think this has been an easy decision for me?'

'I don't know what to think,' she said furiously. 'Oh, God, I wish I'd never let you touch me!'

'Our relationship was hardly as one-sided as you wish to imply,' he said drily. He sat up, his eyes hardening as he looked at her. 'But this alters nothing, Lacey. I have other responsibilities and I cannot afford the sort of distraction that you would present. I am sorry.'

'I'm sorry too.' She moistened her dry lips with the tip of her tongue. 'I hadn't realised of course that all I would be was—a distraction. But I suppose that's all I am to you —a plaything to be pushed aside when you're tired of the game. Just another in the long line of girls you've taken to bed. The fact that you've actually married me is immaterial, of course.'

'It may not be,' he said grimly. 'You may find the fact of our marriage entitles you to a good hiding. Whatever my life has been in the past, it does not concern you. It is over, and you are the only woman in my life.'

'Until the novelty wears off,' she flung at him, hurt and wanting to hurt in return.

The sardonic smile she hated flickered for a moment on his mouth.

'But while I am here and you are on Theros, it will not wear off so quickly—for either of us,' he said lightly, and got out of bed, stretching indolently before he bent to pick up his robe.

Stormily Lacey flung herself over, burying her head in the pillow, and she heard him laugh as he left her.

Even when she was alone, she could still hardly believe it was true. That she had given herself to him, and he had taken all that she had to offer and yet was still bent on the same course as before as if he had been entirely unaffected by their coming together.

She felt hot with shame as she remembered how eagerly she had responded to him. Her low emotional state, her need for comfort had made her an easy conquest, she told herself contemptuously. But in her heart, she knew it was not that simple, that even without the fierce luxury of tears to arouse her, she would have wanted him as soon as soon as his body touched hers. She had known on her wedding night that her capitulation was inevitable, had glimpsed the demands that passion might make of her. Now she was confronted with the reality and she was shaken by the capacity for desire that his expert lovemaking had revealed in her.

But she had been naïve to imagine that their brief time together had aroused similar feelings in him. In fact, if she was honest with herself, he had probably found her total inexperience boring. It was a hurtful thought, but it had to be faced. If he felt as she did, then he could not send her away in the morning, she told herself, bitterness striking at her again.

She was still resentful when she walked into the dining room the next morning and found her husband and Stephanos deep in a low-voiced conversation that ceased on her entrance.

'Oh.' She checked tautly on the threshold. 'Am I interrupting something?'

Troy sighed, rising and holding the chair for her to be

seated. 'Don't be tiresome, *pethi mou*,' he advised succinctly. 'Shall I ring for fresh coffee?'

'No, thank you.' Lacey repressed a grimace as she poured out the remains of the lukewarm brew in the tall silver pot and took a cautious sip, aware of her husband's sardonic gaze. In his dark city suit, with his immaculate white shirt, he seemed totally alien to the lover whose lips and hands had wrought such havoc with her senses only a few hours before. In this daytime guise, he was more the arrogant stranger who had married her as an additional clause in a contract, and easier to hate.

Stephanos leaned forward and addressed her with a friendly smile. 'Is this your first visit to Greece, Mrs Andreakis?'

'Yes,' she replied bleakly, and saw Troy send her a frowning glance.

'Then you have a treat in store,' Stephanos said encouragingly. 'Theros is very beautiful at this time of the year.'

'So is England,' she said stiffly, and there was an awkward pause.

'But you will be glad to see your new home,' Stephanos persevered.

Lacey put down her cup and looked at him. 'Let's be quite clear about this, Mr Lindos,' she said crisply. 'I don't know why you're making this journey today, but I'm going because I've been ordered to, and I'm going under protest.'

'Lacey!' Troy's face was dark with anger, but she went on recklessly.

'Wouldn't you like to protest, Mr Lindos? Isn't having to escort your employer's wife across Europe rather a menial task for someone in your position? I'm sure it doesn't fall within your normal scope of duties.'

'Perhaps not.' Stephanos pushed his chair back and rose. 'But, Kyria Lacey, Troy is not just my employer. He is also my good friend and I am happy to perform this service for him. Escorting you is my privilege, not my duty. And now I will go and make sure that our luggage has been brought down.' And he left the room.

Lacey swallowed, very conscious that her moment of defiance had passed, and had achieved very little. She glanced unwillingly in her husband's direction and his eyes blazed into hers.

'I hope you are satisfied,' he said harshly. 'In future you will kindly ensure that any disagreements we may have remain our private concern. I will have no one else, friend or stranger, involved or embarrassed. Is that clear?'

'Perfectly.' She stared back at him. 'I just didn't want your friend to be under any false impressions about our journey.'

'Nor about your manners, obviously.' He paused for a moment. 'Bad behaviour will not force a change of heart in me, Lacey, any more than bribery.'

'Bribery?' Her frown was puzzled. 'What do you mean?'

His smile was not pleasant. 'Are you saying that charming interlude last night was not intended to persuade me to let you remain in England?'

The hot colour flooded into her cheeks. She sat gazing at him, suddenly mute, unable to think what to say, how to defend herself.

'Poor Lacey,' he said mockingly. 'What a sacrifice—and all in vain.'

She wanted to scream at him, to reach out and claw his face, but she forced herself to self-control, even managed a tight smile to mask her humiliation.

'But at least I shall know better than to make the same mistake again,' she said, achieving the exact degree of carelessness she wanted.

Something seemed to come and go in his eyes, but the impression was so fleeting she decided she had imagined it.

'I hope you apply the same wisdom to all our dealings,' he drawled, then got up abruptly and walked out of the room. Lacey remained where she was. Her heart thudded and her palms felt moist. So he imagined that last night had been merely an act, designed to obtain her own way. That was his estimation of the precious gift she had made him. She shook her head almost blindly. And what of the part he himself had played—the controlled gentleness, the intuitiveness that he had brought to her initiation? Had he been merely cynical, acting the role of the tender bridegroom? She pushed back her chair and got up, pressing a hand to the sudden throb of pain in her throat.

She heard a sound behind her and turned to see Mrs Osborne waiting in the doorway.

'I'm sorry, Miss Lacey. I though everyone had finished.'

'We have,' Lacey forced herself to complete self-control. 'I must go and say my goodbyes. Is—Lady Vernon in her room?'

'Yes, miss.' Lacey sensed the disapproval in the quiet reply. Mrs Osborne hesitated a moment, then blurted out, 'Miss Lacey—do you know what's going to happen? Will her ladyship keep the house on? There are all sorts of rumours, and the staff don't know what to think.'

Lacey bit her lip. 'I'm just as much in the dark as you are, Mrs Osborne, but I'm afraid—very much afraid that the house will be sold.'

Glancing at the older woman, she saw the glint of tears in her eyes.

'I'm sorry, Miss Lacey.' Mrs Osborne gulped slightly. 'It's all been such a shock, that's all. You getting married, then poor Sir James going like that. And now it looks as if we shall all have to look for new posts. I've been here for fifteen years and it will be a wrench, having to work for other people.'

Lacey was touched. She put her hand gently on Mrs Osborne's arm.

'But if the house is sold, then the new family will need a housekeeper. You need never look for another job, I'm sure, Ossie dear.' She paused and said awkwardly, 'If you need a reference—or any of the staff—and you don't like to ask Lady Vernon, then do write to me. I'd be more than happy . . .' She stopped, not knowing how to go on, realising that Mrs Osborne was crying openly now. She kissed her cheek, gave her a brief hug, and went out of the room. Her mood was sombre as she climbed the stairs and made her way towards Michelle's room. It was no use appealing to her stepmother on behalf of the staff, she realised. Michelle tolerated the people who worked for her for as long as they were useful and efficient. As soon as either of these functions ceased, she would be quite ruthless. Probably

112

only Barbara, her maid, would survive the break-up of the household, she thought ruefully.

She had half expected that Michelle would still be in bed, but her stepmother was up, and standing by the window in the tiny, exquisitely decorated sitting room that adjoined her bedroom. She swung round as Lacey entered the room and her eyes narrowed as they went over her. She was smoking a cigarette in quick, nervous puffs and Lacey saw that her face looked drawn and haggard.

Lacey came to a halt a few feet away, feeling gauche as she usually did under her stepmother's scrutiny. The awkwardness of their last conversation still lingered, as she said quietly, 'I've come to say goodbye, Michelle.'

'And to be wished *bon voyage, sans doute.*'

Lacey looked at her levelly. 'You're not obliged to wish me anything you don't mean,' she said.

Michelle laughed, a soft almost excited sound. 'Oh, I shall not injure my conscience by wishing you a safe journey, *ma petite*, believe me. Indeed, you have my sympathy—all that way with only the dull but worthy Stephanos for company. Your husband cannot be very ardent, *ma mie*, to allow you so far out of his sight so soon after your wedding.'

The words were honeyed, but there was malice, bitter as gall, underlying them and Lacey felt herself flinch.

She raised her chin and looked defiantly at her stepmother. 'But journeys end in lovers' meetings, Michelle. Isn't that what they say? And now I must be going. It's a fair drive to the airport. Goodbye.'

Michelle smiled, but to Lacey's relief made no attempt either to kiss her or take her hand.

'*Au revoir, ma fille,*' she murmured, an odd smile quirking the corners of her mouth before she turned away to resume her former stance at the window.

Troy was waiting at the foot of the stairs as Lacey descended, his face a dark mask.

'The car is loaded and Stephanos is waiting,' he said.

'I'm quite ready,' she assured him quietly, and made to move past him to the open front door, but he halted her, his hand on her arm lightly but inflexibly.

'Have you nothing to say to me?' he asked.

'Nothing you would care to hear.' She tried to pull her arm free, but his grip tightened, and she was pulled swiftly but inexorably against the hardness of his body.

'Then say nothing.' He bent and his mouth claimed hers in a slow, erotic onslaught on her senses that drove the strength from her legs and had her clinging to him helplessly, her fingers twined round the lapels of his coat. When he raised his head, she went on leaning against him, her green eyes enormous in her small pale face, her bruised lips still parted as she sought to steady her breathing.

She heard him laugh softly, derisively, but whether he derided her or himself she could not decide.

'Almost you tempt me,' he murmured. 'But I must let you go. *Herete, yineka mou.* Try not to forget me.'

Almost mechanically she went out of the house and down the steps to the car where the driver waited by the open door to help her in. She leaned back on the thickly padded seat, letting Stephanos' softly voiced queries about her comfort wash over her, forcing herself not to look back as the car purred into life and started off smoothly down the drive.

CHAPTER SEVEN

LACEY opened her eyes to a pattern of vines dancing on a sun-drenched wall and lay for a moment assimilating her surroundings and wondering what had woken her.

She had arrived on Theros the previous evening, too tired and too miserable from the sudden attack of sickness that she had experienced on the short helicopter flight from Corfu to notice very much about the villa.

Miss Andreakis, Troy's Aunt Sofia, had been there, a tall, rather frail-looking woman dressed in the inevitable black, who had greeted Lacey in good but heavily accented English. There had also been several young girls in the hall of the villa, but they had turned out to be servants come to peep at their new mistress. When Lacey had asked rather timidly if she was to meet Eleni, Miss Andreakis had burst into a flood of agitated Greek, accompanied by much hand-waving. Stephanos, his eyes twinkling alightly, had inter-preted that the child of wickedness had gone from the villa, without permission, and had not been seen all day. Lacey wondered whether it was the news of her own arrival that had driven Eleni to flight and thought it did not augur well for their future relationship.

But she had been too tired and nauseated to care very much either way, and was thankful to be shown to a large room on the first floor where an enormous but comfortable-looking bed awaited her, and a plump black-eyed girl with a ready smile and the unlikely name of Ariadne helped her undress and get between the lace-trimmed linen sheets, fresh with the smell of sweet herbs. She had been coaxed into drinking part of a bowl of delicious chicken soup, and had fallen asleep almost at once.

She heard a noise like a sandshoe scuffling along a mosaic floor, and, turning her head, saw what had woken her. A young girl, her dark hair drawn into two bunches, sat cross-legged on the bedroom floor a few feet from the bed

115

silently regarding her. She wore a pair of sun-bleached levis which looked as if they had been deliberately shrunk on to her body and a skimpy tee-shirt which revealed plainly that Eleni Andreakis considered the wearing of a bra an unnecessary refinement.

Lacey propped herself up on her elbow and regarded her in turn. Then, hoping her voice would not betray her nervousness, she said, '*Kalimera*, Eleni.'

'For crissakes!' The girl tugged irritably at one of her bunches. 'Do we have to go through all that stuff? And I'd rather be called Helen.'

'O.K.—Helen,' Lacey agreed equably. 'I just thought it would give me a chance to practise my Greek.'

'Well, your pronunciation's lousy,' Eleni or Helen said sullenly. 'And you don't have to speak Greek. Everyone here is bi-lingual, even Aunt Sofia when she remembers.'

'She was a bit upset last night,' Lacey told her carefully. 'She didn't know where you were.'

Helen grinned. 'Oh, I was around,' she said airily. 'But I didn't feel in the mood for formal introductions. Aunt Sofia's so old-fashioned she'd probably have expected me to curtsey or some dumb thing. I thought I'd rather take a look at you in my own time. I'll say this for you,' she went on generously. 'You sure look O.K. when you sleep. I mean, you don't snore or hang your mouth open or anything yuk like that. I guess sleeping with Troy, you wouldn't dare.'

'No,' Lacey agreed meekly, 'I certainly wouldn't.' It occurred to her with a little shock of pain that she had never actually slept with Troy, or woken with him either, but she crushed the thought down.

Helen was speaking again. 'Actually I shall probably never speak to Troy again for the rest of my life because he didn't let me come to the wedding. He kept it all so quiet, I wondered if you had two heads or something, but you look better than I thought. At least he didn't stick some creep on to me.'

'I don't quite follow . . .' Lacey began carefully, but Helen cut in.

'Sure you do. You're supposed to stop me giving Aunt Sofia the run-around. I'm not that dumb, you know. She's

116

been bleating for days about how nice it will be for me to have a sister my own age.'

'I see,' Lacey said carefully, allowing none of her inward dismay to show. 'And how do you feel about it?'

Helen's dark eyes considered her for a moment, and then she gave a faint grin. 'I'll tell you when I know,' she said. 'Are you getting up soon? I thought I'd show you around.'

This was so blatantly an olive branch that Lacey could not help feeling a little suspicious, but she accepted the offer with every appearance of pleasure. After all, she thought, Troy had intended her to be a friend for Helen, and questioning her motives at the outset would not be an ideal basis for any future relationship between them.

Some fifteen minutes later, showered and changed into a slim-fitting cotton shift, she was walking with Helen through the extensive grounds which gave the villa its privacy, and wondering what had happened to the parched wilderness she had imagined. Roses grew everywhere, their masses of fragrant blooms contrasting sharply with the dark, rather sombre green of the cypresses, and the delicate silver of the olive trees. Their scent hung on the air, intermingling with the sharper tang of citrus. Lacey took a deep wondering breath.

'I never imagined anything so lovely,' she told Helen frankly. The younger girl made a slight grimace.

'It's O.K.,' she said off-handedly. 'And it would be even better if there was just something to do once in a while.'

'Where did you live before you came here?' Lacey tried to choose her words with care, but Helen's response was ready enough.

'California,' she said. 'Aunt Dora had a house at Malibu which we used at weekends. Boy, this is some contrast,' she added, jerking her chin discontentedly at the warm stillness all around them.

'It's rather different from what I'm used to as well,' Lacey said gently, and Helen's eyes flew to hers as if the thought had not occurred to her before. As they walked slowly back towards the villa, she chatted with increasing frankness of her life in the States, her friends at High School and the

117

plan to set up a teenage commune which had so badly misfired.

'Aunt Dora thought it was O.K.,' she told Lacey mutinously. 'I don't see why Troy had to play the heavy all of a sudden. He's never worried that much about me before.'

'Perhaps he thought you were safe in your aunt's charge.' Lacey felt bound to respond in some way. 'It may be that it was the first time he'd thought there was any need to interfere.'

'Maybe,' Helen agreed. 'But it was for sure he didn't like Aunt Dora, any more than Papa did. She and Papa had a big row once over the guardianship bit and he accused her of exerting undue influence on Mama when she was dying.'

'But why should she do that?' Lacey asked rather helplessly.

'Money,' Helen said succinctly. 'I guess she thought if she was looking after me, she would have control of my fortune too. Only Papa fixed things so she only got an allowance. Then when he died she tried to get Troy to push it up a little, and there was more trouble!'

Lacey tried to appear non-committal as she listened, but secretly she was appalled at Helen's cynical appraisal of the situation and her apparent acceptance of her aunt's shallow and mercenary set of values.

'How did you get on with your aunt?' she asked eventually.

Helen grinned. 'What do you want me to say—that she used to beat me and starve me and lock me in the cellar? She didn't. We got on fine. She couldn't help the way she was about money. She and Mama never had any when they were girls, but Mama didn't care about things like that. And when she married Papa, nothing changed. She never wanted to become part of the jet-set crowd. That's really why they built this house, so they could have an ordinary home and an ordinary family. Aunt Dora always said she should have married the millionaire, not Mama. She said she would have made better use of the potential.'

Lacey had to smile in spite of herself. Helen's Aunt Dora might be a gold-digger, but at least she was almost naïvely open about it, whereas Michelle ... but she closed her mind to thoughts about her stepmother, relegating them to a corner of her consciousness.

'What about you, Lacey?' Helen said. 'Of course it's not really so different for you, is it, your folks being wealthy too.' She stopped, her eyes, suddenly, round with dismay. 'What am I saying? Gee, Lacey, I'm sorry. I forgot all about your father. Me and my big mouth,' she added contritely.

Lacey forced a smile. 'Don't worry. I—I have to face up to it some time.'

Aunt Sofia was out on the tiled patio looking for them as they approached the house, but her brow cleared slightly as she saw them approaching the house in apparent amity and Lacey agreed eagerly to her suggestion that they should have breakfast in the open air. Two dark-clad maids carried out a table and chairs, and proceeded to set out freshly squeezed orange juice, hot rolls and a pot of the dark, strong Turkish coffee. Lacey was not enamoured of this brew, but she told herself that, like everything else in her new life, she would have to accustom herself.

When breakfast was over, Helen took her round the villa. Lacey found that the rooms were spacious and airy, and far less ostentatious than she had privately feared. The room in which she had woken up that morning, together with its adjoining bathroom, were among the most luxurious, and she was not altogether surprised when Helen told her that Troy had had the suite entirely redecorated before the wedding. Perhaps this was the surprise he'd said was waiting for her on Theros, she thought vaguely. But when they arrived finally at the big *saloni*, Lacey realised how wrong she was. For there, dominating the quiet comfort of its surroundings, stood a brand new baby grand piano, and she knew without a second's doubt that this was her wedding present, brought from where? Corfu? the mainland? at heaven only knew what expense and difficulty. Her vision blurred ridiculously, and she had to shake her head impatiently to regain her self-control.

It did not take much urging from either Helen or Aunt Sofia to persuade her to sit down and try the instrument. Its tone was perfect, she thought, as her fingers discovered familiar chords. It was not until she was well embarked into

119

the piece that she realised she was playing Liszt's *Liebe-straum* and her fingers faltered slightly as the significance of her choice came home to her. A glance at Aunt Sofia's benign smile revealed that she too was perfectly familiar with the evocative music and thought it a perfectly suitable piece to be at the forefront of a young bride's mind. Lacey could have screamed with vexation, but she forced herself to play to the end and accept the admiring applause.

'Meet the girl who has everything.' Was there a sour note in Helen's congratulations? Lacey found herself wondering. 'She has looks, she has money and now she even has talent. I bet you just never put a foot wrong, do you, Lacey?'

'Yes, very often—and both feet,' Lacey hastened to assure her, but she felt that the hoped-for camaraderie had received a setback, and was not totally surprised when Helen disappeared after lunch, leaving her to her own devices. Aunt Sofia retired to her room for a rest and Lacey found herself at a loose end. She could not even occupy herself by unpacking her clothes as this had been done for her by one of the maids, she thought, wandering into the master bedroom and staring round with a critical eye. Not that she could fault any of the arrangements, from the king-size bed with its luxuriously padded headboard which dominated the large room to the fitted wardrobes with their louvred doors which ran the length of one wall. It was odd, too, to compare them with the modest amenities that had been hers at the convent not so long ago, and to realise that that part of her life was over and that she could not, even if she wanted to, go back to being the girl she was then. That brief, magical time in Troy's arms had changed all that— transformed her from a child into a woman and a wife. It was no use pretending to herself that this had been simply an isolated incident born of her distress either. Troy had always had the power to make her aware of her body. She could acknowledge this now and admit too that that aware-ness had been overtaken by sheer physical need and that until he came to her again, she would know an aching loneliness in that huge bed which had never been intended for single occupation.

With a little sigh, she wandered across the room and pushed open the door that led to his dressing room. She did not know what she was seeking. There wasn't even a whiff of the familiar cigar smoke left hanging in the still air to evoke his presence. The rows of formal suits hanging in the clothes cupboard seemed blank and anonymous and gave no clue to the man who owned them and who now counted her as another of his possessions. There were no jarring notes. Everything was of the finest materials and fastidiously kept, she thought, almost pettishly slamming shut one of the drawers of the dressing chest. As she turned away, her arm brushed an onyx box standing on top of the chest, and sent it tumbling to the carpet.

'Oh, no!' Lacey knelt down beside it ruefully. This was the retribution that fate dealt out to snoopers, and it would serve her right if the box was broken and she had to explain to Troy that she had caused the accident while she was going through his things.

But the box was intact, although it had opened during its fall and the cuff links and studs it contained were now strewn on the floor. Lacey replaced the velvet-lined partitions, and began to sort the contents into matching sets. There only appeared to be one casualty—one of the cuff links was broken, and she began to search around on the floor for the missing half, the broken piece clutched in her hand. Where on earth was it? It was the wrong shape to roll and it would be such a shame if it was lost because it was such an attractive pattern, chequered in gold and enamel . . . She suddenly felt very cold as she stared down at the cuff link. She knew quite definitely that her search was useless, and that she would not find the rest of the broken trinket on Troy's dressing room floor. She knew, because she had found it already in the bathroom of the suite she had occupied with Michelle in Paris all those weeks ago—where Troy had lost it.

She sat back on her heels and stared down at the broken piece until it blurred under her eyes. Such a tiny thing, she found herself thinking, and yet it was the missing piece in the jigsaw which made everything else fall into place.

It showed her Troy and Michelle—together in Paris. Pain

121

and bitterness fought with disbelief making her feel almost physically sick. No wonder Michelle behaved with such hostility, seeing herself cynically jettisoned by her lover in favour of her own stepdaughter. What had Michelle said to her that night about her marriage? 'Not now—not to you.' Had she then expected Troy to marry herself? Like Michelle, he must have known it was only a matter of time before she was a widow and free to marry him. Why hadn't he waited for her?

Or did he draw the line at making his wife the woman who had already betrayed one husband? Lacey found she was shivering uncontrollably. Instead he had chosen her— the inexperienced girl whom he could mould into the docile fidelity that his double standard of morality no doubt demanded.

How could she have been such a fool? she asked herself despairingly. She had been so abysmally easy to beguile with his expert lovemaking, so ready to be blinded to everything but her awakening desire for him. She had not even recognised his voice as that of the man who had telephoned the suite that night. Was that part of her attraction as a wife, she wondered, that she was so pitifully easy to dupe?

The thought stung and tormented, to be succeeded by the even more bitter realisation that she was now here, safely disposed of on Theros, while Troy was still in England. With Michelle. The marriage of convenience had suddenly become an inconvenience, she thought, biting her lip savagely, trying to blot out the memory of his lovemaking. He had simply used her because it was his right to do so, and as soon as she was out of the way had no doubt turned in relief from her inexperience to the practised charms of his mistress.

Her eyelids were closed so tightly that they hurt, and her heart was thudding unpleasantly, nauseously and so loudly that it seemed to fill her ears. And then she realised that it was not merely her own tumultous pulses that she heard, and that someone was knocking at the bedroom door with a soft persistence.

She dragged herself up off her knees and still holding the

122

cuff link clutched in her palm went out of the dressing room and across the bedroom to the door.

Stephanos was standing there smiling, but his eyes grew suddenly anxious as they took in her over-bright eyes and pale face.

'I have come to take my leave of you, Mrs Andreakis,' he said gently. 'I shall join Troy in London some time tomorrow, and I was wondering if you would care to send any messages to him.'

Lacey stared at him, for a moment hardly comprehending what he was saying. He had been a courteous and considerate escort, but she knew he had been shocked at the utter chill which had attended her scene with Troy in the breakfast room, of which he had been an unwilling witness.

'No,' she said, her throat constricted. 'There's no message.'

'Mrs Andreakis—Kyria Lacey.' He looked at her almost beseechingly. 'If you do not wish to send a verbal message, I quite understand. I would be happy to wait while you wrote a note.' He paused, but she remained silent. 'Forgive me, but this cannot be a happy time for either of you. So much sorrow so soon after your marriage and now this separation. I have been a friend of Troy's for many years and I know it would comfort him to hear from you.'

She smiled then, a brilliant artificial smile without meaning or emotion behind it.

'I'm no longer a child, Mr Lindos,' she said quietly. 'I don't imagine Troy will be lacking comfort—do you?'

She stepped back and closed the door quietly but firmly before he could intervene again. There was a pause, then she heard his footsteps going slowly down the corridor. She waited until she could hear them no longer, then threw herself across the huge barren width of the bed, pummelling the quilted bedcover with her fists while tears of rage, jealousy and hurt rained wildly down her white face.

It was a subdued trio of women that assembled for dinner that night. Helen arrived at the table with an air of bravado. She had been returned protesting to the villa some

123

time before by the annoyed father of one of the younger fishermen who had allowed Helen to persuade him to take her out on his boat. But Yanni's *babas* had reacted with vigorous disapproval. Apart from the fact that her behaviour was unseemly for a girl of her age, he had no wish to arouse the wrath of the Kyrios Troy, he had told Aunt Sofia flatly.

The poor woman was so outraged by Helen's behaviour and the thought of Troy's probable reaction if he learned of her conduct that she spent most of the meal moaning softly to herself and addressing reproachful remarks in a mixture of English and Greek to the patently unrepentant Helen. And so it was that Lacey's wan appearance and almost utter lack of appetite passed almost unobserved. In fact, Lacey felt that Aunt Sofia held her partly to blame for the incident by failing to keep a proper eye on her errant young sister-in-law.

'Oh, God, everything's such a drag.' Helen cut irritably across her aunt's mutterings. 'I'd never have asked Yanni if I'd guessed he'd let his old man push him around like that. There's just nothing to do on this place.'

'Don't you swim?' Lacey hastily forestalled another outburst of wails from Aunt Sofia.

'Oh, sure, but that's not much fun on your own.'

'But there must be girls of your own age on the island. Aren't there any families in the village with daughters?' Lacey asked.

Helen nodded, an impish grin lifting the corners of her mouth. 'But they're all too busy learning to be good little wives to have fun. Any swimming that goes on is a strictly masculine affair. Besides,' she shot an oblique glance at Aunt Sofia, 'I like to do my swimming in the raw.'

Lacey felt her lips tighten in annoyance. Helen seemed to go out of her way to say and do things that would distress and disturb the older woman.

'In that case,' she tried to speak lightly, 'it's probably just as well that the bathing isn't mixed.'

After all, she thought, this was one of the main reasons for her being here, to try and win Helen over and give her some sort of companionship. She would not achieve this by joining Aunt Sofia in overt disapproval of the girl's every action.

She had done a lot of hard thinking alone in her room during the long afternoon hours after that first passionate outburst of misery had abated. Her first plan had been flight at any cost, but sane consideration had convinced her that this course of action was impossible. Catching the ferry to Corfu would be easy enough, but once there her plans fell to pieces. The fact was she had very little actual cash at her disposal and no means of obtaining any more. It was hardly likely that Aunt Sofia would be inclined to finance her precipitate departure, she thought, her lips twisting slightly.

It seemed she was obliged to remain, at least for a while, and she was prepared to abide by the terms of the contract that had brought her to Theros. It had been a business arrangement, after all. Troy Andreakis had never pretended that he was stirred by an emotion deeper than the normal desire a virile man might feel for an attractive girl. The fact that his indifference and betrayal had wounded her so deeply would remain her secret and she would conduct their relationship on the level of the sterile bargain it was and always had been.

She would learn from Aunt Sofia how to run the villa and manage the servants; she would try and win Helen over to at least an outward show of conventional behaviour. As for the rest of the bargain—she swallowed convulsively —he had the proof of her innocence which he had demanded. He could expect no more. She would not share his bed or his attentions.

She made herself smile at Helen, concealing the anguished turmoil that possessed her.

'I'm sorry you think Theros is such a drag. I was rather hoping you might show me around—the village, the beaches.'

'Mm.' For a moment Lacey thought she saw someone much older peep at her from behind Helen's long lashes. 'Maybe that's not such a bad idea, and at least we'll both get a pat on the head from Brother Troy when he finally shows up.' And with a smile that Lacey found hard to decipher, she began to serve herself from a bowl of previously rejected fresh fruit salad.

The next few days passed quietly. Lacey familiarised herself with the villa's layout and ventured into the kitchen regions to meet Maria, the genius who presided over the cooking stove. She had wondered if any of the servants would resent a new mistress being suddenly pushed on to them, but the opposite seemed the case, and Aunt Sofia made it more than clear that she was happy to resign the housekeeping reins into Lacey's hands whenever she wished. She learned that much of the produce used by the house was grown on the Andreakis estate itself, and sampled the island wine, richly red and rather too sweet for her taste.

The villa itself she found a delightful place with its big low-ceilinged rooms, and the wide terrace which ran the full length of the house. The big entrance hall and passages were coolly tiled, but most of the main rooms had elegantly blocked parquet floors only partly covered by thick goatskin rugs. The interior walls were washed in pastel colours, blues and yellows predominating, and local, heavily textured fabrics had been used extensively for upholstery and curtaining. It was beautiful, Lacey thought, but at the same time it was a family home, not a showpiece. She tried to say as much to Aunt Sofia, who nodded and smiled approvingly.

'But above all it is a house for children, *pethi mou*,' she declared to Lacey's embarrassment, her eyes sweeping the slender figure of her new niece with a trace of regret, as if she expected her to be pregnant already. 'There are many rooms which can become nurseries when the time comes.'

It was a curiously appealing picture and Lacey felt a pang as she firmly shut it out of her mind. Providing occupants for potential nurseries did not come within the terms of the bargain with Troy Andreakis, she told herself bleakly.

The afternoons she spent mainly with Helen. Sometimes they lay on the terrace, while Lacey acclimatised herself to the strong sun, at others they played tennis on the sheltered court that occupied one corner of the garden.

She had been on Theros almost a week before she submitted to her sister-in-law's promptings and set out to walk to the village.

The road was longer and dustier than Lacey had envisaged, but Helen assured her emphatically that most of the villagers were pedestrians. No one used a car on Theros, she declared, and donkeys were the most usual form of transport.

'Has no one ever thought of improving the roads?' Lacey asked ruefully, detaching a pebble from inside her sandal.

'If so, they've rapidly thought again. I guess the islanders think they're O.K. the way they are,' Helen said breezily. 'Besides, better roads mean more tourists and hotels and gas stations—the whole bit. I don't think Theros could take that.'

'I'm surprised to hear you say that.' Lacey gave her an ironic look. 'I thought you wanted the island to be made livelier.'

'Don't fool yourself, sister dear. I want out.' Helen scuffed her feet moodily as she walked along. 'Aunt Dora would have me back, I know. If only Troy would say the word.'

'Do you think that's likely?'

Helen shrugged. 'People do change their minds,' she replied vaguely.

But not Troy, Lacey thought bitterly, the humiliating recollection of how she had begged him to let her remain with him after he had made love to her fiercely in her mind.

The village, she found, was unexpectedly modern in its appearance with attractive, spotlessly whitewashed houses in an easy sprawl around the small harbour with its bobbing caiques. When she commented on this newness to Helen, she learned that much of the village had been destroyed in the earthquake which had swept the area in the early fifties, and that the villagers had patiently rebuilt their homes on the same site, showing, Lacey decided wryly, a touching faith that the Earthshaker would not strike again in the same place.

Although it was relatively early in the day, the harbour side was alive with activity and the small tavernas dotted along its length were busy with custom.

Helen pointed to a large boat heading out to sea. 'The ferry's just left—today's high-spot,' she said.

Lacey found the brief circuit of the harbour something of an ordeal. She soon realised that as the new-made wife of the richest and most influential man in the area she was the target for all the local eyes. Helen, of course, seemed perfectly at home in the village and at her prompting Lacey began to respond with diminishing shyness to the greetings which came their way. As they strolled along, Helen nudged her.

'We're coming to Niko's place,' she said in an undertone. 'He's Spiro's brother—the guy that does the gardens at the villa—so I guess Troy would like us to stop and say hello at least.'

But as they approached it was obvious that the news of their arrival had preceded them. Niko, large and benignly smiling, was already dusting off the chairs outside the taverna and his wife Melina was waiting with a tray of freshly crushed fruit juice. It was impossible to refuse this friendly hospitality, even though Lacey soon found she had exhausted her few words of Greek and had to rely on Helen to act as interpreter for her thanks for the couple's good wishes.

It was a delightful relaxation, she found, to sit in the sunshine looking out over the sea and the faint gauzy haze which seemed to shimmer above it. The air was full of scents, and the sounds of voices and laughter, interspersed with the cooing of doves from a dozen alleys opening off the street along the harbour and the occasional bleating of a goat. Lacey half-closed her eyes, feeling a sudden peace insidiously invading her being, and then sat up, nearly spilling her drink with a nervous jerk as Helen exclaimed joyously, 'Evan! Well, what do you know?'

He was a tall, brown-haired young man, the lower part of his face hidden under a beard. He wore rather tattered shorts, and a safari jacket hung over his bare chest revealing a varied selection of chains and medallions. A professional-looking camera was slung round his neck and a large camera case hung from his shoulder. He was grinning at Helen.

'I thought you said this place didn't exist,' he accused, and hitched forward another chair, before turning with rather studied politeness to Lacey. 'Er—you don't mind?'

Lacey felt she could do little but allow him to join them. He and Helen were obviously well acquainted and she wondered with alarm whether Evan Kent, as Helen rather triumphantly introduced him to her, had anything to do with the commune which had been the cause of Helen's removal from her aunt's sphere of influence in California.

Troy would hardly be pleased, she thought, if Helen's hippy friends began arriving on Theros for a grand reunion, and she felt rather helpless and inadequate when she considered her ability to cope with such an eventuality.

But Evan, she soon gathered from the conversation, was far from being a hippy or a beachcomber as his appearance suggested. In fact, he was a professional photographer employed by a leading American magazine.

'You're on holiday, Mr Kent?' she asked on one of the few occasions when Helen paused for a breath.

'You could call it that.' He paused. 'I do have—an assignment of sorts, but it may not work out.'

Lacey immediately felt uneasy. She hoped that this assignment was not connected with Troy in any way. He had never made any secret of his loathing of personal publicity, and the fact that Evan Kent was a friend of Helen's would not influence him in his favour, rather the contrary, she thought unhappily. But this was surely one problem that she could not be expected to deal with unaided.

'Where are you staying?' Helen inquired. 'We don't run to the Hilton here, but I guess Niko could find you a room. How long do you plan to be around?'

Evan Kent's shrug was negligent. 'A few days, or as long as it takes.' He studied the glass of ouzo Melina had brought him through slightly narrowed eyes. 'Is Big Brother in residence?'

'Not at the moment,' Helen said lightly. 'But he shouldn't be away for very long. After all, this is supposed to be his honeymoon.'

Evan Kent turned and gave Lacey a long, deliberate look. 'In his shoes, I don't think I'd ever have left,' he drawled, and she felt the colour flame in her cheeks. She reached rather clumsily for her bag and got up, murmuring something confused to Helen about the need to return to the villa. She expected an argument, but Helen was unreservedly co-operative. She chatted casually about the village and the toll the earthquake had taken on the way back to the villa, and they were nearly at the house before she said almost idly, 'Could Evan come to dinner one night, do you suppose, Lacey?'

Lacey hesitated, but reason suggested strongly that she should agree. After all, there could be little harm in this young man spending an evening at the villa with Aunt Sofia as chaperone, and if she refused Helen could well take matters into her own hands by meeting him in the village and causing more gossip.

'I don't see why not,' she said slowly. 'Have you known him long?'

'Oh, for ever,' Helen replied largely. 'His brother and I were in high school together. The only thing is,' she gave Lacey a sideways glance, 'I wouldn't tell Aunt Sofia he works for a magazine. I mean, she might get all uptight about it and tell Troy, and what he doesn't know won't hurt him.'

Lacey was conscious of that strangely troubled feeling again, but Helen's gaze seemed candid enough. 'I suppose it will be all right,' she acknowledged with a faint sigh. 'But perhaps you'll make it clear that no pictures or stories are to be done about the villa.'

'No problem,' Helen assured her, a satisfied smile playing about her lips.

When Evan did arrive at the villa for dinner a few nights later, Lacey was relieved to find him rather more conventionally dressed in dark slacks and a silk shirt and even Aunt Sofia seemed to find him acceptable. No word of his controversial profession passed his lips, and he talked knowledgeably of other Greek islands he had visited in the Aegean Sea and the difference he had found between the landscapes and temperaments of the people in the Aegean and the Ionian areas. Lacey found herself warming to him. She had known few young men apart from Alan, and she told herself it was just a general unhappiness about her situation that had caused her initial uneasiness about him. He didn't embarrass her by any further references to her honeymoon, and he treated Aunt Sofia with a charming deference. His behaviour to Helen was affectionate in a casual, fraternal manner and Lacey found she was dismissing her fears that they might have been involved in a closer relationship in California.

Moreover, his visit proved a welcome break in the quiet routine of her life on Theros. She was trying to concentrate all her interest on the villa and its gardens and learning about the vines and olive groves which gave the island its main exports, anything in fact that would divert her attention from her husband and the confrontation that sooner or later would come between them. She still had no idea when to expect him. The 'complications' he had referred to in England must be proving even more absorbing than he had expected, she thought, fanning her smouldering anger into a blaze again as she visualised him with Michelle. In some ways she wished she had never found the broken cuff link and realised its significance. She might have been living in a fool's paradise, but wasn't that better than the hell in which she now found herself?

She was glad to escape from her unhappy thoughts in the hilarious game of Scrabble that followed dinner, and later, as she said goodbye to Evan, she realised she had enjoyed the evening more than she would have thought possible.

As the days lengthened into her second, and then her third week on Theros, Evan became a regular visitor at the villa. The midday meal developed into a picnic, usually in one of the rocky coves below the villa where they swam and lay on the rocks, soaking up the sun like lizards. Lacey's skin was beginning to acquire a smooth honey-coloured tan and her too-slender curves were becoming more rounded, thanks to Maria's declared intention of feeding the Kyria up on the somewhat specious grounds that a skinny woman was no good to a man.

Judging by the appreciative gleam she had seen in Evan's eyes a few times as he looked at her, Lacey thought wryly that Maria might have a point. Occasionally she found herself wondering how Troy would react if he returned unexpectedly, but she told herself defiantly that his own conduct gave him no grounds for complaint. Besides, and she had to face the fact, although she liked Evan, was amused by him, and looked forward to his visits, her feelings went no deeper than that. She did not want him as a lover. If her body ached with longing and loneliness as she lay unsleeping in the big bed at night, she was only too aware that only one man could satisfy her need. It seemed that brief time of darkness with Troy had spoiled her for other men, she thought drearily. But however much she might want him, and there were times when she was tormented by desire, she vowed to herself that she would never allow him to possess her again. She would not share him with Michelle.

At the same time, she found his total silence unnerving. Perhaps he had been angered by her failure to send him a message by Stephanos, she thought bleakly. But, as his wife, she felt she was at least entitled to some advance warning of his plans, and she knew that Aunt Sofia thought it was strange that there were never any letters or telephone calls for her. Just fresh evidence of his indifference to her, she told herself, but this confirmation of the barrenness of their relationship gave her no satisfaction.

It did not occur to her that Aunt Sofia's concern might be extended to other areas until Miss Andreakis tackled her one morning as she was about to join Helen and Evan on the terrace where Spiro had set up an old table tennis table he had found in one of the basements.

'Is it wise to see so much of this young man, *pethi mou?*' Aunt Sofia's dark eyes were full of real anxiety as she looked at her. Lacey smiled at her confidently.

'Oh, you don't have to worry,' she said. 'He's much too old for Helen anyway. She told him yesterday that he was a drag because he said the water was too shallow to dive from the rocks. And I'm keeping a close eye on them.'

'And who is keeping an eye on you?' Aunt Sofia asked carefully.

Lacey stared at her as the older woman went on, 'You

are no longer a free agent, Lacey. You are a wife, and whatever is the custom in your own country, here on Theros the
women do not seek the company of men other than their
husbands.'

'And what about the men?' Lacey asked tonelessly. 'Do
they never seek the company of women other than their
wives?'

Aunt Sofia flushed slightly. 'It is not always a man's
nature to be faithful for the whole of his life.'

'No?' Lacey asked drily. 'And when does the normal
straying period commence? A week after marriage—a
month, a year?'

She saw she was distressing Aunt Sofia and bit her lip.

'I'm sorry, but this—double standard for men and women
irritates me. But you really have no need to worry. Evan is
Helen's friend and I have no intention of being unfaithful
with him or anyone else. Besides,' she chose her words with
care, 'Troy has spent a lot of time in Britain and the States.
He should have a slightly more liberal attitude.'

'Oh, no doubt he has—for other people, *pethi mou.*'
Aunt Sofia's tone was dry in turn. 'Whether he is prepared
to be so—liberal where his own wife is concerned remains
to be seen.'

As she went to join the others, Lacey told herself
vehemently that Aunt Sofia was simply making mountains
out of molehills. There was nothing in her relationship with
Evan that could cause even the most jealous husband a
minute's anxiety. All the older woman's warning had done
was make her more conscious of him and introduced an
awkwardness into the casual camaraderie that had existed
up to now.

'What's the matter, Lacey?' Evan asked eventually. They
were lying on one of the few sandy beaches Theros boasted,
reached by a steep path from the villa grounds, and they
were temporarily alone, Helen having decided to go for
another swim.

'Nothing.' She picked up a handful of sand and let it
drift through her fingers.

'Now you've made the conventional reply, how about telling me the truth?' he suggested. He put out a hand and

133

touched her ankle. His fingers were warm and they sent a disturbing current through Lacey, who sat up, pushing her pale hair impatiently off her face.

'Oh, it's too stupid for words,' she said at last. 'Troy's aunt thinks—at least she says—she doesn't think I ought . . .' she faltered to a halt.

'I get it. The lady thinks the chaperone needs a chaperone.' He picked up a pebble and shied it moodily in the general direction of the sea. 'Could be she's right, Lacey.'

She glanced at him startled. 'Oh, Evan, no!'

'Oh, Lacey, yes,' he mimicked. 'Just because you're Andreakis' property it doesn't mean other men won't want to look—especially when the owner himself doesn't seem particularly interested.'

'You have no right to say that!' Her face flamed.

'I'm giving myself that right.' He reached out, gripping her shoulders. 'You're a beautiful girl, Lacey, and you deserve to be treated like one—not like some block of shares in a corporation to be filed away until needed. What kind of marriage have you got, for heaven's sake?'

'Please let me go,' she said unhappily. 'Troy and I have—an understanding.'

'I hope it keeps you warm at nights. Does it, Lacey?' He tried to look into her eyes, but she kept them fixed on the ground. 'You don't need an understanding, Lacey. You need to live and to love the way you were meant to.' He began to caress her shoulders and arms with light stroking movements. 'Let me show you, Lacey, sweet baby.'

His face was only inches from hers when she twisted out of his arms and stood up.

'I'm sorry, Evan. I never intended to let you think I was available.'

'I don't think that,' he said violently, staring up at her. 'But I think you're lonely.'

'If I am, it's something I have to work out for myself.' She crossed her arms across her breasts and stared out over the shimmering expanse of hazy sea. Just for a moment, she had been tempted. It would have been so easy to let Evan press her back into the sand, but it was not just the thought that Helen might return and find them that had stopped her. Nothing had changed after all. If she let Evan make love to her she would simply be exchanging loneliness for guilt, and that would be madness when she did not really want him. Her only motive for giving herself to him would be to revenge herself on Troy, and that was an ignoble reason for doing anything and would just bring her down to Troy's level, she thought bitterly.

'I can't figure you, Lacey.' Evan's voice was almost reflective. 'The guy dumps you here. He doesn't write, he doesn't phone—Helen didn't realise she was giving away any state secrets,' he added hastily, intercepting her look of indignant surprise. 'And yet you sit here with your hands folded, waiting for him to come back to you. Well, you're on the wrong island, baby. The faithful Penelope waited on Ithaca.'

'The geography isn't important,' she said gravely.

'No.' He looked at her resignedly. 'I guess if you love the guy, you love him, and there's nothing anyone can do about that except wait for you to get over it.'

'You talk about love as if it was some infectious disease,' Lacey said calmly, while her mind ran riot. What was she doing talking about it at all in connection with Troy and herself? She didn't love him. Love was good and simple and included things like knowledge and respect—everything she didn't share with Troy. What she felt for him was too complex and too contradictory to bear the sweet name of love—wasn't it?

'If it is, marriage is generally regarded as the cure. You must have a bad case,' he said wryly. He stood up, his lips compressed. He looked suddenly older and harder. 'Of all the guys in the world, and it has to be him.' He sighed. 'I suppose that's the way it goes.'

Before Lacey could prevent him, he reached for her and pulled her into his arms, kissing her hard on the mouth. When he let her go, she wanted to wipe her hand across her lips, but she knew it would be hurtful, so she stood motionless, her hands balled into fists at her side.

'I think you'd better go, Evan,' she said.

'Maybe you're right.' He stood for a moment regarding her, his hands on his hips. 'Suddenly the lady turns into Mrs

Andreakis. It's quite a transformation, baby.' He smiled and he was the old Evan again. 'Don't let's part bad friends, Lacey. I'm going over to Corfu for a couple of days. When I get back, I'll be in touch.'

She wanted to tell him that was not a good idea, but he had gathered up his things and was scrambling up the steep path towards the cliff top before she could collect her scattered thoughts. Lacey was not sorry to see him go, but sorry for the circumstances which had made it necessary that he should. Aunt Sofia had been wiser than she gave her credit for, she thought ironically.

She sank down on the sand again, leaning back against a sun-warmed rock while her mind tried to deal coherently with the new and unwelcome thoughts about her relationship with Troy that Evan had put there. In spite of everything that had happened was she—could she be in love with this stranger who had married her? If she had really hated him, might she not have welcomed the knowledge of his intimacy with another woman because it would inevitably mean she would see less of him? In fact, the discovery of his relationship with Michelle had been a nightmare of agony and hurt which the passing days only served to deepen.

She shivered and looked up startled as Helen's shadow fell across her.

'Hi.' Helen reached for a towel, glancing round. 'Where'd Evan go?'

Lacey sighed. 'He's gone to pack, I think. He said something about going to Corfu for a while.'

'Already?' Helen's reaction was sharp and Lacey looked at her in some surprise. The younger girl looked thoroughly upset, and Lacey felt a twinge of alarm. Had her initial forebodings been correct? Helen had dismissed Evan as the brother of a friend, but this might simply have been a ploy to reassure Lacey. He was very attractive, as she had been made only too aware. Had Helen also succumbed to this attraction? Certainly the unguarded expression in her eyes suggested that his departure came very close to being the end of the world. She groaned inwardly. She had been spectacularly unsuccessful as a chaperone on two counts, it seemed.

'Oh well, that's that, I guess,' Helen said, and she gave a short laugh. 'Maybe we'd better get back before Aunt Sofia thinks we've drowned.'

Her manner was odd as they walked slowly back to the villa in the sun, and Lacey decided regretfully that the old Helen, moody and resentful, seemed to have returned because of Evan's defection. Her returns to any conversational ploys Lacey began were monosyllabic, and eventually Lacey too fell silent. The day was suddenly shadowed, she thought and with mounting irritation, 'Damn Evan. He's spoiled everything.'

CHAPTER EIGHT

HELEN seemed to have recovered her spirits the next day and was back to her old buoyant self, on the surface at least. If she was missing Evan, she was hiding it remarkably well, Lacey thought. She herself had spent a restless night and had fought a headache most of the morning. It was pleasant to lie on the terrace after a light lunch, and her heart sank a little when she heard Helen suggest a swim.

'You go,' she urged, staring up through the leaves and petals of the climbing rose that festooned the trellis above her.

'It's no fun alone,' Helen protested. 'And you know Aunt Sofia throws a blue fit every time I go to the beach on my own. She thinks I'm going to be eaten by a giant squid or washed away by a tidal wave or something.'

Lacey smiled unwillingly. 'But our little beach is perfectly safe,' she argued. 'There isn't even a current to make it dangerous,' then as she saw the only too familiar mutinous pout begin to appear on Helen's face, she hastily capitulated. 'O.K., I'll come, but I don't promise I'll come in the sea.'

'Oh, you will when you get there,' Helen promised. 'You won't be able to resist it.'

Certainly the little beach was at its inviting best, Lacey had to admit as she climbed over the tumbled rocks at the base of the cliff and jumped down on to the stretch of sand. The air was still and seemed to hold a faint scent of lemons, and the sea whispered and lapped at the sand.

She turned to Helen. 'I wish I'd brought my swimsuit after all.'

'Well, don't let that stop you,' Helen said calmly, pulling off her tee-shirt and unzipping her jeans. She caught Lacey's glance and grinned. 'I told you I liked swimming in the raw. I wasn't kidding. How about you, Big Sister? Ever tried it?'

'Er—no.' Lacey tried unsuccessfully to conceal her faint

138

embarrassment and felt a complete fool.

'Well, now's your chance,' Helen said mockingly. 'Hell, Lacey, who's going to see you? This beach is private, after all, and Aunt Sofia isn't likely to come down. Besides, when Troy shows up, you can surprise him with your all-over tan. Don't tell me he wouldn't like that.'

Lacey's cheeks grew warmer still. She looked uncertainly from the cliffs behind them to the dark blue expanse of the little bay.

'Oh, for heaven's sake!' Helen slipped out of her briefs and ran slim and long-legged to the water's edge. 'Come on in,' she called over her shoulder. 'The water's fine.'

Lacey hesitated, then told herself she was being ridiculous. She was reluctant to jeopardise any success she might have had in building a relationship with Helen by suddenly turning into a wet blanket over an innocent diversion like swimming without clothes. With sudden determination, she reached for the zip of her sundress and within moments had joined Helen in the sea, revelling in the sudden coolness of the water against the warmth of her flesh.

'Isn't it a great feeling?' Helen called, and Lacey was forced to agree. All her anxieties, even the slight headache seemed to fall away with her clothes, and she felt completely free. They spent nearly half an hour swimming, diving and floating and playing noisy splashing games in the shallows. It was like the best days of childhood, Lacey thought, but with all the feelings intensified. She was breathless by the time they got back to their clothes. Helen shook the surplus water off her body like a puppy and spread out her towel, obviously intending to sunbathe. Her eyes widened when she saw Lacey reaching for her sundress again.

'Boy, you sure have a hang-up about wearing clothes,' she commented. 'Are you afraid the sun's going to be shocked and go behind a cloud or something?'

Lacey sighed. 'Something like that,' she admitted with a faint smile. 'Blame my convent upbringing.'

'Well, I just don't know what you're afraid of,' Helen argued. 'If a boat comes round the headland we'd have time to get into evening gowns before they spotted us.' She wriggled her shoulders luxuriously. 'Doesn't the sun feel good?'

'Yes, it does,' Lacey yielded, stretching herself out on the sand.

'Don't go to sleep,' Helen warned. 'Troy won't thank you if you welcome him back with a bad case of sunburn.'

Lacey moved restlessly, brushing a hovering insect away from her face. She did not wish to be reminded of the scene that would have to be faced when her husband did arrive on Theros. It was bitter to reflect how different her attitude might have been to his return if she had not found that cuff link. She turned on her side, pushing her hair back from her face, and paused, her attention suddenly arrested.

'What was that?' she queried sharply.

'What was what?' Helen demanded drowsily.

Lacey sat up, reaching for her dress. 'I saw something on the cliff top over there—like a light flashing.' She shaded her eyes with her hand and stared up at the cliff. But it seemed deserted. There wasn't a sound or a flicker of movement to be seen and Lacey began to wonder if she had imagined that brief glimmer of light as if the sun had caught a polished surface and flung its brilliance back momentarily.

'Oh, relax,' Helen said irritably. 'That must be nearly a quarter of a mile away. If there was anyone there, what could they see?'

'I prefer not to think,' Lacey said tartly, wriggling back into her clothes. 'I think I'll go back now. Enough is enough, and I'm sure there was someone up there, even if there isn't now.'

'Then I may as well come too.' Shrugging, Helen reached for her own things. 'Boy, are you jumpy!' Her face was flushed and she looked moody again as they trudged back up the path to the villa. Lacey felt a pang of self-reproach.

'I'm sorry, Helen.' She touched her sister-in-law's arm gently. 'I suppose I spoiled your afternoon. I don't mean to be a killjoy. We'll go again—tomorrow, perhaps . . .'

'Oh, forget it. I should have remembered you were little Miss Perfect,' Helen said abruptly, and Lacey felt snubbed. They walked in silence, a silence eventually dispelled by a distant hum growing louder and more vibrant by the second.

Lacey glanced up into the sky. 'That sounds like a helicopter.'

'Bright girl!' Helen sounded sarcastic. 'And now for the sixty-four-thousand-dollar prize, can you tell me who'll be in it?' She saw Lacey's lips part incredulously on the name and nodded. 'Right again. I'll say this for Big Brother Troy, he has a great sense of timing.'

There was an odd note in her voice, but Lacey disregarded it, too absorbed in the turmoil of emotion that had suddenly gripped her to pay any heed to Helen's reactions.

Her legs felt weak and her stomach churned agonisingly. All her sense of well-being and contentment had gone. If there had been anywhere to run to, any place of refuge that would have accepted her, she would have gone. But this was his island, too small and too familiar to shelter her against him. Anger began to build up inside her. It was typical that he should do this—literally descend on them out of the blue without a word of warning, so totally arrogant, so certain of his welcome.

She realised that her footsteps had slowed perceptibly, and that Helen was watching her in obvious surprise. She forced a smile, pressing one hand against her side

'I—I've got a bit of a stitch. I think I must have come up the path too fast. You go on ahead.'

'Well—O.K.,' Helen said dubiously. 'But I wouldn't hang around. Troy doesn't like to be kept waiting. Be seeing you.' And she broke into a run, disappearing between the tall hedges of flowering aloe.

Lacey stood quite still, trying to subdue her racing pulses into tranquillity. She had no idea what she was going to say to Troy when they finally came face to face and she was dreading the actual moment of confrontation. Ever since their first meeting, she had been either trying to elude him or get the better of him, and she had succeeded in neither. It was all very well to rehearse dignified scenes in one's mind which would bring down the curtain on this farce of a marriage almost before it had begun, but she knew if she was honest she had always discounted one important factor in these imaginary debates—the overwhelming physical attraction he had for her. It was simple enough to deny it in his absence, but now that he was here, she knew it would be hard to fight and impossible to ignore.

In her constant heart-searchings over the past days, one thing had been brought home to her more and more forcibly —that her prime emotion about the situation had been jealousy. She might tell herself she was outraged by his duplicity, by his betrayal not only of herself but of her father, but in reality it was the mental image of Michelle lying in his arms as she had once lain, sharing the intimacies of lovemaking, the kisses and caresses that had awoken Lacey to what fulfilment could mean, that tortured her.

And she knew without further doubt that her real feelings for Troy went much deeper than mere physical attraction alone.

She walked through the grounds towards the villa, her heart like ice within her. The trim scarlet and black helicopter, its whirring blades motionless, stood on the wide lawn in front of the terrace like some strange mechanical bird. She walked up the terrace steps and entered the house by the *saloni*. To her surprise Stephanos Lindos was sitting on one of the low cushioned seats reading a newspaper. He threw it aside when he saw Lacey and rose.

'My dear Mrs Andreakis! You look most well. The air on Theros must agree with you.'

Lacey decided drily that he was simply being gallant. She might have gained a little superficial weight, but there were shadows denoting restless nights under her eyes. The sun might have taken the pallor of an English winter from her skin, but it could not hide the look of strain which had come to inhabit her face.

'*Kalostone, kyrie*. Welcome,' she tried diffidently, and he smiled at her delightedly.

'Such progress in such a short time,' he approved. 'But I promise I will not outstay your charming welcome. I remain here for this evening only, and then you will have privacy to continue with your honeymoon.'

'Er—where is everyone?' She looked around, trying to

appear casual, but he was not deceived.

'Troy has gone up to shower,' he said. 'He has had nearly forty-eight hours travelling and business meetings. The last was in Athens this morning, but he would not rest. He was determined not to delay your reunion for a moment longer than necessary.'

Lacey had been considering waiting in the *saloni* so that her first meeting with Troy would be in the presence of a third party, but she knew with a feeling of resignation that it was impossible. Stephanos was so obviously expecting her to join Troy upstairs in the privacy of their suite, and she supposed this was why Aunt Sofia and Helen were also keeping out of the way—to spare the bride's blushes as she raced to meet her groom, she thought ironically.

It took all the courage she possessed to get her across the hall and up the short flight of gracefully curving stairs to the first floor. She paused at the door of the suite, mentally bracing herself, then she twisted the handle of the door and went in. The bedroom itself was empty, but the bathroom door stood slightly ajar and she could hear the splash of water from inside.

Feeling at a loss, she wandered over to her dressing table and picking up her hairbrush began to smooth her hair, still dishevelled from her time on the beach.

'Making yourself beautiful for me, *yineka mou?*' His voice, low and teasing, made Lacey whirl hastily towards the bathroom, her brush dropping unnoticed to the floor. He was draped against the door jamb, his dark hair dripping wet, a towel hitched negligently around the lower part of his body. She stood completely tonguetied as his eyes went over her with a sensual reminiscence that turned her bones to water.

'Well?' He smiled at her with only a shadow of the mockery she was used to. 'Aren't you going to say you're pleased to see me? That you've missed me?'

She moistened her lips desperately. 'Welcome home.'

His smile widened slightly. He came away from the door in one swift, fluid movement and started across the bedroom towards her. She stepped backwards hastily and found herself pinned against the dressing table. He reached for her, drawing her taut body into his arms, holding her so closely against him that she was aware of every pulse beat in his damp skin. He bent his head and put his mouth to the curve of her neck and shoulder, pulling a handful of her hair almost savagely against his face.

'You are the sea, the sun and the roses.' His voice sounded ragged. 'What more welcome could a man desire?'

His hands moved to the fastening of her dress and she pulled away from him. 'No!'

'Shy?' His fingers trailed fire along her throat and down to the curve of her breast. 'My sweet one, don't you realise that everyone in this house is exercising such tact that they have practically become invisible? If we don't appear downstairs tonight—tomorrow—next week, it will not be thought in any way strange. We cannot be so ungracious as to disappoint them.'

'Stephanos said you would be tired. I'll let you get some rest.' She tried to control her hurried breathing. His nearness, the warm scent of his skin, some cologne he had used acted on her senses like a drug.

'Lacey *mou*.' He let exasperation show. 'I have travelled many hundreds of miles in the past hours, gone without sleep, hurried through meetings, possibly lost on business deals because I knew I could not exist any longer without you. When I need rest, you will know because I shall sleep in your arms. But for the present, my needs have nothing to do with sleep and my patience is limited.'

He reached for her again, but she eluded his embrace, afraid that his lips and hands would seduce her into compliance before she could confront him with her knowledge. Her hand shook slightly as she pulled open the drawer in the dressing table and extracted the small tissue-wrapped bundle she had placed there, awaiting his return.

'Do you recognise this?' Her voice sounded breathless.

He gave the cuff link an impatient glance. 'Of course. It is mine. Where did you get it?'

'I found it,' she said. 'On a bathroom floor in a Paris hotel—months ago.'

His eyes narrowed, then he turned on his heel and walked towards his dressing room. Lacey waited, a tight knot of fear and excitement impeding her breathing. When he emerged from the dressing room, he was carrying the onyx box, and it was open.

'You are a liar,' he said dispassionately. 'You took that broken piece from this box for some reason. I am waiting to hear it. What were you doing? Making an inventory of my things in my absence?'

Put like that, it made her action seem sly, the satisfaction of an idle curiosity. And this was not the time to try and explain that she had gone into his room only in an attempt to discover more about his personality, to try and learn about him from the intimate possessions with which he surrounded himself.

'I found it by accident,' she said slowly. 'Just as I found the other piece in Michelle's bathroom. You lost it there, didn't you? And you telephoned the suite later to see if she had found it?'

'Yes.' He put the box down on her dressing table and studied her as if he had never seen her before. 'And what does that prove?'

'Not a great deal—by itself.' She pushed her hair back from her face, wishing suddenly that she had never started this. She had expected to see guilt and uneasiness, but the eyes that watched her so steadily held nothing but a bleak anger that chilled her and made her fumble for her words. 'But there was more, you see. It was Michelle. She was so angry about our marriage, and yet she had no reason to be unless she was—jealous, or felt she had first claim on you as a husband.' She moistened her lips again. 'Did she—think that you might marry her?'

'Yes.' Grim-mouthed, he folded his arms across his bare chest and stared at her. 'Well, continue, my dove. You've poked and pried and racked your brains, and no doubt you've fed the results of all this effort into that twisted little computer you call a mind. What conclusions have you come up with?'

Lacey lifted her shoulders almost despairingly. There was no way in which he was going to make this easy for her. He was going to make her say the unsayable, utter the thought that had tormented her days and nights.

145

'You are Michelle's lover.' The words fell, heavy as stones, between them. She only had to raise her hand and she could have touched him, yet they were miles apart and she began to shiver.

'And if so—what then?' His voice was soft, but there was a note in it which menaced her.

She stared at him in disbelief. 'Is that all you have to say?'

'No—I could say a great deal, but I'm not sure there is any point.' His voice, even the expression in his eyes, seemed almost objective. 'You have so obviously made up your mind already that I feel I would be wasting my time if I embarked on any kind of defence.'

'What defence is there?' she said wearily. The hurt was harsh in her throat, but what had she expected, after all? A plea for forgiveness, a promise of eternal fidelity in the future when everything she knew about him told her that he considered himself above the laws of conventional morality. The way he had forced her into marrying him should have taught her that, she supposed bitterly.

'Very little, it's true,' he drawled. 'Yet I suppose I could plead Michelle's beauty quite apart from her utter willingness—a temptation to any man.'

'My father's wife,' she said slowly.

'Do you really suppose your father was under any illusions, before or after he married her?' he asked brutally and saw her wince. 'When a man takes a woman like your stepmother for his wife, then he accepts that his marriage will be a series of compromises. He puts his ideals, if he has any, behind him.'

'As you have done?' she whispered.

'I?' He smiled mirthlessly. 'Don't deceive yourself, *pethi mou*. There will be no compromise in my marriage. You belong to me and only to me.'

'Not any more.' Somehow she forced the words out of her throat. 'I—I can't compromise either.'

There was a long silence. He stared down at her, his eyes narrowed, a frown drawing his dark brows together.

'I suggest you explain yourself,' he said softly.

'It's quite simple really.' She made herself meet his gaze.

146

'We had a bargain. As far as I am concerned, its terms have been fulfilled. I'll go on living here as long as you need a companion for Helen, and then we can make some kind of arrangement—an annulment or a divorce—it doesn't matter which . . .'

'Doesn't matter?' His interruption cut savagely across her stumbling words. 'Perhaps not to you, my dove, but it matters to me. You're my wife, Lacey, and you'll live in this house as my wife. You may have tried and sentenced me in your own mind, but I still have the right to appeal.'

He reached for her, jerking her into his arms with such force that her instinctive cry of protest was cut off in her throat. His mouth crushed hers relentlessly, sweeping away the defences of pride, jealousy and resentment that she had thought would be so impregnable against him. Her lips parted helplessly, acknowledging the totality of her surrender to the sheer wanton desire that was sweeping her body. Her blood ran fire, meeting his urgency with her own as his hands moved on her in intimate demand. But as he picked her up and started with her towards the bed, sanity returned and with it at last, desperate determination to salvage at least something of her self-respect and she began to struggle against his imprisoning arms.

'No,' she gasped, twisting away from him across the quilted coverlet. 'No, you'll make me hate you.'

'Meaning you don't already?' There was derision in his voice and he twisted one hand in the smooth fall of her hair, forcing her brutally to stillness. 'What is more to the point, Lacey *mou*, you might make me hate myself.'

He released her almost contemptuously and rolled away from her across the width of the bed. She lay for a moment hardly daring to move, then sat up slowly, pushing her dishevelled hair back from her face. But he made no move to prevent her as she climbed off the bed and, moving like an automaton, walked across the room to the bathroom, closing and locking the door behind her. She stripped off her torn dress and underclothes and stood under the shower, letting a torrent of warm water pour over her body as if she was performing some ritual cleansing ceremony, while the

147

drops mingled and fused with the tears of self-loathing that ran unchecked from beneath her aching eyelids.

Lacey never knew how she managed to get through the evening that followed. When she emerged from the bathroom, it was to find the rest of the suite empty. The only sign of Troy's presence was the damp and crumpled towel he had been wearing which now lay discarded on his dressing room floor.

Lacey was tempted to stay in the suite and avoid going downstairs altogether, but she did not know what Troy's reaction might be to this and she felt it would cause gossip in the household if the breach between them became open knowledge. It would be better, she decided, to go down to dinner and try and behave with at least a semblance of normality, so she dressed with care in a long hostess gown patterned in blues and greens and tied her hair back with a floating chiffon scarf in the same shades. As she gave herself one last critical look before turning away from the mirror, she thought ironically that at least on the surface she resembled the glowing bride everyone would be expecting to see. The dress with its soft, clinging lines was both seductive and feminine, the perfect choice, she decided with a sigh, for any new wife dressing to please her husband.

When she eventually arrived downstairs, she found Helen and Aunt Sofia occupying the *saloni* and learned that Troy was shut away in his study with Stephanos going through some papers. It was evident from Aunt Sofia's expression that she thought this a strange occupation for a man still virtually on his honeymoon and Lacey hastily decided she was going for a stroll before dinner before the older woman's curiosity caused her to start probing into this unusual state of affairs.

Somewhat to her dismay, Helen immediately offered to accompany her. Lacey wanted to think, away from the frankly stifling atmosphere of the house and she did not want to undergo a cross-examination on her relationship with Troy by her young sister-in-law. But Helen seemed oddly quiet again as they walked through the garden, as though she too had things on her mind, and the conversation was of a desultory nature and safely kept to impersonal topics.

Lacey had just reluctantly decided it was time they retraced their steps back to the house, when a boy's voice called, 'Kyria Eleni!'

Lacey recognised the lad approaching her as Petros, the younger son of Spiro who looked after the villa's garden and grounds with the help of the older male members of his family, but she knew they had normally finished for the day long before and she waited rather curiously to see what he wanted.

He came up to them beaming and poked a rather crumpled envelope at Helen. 'I bring a letter from Kyrios Kent,' he announced.

'Oh—er—thanks, Petros.' Helen seemed oddly taken aback and Lacey felt a resurgence of her old uneasiness about Helen's relationship with the young photographer.

'I thought Evan was in Corfu,' she said, and Helen looked almost startled for a moment.

'I guess he must have written this before he went,' she said at last, gazing almost frowningly at the envelope which she made no attempt to open. It was clear she wanted some privacy, so, stifling her misgivings, Lacey wandered on ahead, expecting that Helen would catch her up once she had read her letter. She was a little concerned about the situation. Helen's reluctance to open the note suggested that it might be some sort of love letter, and Lacey had no illusions about what Troy's reaction to that would be. Yet had she any choice but to tell him? She groaned inwardly. At the time it had all seemed so innocent, but Aunt Sofia's warning and Evan's own behaviour had destroyed that innocence. She did not relish the thought of telling Troy that she had encouraged Evan's visits to the villa. In retrospect she could see that this had been a mistake from every point of view. She might even have unconsciously given Evan the impression that she was a neglected wife, eager for consolation.

She bent and restlessly picked one of the flowers that grew beside the path, holding it to her face so she could inhale its fragrance.

What, after all, did she really know of Evan, apart from

149

the fact that Helen had been acquainted with his family in California, and that was not a fact that was likely to recommend him to Troy, she thought ruefully. It seemed hardly likely that he should attempt to make love to herself, if it was Helen he was really interested in. On the other hand it would be some years before Helen would be considered adult enough to conduct a serious relationship, and she would probably have fallen in and out of love several times before then. Did Evan really think he could make an impression on her sufficiently lasting to carry through to Helen's maturity? Lacey shook her head doubtfully. She did not care to contemplate the other possibilities which kept thrusting themselves to the forefront of her mind, reminding her that Helen would be a very rich girl some day, and even more disturbingly that the guardians of very rich minors had been known to pay out large sums to keep away undesirable suitors.

She sighed. She did not want to think badly of Evan, even now, but his attitude towards herself and the ambiguity of his relationship with Helen had raised serious doubts in her mind which could not easily be dispelled.

There was still no sign of Helen and rather impatiently Lacey walked back to the bend in the path where she had left her sister-in-law. But the girl seemed to have vanished, and there was no response when she called.

Her heart sank. Helen's behaviour had on the whole been so much more reasonable and predictable of late that it seemed barely credible that she should have chosen Troy's first evening at home to do another of her disappearing acts, she thought despairingly. Now what was she to do? Make some excuse for Helen's absence at dinner or inaugurate a search party for the girl, adding further stress to an already unhappy situation? She groaned inwardly. Explaining Evan's visits was probably going to be difficult enough without having to reveal the existence of secret letters. If it hadn't been for the fact that Evan was in Corfu, she might have thought Helen had gone off to meet him clandestinely.

And she had really thought she was making progress with Helen, and that at least this aspect of her bargain with

Troy was working out as he wished. Now it seemed she had yet another failure to cope with.

A feeling of guilt at having let the situation develop added to her depression as she walked across the terrace and entered the *saloni*, and it did not help that the first person she saw was Troy, sardonically attractive in a white dinner jacket, pouring drinks for himself and Stephanos at the cocktail cabinet.

He gave her a level, unsmiling glance before asking with chilly formality whether or not she wanted an aperitif before her meal. Lacey shook her head, feeling the colour rise in her cheeks, and was glad to sink into the nearest chair, her legs trembling. She could see Aunt Sofia looking anxiously around, obviously in search of her errant niece, and was relieved when Stephanos came over and began to chat with his usual friendliness. It meant she could turn her attention to him and avoid Aunt Sofia's questioning and increasingly accusing look as the minutes ticked by and Helen failed to appear.

Dinner had just been announced when there was a rush of feet across the terrace and Helen almost fell into the *saloni*. She looked hot and breathless as if she had been running a long way, and the hem of her long cotton dress was caked with dust. Aunt Sofia clucked disapprovingly, but if Troy noticed there was anything amiss, he had obviously decided to ignore it. As they went in to dinner, Lacey hung back and spoke to Helen in a low voice.

'Where did you get to? I was worried about you.'

'Oh, for God's sake!' Helen hunched her shoulders petulantly. 'I just didn't feel like coming back to this morgue before I had to, so I walked some more. There's no need to make a federal case out of it.'

Lacey flushed and relapsed into silence, but she was not convinced. The very tone and nature of Helen's reply had revealed that something had upset her badly, and she wondered what it could be. Lacey had little appetite for the meal that followed and she noticed that Helen, too, was picking at her food in a most uncharacteristic manner. Lacey found herself wondering whether the letter from Evan had been a farewell note to say that he was on his way out

151

of her life and back to the States. If Helen really thought she was in love with him, that would explain her despondency, but Lacey herself could not avoid a tinge of relief. If he had gone, this was at least the solution to one of her problems and perhaps Troy need never know anything about it at all.

She felt sad for Helen, drooping so visibly in her chair. Lacey had never been tormented by adolescent passions for young men at Helen's age—she supposed vaguely that all her emotional energies had been used by her music—but she could remember what some of her friends had suffered and she was determined to treat Helen's young feelings with respect. After all, love was love no matter what age you were, and if the man you wanted with all your heart, body and soul didn't want you, the hurt was still intolerable, she thought, her throat aching suddenly.

Her fork clattered noisily to the floor and she bent to retrieve it before one of the maids could move to her side, glad that the action gave her an excuse for the sudden flame of colour in her face. What use was it, trying to deny her feelings for Troy any longer? If she was really content merely to be bound to him legally, then she would not care how many mistresses he had. She would be content to be the figurehead in his home, the hostess when he required one, the companion for his sister, glad to be cut off from any real intimacy in his life. But now she knew the truth, knew that she craved to be first with him in every way, not just in his bed, but in his mind and heart too. She bit on her lip until she could taste blood.

Her fingers shook uncontrollably as she forced herself to pick up her glass and sip some of the wine it contained. She was still stunned at the implications of the discoveries she was making about her own feelings, but she was rational enough to concede that nothing had really changed. Michelle was still Troy's mistress, and he had lingered on in England to be with her. She recalled how he had spoken of Michelle, of her beauty and 'utter willingness'—a woman's weapons to win the man of her choice. Was that what she herself should have done? Would it have been wiser to have pretended ignorance of the affair and set out to win him for herself? Whatever other relationships he might enjoy, he had come to Theros wanting her. If her anger and bitterness had not got the better of her, they could have been together now in the peace and intimacy of the big room upstairs.

But that would be little comfort, she told herself miserably, if at the end of the honeymoon he simply resumed his old life. No matter how much she might want him, she knew she could never be content to be second best in his life, the docile wife waiting patiently in the wings for the few cherished moments he could spare her.

At least if they went on in the way they were, she would still have her pride, but that seemed a poor substitute for all the other emotions that she would be denied. For the first time, she found herself wishing that she was going to have a child. She had no doubt that the mother of his baby would arouse all Troy's latent tenderness and protectiveness. But afterwards? She leaned forward to replace her wineglass and as she did so the room seemed to sway crazily in front of her eyes as if the world was out of focus. She gripped the arms of her chair, afraid she was going to faint, when a scream from Aunt Sofia and the crash of breaking crockery as Ariadne who was clearing the main course dropped some plates made her realise that the phenomenon had not been the result of her own overcharged emotions but a rather more potent physical force.

She was terrifyingly aware that the whole house was shaking slightly, causing light fitments to sway backwards and forwards and setting the pieces of statuary and rare china with which the dining room was decorated sliding and dancing.

The tremor could only have lasted a few seconds and as it died away, it was succeeded by an almost uncanny stillness as if the earth was holding its breath.

'Gee!' Helen's attempt at a light laugh held a distinct quaver. 'I think it was safer in San Francisco.' There was a pause, then Troy gave her a reluctant grin and Stephanos laughed out loud before they turned their attention to calming Aunt Sofia, who seemed almost on the verge of hysteria and who was having a bad effect on the equally frightened

Ariadne. Troy went to the *saloni* to fetch a glass of brandy for his aunt, and on the way back he halted briefly by Lacey's chair, his dark eyes searching her face.

'Are you all right?' he asked crisply, and she nodded, unable to trust herself to speak.

By a kind of mutual consent the rest of dinner was abandoned and they all went into the *saloni*. Aunt Sofia, weeping a little, and apparently prophesying doom, was led off to her room by Ione, another of the maids, and Lacey began almost imperceptibly to relax.

Stephanos came across to her carrying a cognac. 'You must drink this, Mrs Andreakis. Even those of us who are used to these tremors do not find them a pleasant experience. We must hope there will be no more.'

'Do they happen often?' Lacey accepted the glass from him.

'There has always been a certain amount of activity in this region, but it is rarely felt on land. The last real trouble was over twenty years ago.'

'Yes, Helen told me about it.' Lacey sipped at the cognac, feeling its reassuring warmth stealing through her veins.

Stephanos laughed. 'She has a vivid imagination, that little one. All this was before she was born, you understand, so do not let her frighten you with any horror stories. Theros did not suffer as badly as Levkas or Ithaca.'

Out of the corner of her eye, Lacey saw that Troy was moving across to join them and a sudden tension invaded her limbs.

He looked at her unsmilingly before transferring his attention to Stephanos.

'I have telephoned Father Alexis, but he says there has been little damage in the town, and certainly no panic. We must hope this was just an isolated incident.'

Stephanos nodded and said something to him in Greek, which brought a noncommittal shrug in response from Troy. Lacey was sure that some reference to herself had been made, but she did not wish to appear foolish or inquisitive by asking, so she remained silent, staring down at the remainder of the brandy in her goblet.

The men continued to converse in low voices and eventually Lacey put down her brandy and, getting up, wandered over to where the piano was standing. She sank down on to the wide seat and lifted the lid. She had no clear idea of what she was going to play, but she felt she needed the soothing quality that her music invariably provided. For a while she let her fingers stray idly over the keys, recalling odd chords and phrases, but none of them seemed to hold any great appeal. One fragment of melody teased at her memory and she began to pick the notes out as they came back to her, humming the tune under her breath as she did so. It was totally familiar yet oddly elusive, and as she hesitated, puzzled, the opening phrase suddenly took shape in her mind. Of course she knew what it was. It was the quartet from *The Yeomen of the Guard*, and she added the words softly to the melody as she played it through again. 'Strange adventure, Maiden wedded to a groom she's never seen ...' Her fingers stumbled into discord as she realised the significance of what she was playing, that almost forgotten conversation with Vanessa before her wedding stinging back into her mind. What had Vanessa said? 'Rather a fairy tale.'

Lacey bit her lip as she bent over the keys. Well, all the elements were there, she thought with a bitter little sigh welling up inside her, even the beautiful stepmother, but there was no sign of any happy ending.

She came out of her reverie with a start to find Troy standing, looking down at her. The lines on his dark face seemed more deeply accentuated, but that might be just a trick of the lamplight, otherwise he was the enigma he had always been. It seemed impossible that this cool, impassive stranger had been the man with whom she had quarrelled so violently only a few hours before and whose totally devastating lovemaking had carried her beyond decency, beyond reason almost to the edge of rapture.

'Won't you play something for us?' It was the courteous query that any host might make of a guest with a talent for music.

She shook her head quietly, closing the piano lid over the keys. 'Not tonight. I'm—I'm not really in the mood.'

'I see.' He paused for a moment. 'But the piano is—satisfactory, is it?'

She looked up at him, stricken. She had completely overlooked the fact that this was his gift to her, the thing he had known she would prize above the jewellery, the cars, the yachts that rich men often bestowed on their wives. and she had not even thanked him.

'It's beautiful,' she assured him rather huskily. 'I—I don't know what to say . . .'

He lifted his hand, silencing her. 'There is no need to say anything. If you are content, then I must be so too.'

'Troy.' Impulsively she put out her hand and touched his as he made to turn away. For a moment he stood rigid, then he slipped his hands into the pockets of his dinner jacket, deliberately avoiding the contact with her. His mouth twisted slightly as he looked at her.

'It's all right, Lacey *mou*. You have convinced me of your gratitude. There is no need to outrage your feelings any further. Besides, it is not in my nature to be satisfied with—crumbs, from anyone's table.'

He turned and walked away, rejoining Stephanos who was with Helen at the opposite end of the room going through the well-stocked cabinet of long-playing records that stood beside the hi-fi system. Lacey sat staring down at her hands, her cheeks burning. She might have known her gesture would have been misunderstood, she thought bitterly, but that sudden craving to touch him, to feel her skin against his however fleetingly had overwhelmed her, blinding her to all other considerations.

She got up and walked over to the long windows that led on to the terrace, pulling aside the heavy curtains and staring out into the darkness. Almost immediately the glass was bombarded by moths and other insects, flinging themselves against it in a vain attempt to reach the light. Lacey stood for a moment watching their useless struggle with brooding eyes, then with a sigh, she let the curtain fall back into place. The barrier between Troy and herself was an intangible one, but it would prove no less difficult to cross.

After a while, she excused herself and went to her room. She had wanted to have another talk with Helen, to find out where she had really disappeared to before dinner, but her sister-in-law seemed determined to keep out of her way, insisting with almost hysterical gaiety on demonstrating all

156

the latest dance movements that she had learned at beach parties in California and trying to persuade a reluctant Stephanos to attempt them as well.

Alone in the big bedroom, Lacey felt restless. She bathed and put on her white chiffon nightdress, but in spite of these preparations, she did not get into bed. She wandered round the room, bare-footed, rearranging the bottles and containers on her dressing table, adjusting the placing of the roses that stood in a silver bowl on a table beside the bed. After a while she made herself sit down on the softly upholstered couch that stood near the window and pick up a book she had been reading, but the words whirled round in her brain making little sense and after a few minutes she threw it aside.

The sound of a door closing nearby brought her to her feet, and she saw that a thread of light was showing under the communicating door that led from the bedroom into Troy's dressing room. Moving silently, she slipped round the room, turning off the lights, then climbed into the wide bed and lay there motionless, her breathing oddly constricted. Her eyes strained towards the door in the darkness, waiting for it to open. She was so sure that he would come to her, in spite of everything that had happened, that she could hardly believe it when the thread of light disappeared and the door between them remained inimically closed.

She sat up, sudden determination banishing the turmoil that had raged inside her all evening. Michelle might still win in the end, but she did not have to make it easy for her by not even putting up a token resistance on her own behalf. She too would fight for what she wanted.

She slipped noiselessly out of bed and walked softly across the room to the door. The handle twisted easily under her fingers as she turned it, but the door did not move. Surprised, she turned the handle again, this time applying the pressure of her weight against it, but it still did not budge, and it was then that the humiliating truth burst on Lacey. His door was locked. Her fight was over, before it had even begun.

CHAPTER NINE

Lacey slept late the following morning and woke feeling unrefreshed and on edge. Not even the earth tremor and its aftermath had had the shattering effect of the discovery that Troy was apparently quite prepared to accept the terms she had flung at him and shut her out of his life. She could only hope he was not aware of her abortive attempt to get into his room. That would be the final humiliation.

The villa seemed deserted when she eventually arrived downstairs, and Ione, who insisted on bringing her fresh rolls and coffee in spite of assurances that she wanted no breakfast, told her that Kyrios Troy and Kyria Eleni had gone down to the boathouse to make sure there was no damage from the previous night.

'I see.' Lacey sipped at her coffee. 'Was there—did much get broken in the house? Upstairs seemed totally untouched, as if nothing had happened.'

Ione's broad shrug indicated that in her opinion, very little had occurred. '*Ligho*, Kyria Lacey. A few dishes in the kitchen and the plates which Ariadne dropped, as you know. She is not of Theros, that one,' she added pityingly.

Lacey grimaced. 'Neither am I, Ione, and I'm afraid Ariadne has my sympathy.'

Ione looked shocked. '*Po, po, po.* Such a little shake, Kyria Lacey. No one could really be frightened.' Her eyes brightened. 'Now, twenty years ago . . .'

'Yes, I know,' Lacey interrupted hastily. 'And if you're going to tell me I should have been here then—please don't.'

Ione tutted. 'That would be foolishness, Kyria Lacey. I was not even here myself.'

Her breakfast over, Lacey walked out on to the terrace, and strolled through the gardens towards the path leading to the beach. As she came out on to the road above the bay, she hesitated. The path to the beach where she and Helen had bathed the day before lay straight ahead; the fork leading down to the adjoining cove where the boathouse was situated went off to the left. She knew she would have to face Troy sooner or later, but just at the moment solitude seemed preferable and she took the path down to the beach. But as she scrambled down the last sharp incline, she realised she was not alone as her eye caught a swift flash of colour among the rocks over to her right. She stood up and shaded her eyes, but she could see no one. She discarded the light sandals she was wearing and began to climb over the rocks towards where the patch of colour still showed. She recognised it as soon as she got close. It was one of the cotton scarves that Helen often wore round her neck, caught on a projecting piece of rock. Lacey detached it without tearing it any further and stood looking around, convinced that she was being watched.

'Helen!' she called in some exasperation. 'Helen, where are you?'

But there was no reply, but somewhere not too far away there was a subdued rattle and a chink as if a pebble had been dislodged by a careless foot.

'Helen!' she tried again. 'Please don't play silly games. I'm not in the mood. I've got your scarf. Don't you want it?'

Silence.

'Oh, be like that, then!' Lacey laid the scarf across the top of a flat rock, and put a stone on top of it to keep it from blowing away in the slight breeze. As she gave one last glance round, she noticed that at the foot of the cliff, overshadowed and partly protected by a massive overhang, there was a dark slit, suggesting a cave of some kind. It seemed more than probable that Helen had gone to ground there, and there she could stay, Lacey decided with a fair amount of rancour. She could not help feeling a little hurt as she turned away. After all, Helen had no reason to shun her company.

She walked down the beach to the water's edge and stood, letting the creaming shallows curl slowly round her bare feet, then she turned and began to make her way slowly over the rocks guarding the promontory that led to the boathouse. Here, the natural curve of the cliff had provided a deep rocky basin and as well as the large wooden boathouse, a small jetty had also been constructed. A dinghy was tied up to the jetty and Stephanos was seated in it, tinkering with its outboard motor. He caught sight of Lacey perched precariously on her rock and gave her an encouraging wave, pointing to where she could scramble across to the side of the boathouse.

'Kalimera,' he called. 'You are looking for Troy, ne? You are just too late.'

He gestured towards a superbly built white racing dinghy with scarlet sails tacking out of the cove towards the open sea.

Lacey shaded her eyes to watch its progress. 'Does—does he sail alone?' she asked, coming to sit on the edge of the jetty and declining the cigarette Stephanos offered her with a shake of her head.

'Not usually.' Stephanos wiped his fingers on an oily rag. 'But today he did not seem to wish for company,' he added, sending her a sideways look.

'I just wondered if it was safe,' she said lamely.

He smiled at her. 'Troy has sailed these waters since he was a small child, Kyria Lacey. You need not concern yourself.'

'Oh no, I'm sure I needn't.' To her own annoyance Lacey heard a quiver in her voice. 'I'm sure he is—quite capable of looking after himself.'

She was aware that Stephanos was looking curiously at her and made an attempt to regain her self-control.

'I'm sorry.' She tried to smile. 'I think living on the edge of an earthquake must be making me nervous.'

'My dear Mrs Andreakis, please believe me, if there was real danger Troy would not permit you to stay here.' He gave her an anxious look. 'Do you wish me to speak to him for you? Perhaps the trip to Nassau can be brought forward . . .'

'Oh, no!' Lacey was appalled at the thought. Things were bad enough at the villa, she thought. What they might be like in the more cramped conditions of the Artemis, she did not dare think. 'I'm—I'm just being silly. It was just so un-

160

expected. Besides, I'm not at all sure we shall be going to Nassau now.'

'*Ohi?*' Stephanos studied her for a moment. 'That is not the impression I had. Have you spoken to Troy about this?'

'No.' Lacey paused. 'There hasn't really been a great deal of opportunity,' she added, choosing her words with care.

'He has been preoccupied,' Stephanos admitted. 'The last months have not been easy for either of you, I think, and for Troy there has been the added problem of his sister.'

Lacey sighed. 'Now I thought I was really making progress there,' she said ruefully. 'Yet I'm sure she was deliberately avoiding me in the next cove just now. I feel as if I'm back to square one again.'

Stephanos smiled. 'I do not think Eleni understands herself very well. There are two different cultures at war in her, even more so than they are in Troy—the old world and the new. Part of her wishes to be the Liberated Woman, and the other half longs for the sheltered life that girls normally lead on these islands. Somehow she will have to find a compromise, and I think it is something that only she can do.'

'It's something we all have to do.' Lacey gave a little sigh again. 'But that's not all. There's been a young man staying on the island—someone she knew in the States. I—allowed them to meet because I saw no harm in it, and Troy's aunt didn't raise any objections either,' she added rather defensively as she saw Stephanos' eyebrows shoot up. 'But now I'm not sure I've done the right thing. I think she's fallen for him rather hard—and now he's gone.'

Stephanos frowned slightly. 'You speak of the young man who is renting a room at Niko's taverna?' he inquired.

'Why, yes. You mean he's still there?'

'I understand he is spending a few days in Corfu, but means to return,' Stephanos said blandly. 'There is no urgent necessity for Eleni to pine for him just yet.'

Lacey stared at him. 'You seem remarkably well informed about his movements,' she said slowly.

Stephanos shrugged and spread his hands. 'We are always interested in strangers who spend any length of time on Theros—especially when they are professional photographers.' He paused. 'Perhaps it might have been wiser to keep him at a distance, Kyria Lacey.'

'Oh, he hasn't taken any pictures anywhere near the villa,' Lacey assured him. 'I was adamant about that.'

'Hm.' Stephanos sounded noncommittal. 'But to return to Eleni. I agree she seems to have something on her mind, but I would not myself have diagnosed it as an affair of the heart. I too have younger sisters, so I am not without experience in these matters,' he added modestly.

'Then what is your diagnosis?' Lacey could not help being amused, in spite of her own unhappiness.

'I would say she has a guilty conscience.'

'What?' Lacey gave a little frown. 'Oh, I'm sure you're wrong. I mean, she has no reason—she's hardly been out of my sight, really.'

'Oh, I am not suggesting she has committed any sexual misdemeanour.' Stephanos sounded quite shocked. 'In spite of the laxity of her aunt's upbringing, Eleni is sufficiently Greek to value her own purity. But there are other forms of mischief.' He hesitated. 'I do not know whether I should tell you this, Kyria Lacey, but there was a quarrel between Eleni and your husband after you went to bed last night.'

'I had no idea.' Lacey stared. 'What was it about?'

'She told him she wished to return to the States—for a holiday. Troy said it was impossible and she became very angry. There was a lot of wild talk about having the means at her disposal to make him do as she wished. You have no idea what she could have meant?'

Lacey shook her head slowly. 'None. But she probably wasn't serious.'

'Troy thinks differently. She came with us this morning. He had asked her if she would like to crew for him and she was pleased, but when he tried to question her—quite gently—on what she had meant last night, she became furious and flounced off. We both felt that she was angry with herself for having said too much, too soon.'

Lacey gasped. 'But—but you're talking about blackmail! Helen's barely more than a child.'

'But a child who has been spoiled almost to the point of recklessness by a giddy selfish woman who has taught her

162

to consider only her own desires,' Stephanos remarked quietly. 'In such an environment, a more stable personality than Eleni might acquire—strange values.'

Lacey got up, twisting her hands together nervously. 'I don't think her aunt can wholly be blamed for that,' she said shortly. 'Helen may be more like her brother than she realises.'

She walked away before he could reply, aware that growing tension had forced her into saying more than she had intended. Depression hung over her like a cloud all the way back to the house.

The next few days seemed to crawl by. Lacey thought she would never have believed it possible to feel so alone in a house full of people. She was thankful that Stephanos' projected departure had not in fact taken place. His presence at the villa ensured that at least an appearance of normality was presented when the various members of the household gathered together at mealtimes and in the *saloni* during the evenings.

Troy spent much of the time working in his study, often late into the night, and did not appear for meals. Lacey would lie awake watching for the tell-tale gleam of light under the communicating door, unable to sleep without the sterile reassurance of his presence a few yards away. The door between them was still locked. She had not tried to open it since, but she knew it just the same, and the hurt of it scalded her as she lay in the darkness.

Her anxiety about Helen, too, was growing. The younger girl had become almost morose, snubbing every overture and disappearing alone to the little beach below the villa first thing in the morning until evening. Aunt Sofia seemed the only person oblivious to the undercurrents and tensions around her. She was planning happily for the time when she could leave Theros and return to the house Troy had purchased for her near Athens where she could be with her friends, and she embarrassed Lacey by promising to return to look after the household when her babies were born. Troy had been present when she had made these remarks, and it was obvious to Lacey from the coldly sardonic glance

163

he sent her that he had heard every word.

How much longer could they go on like this? she asked herself wearily. Just what did he intend? This stalemate in their marriage could be no more satisfying to him than it was to her, but how was it going to end? She supposed that in spite of what he had said about her continuing to live with him as his wife, he would want a divorce eventually, but she had no doubt it would be in his own good time. After all, he would not want the undesirable publicity attached to such a speedy breakdown of his marriage as would undoubtedly occur if they parted now. It was poor comfort to know that she was being allowed to live with him, almost on sufferance, as if she was the one to blame instead of himself for the failure of their relationship.

She heard footsteps approaching across the terrace where she was lying on a sun-lounger, shaded from the full heat of the afternoon sun, and she looked up, almost glad of an interruption to the unwelcome tenor of her thoughts.

'Kyria Lacey,' Ariadne stood in front of her, 'Kyrios Kent is here. He brought a package for Kyrios Troy and when I told him he was sailing with Kyrios Stephanos, he asked for you.'

Lacey hesitated. She had not realised that Evan had returned to Theros, and she did not particularly want to see him again, but she supposed she had little choice.

'Are you sure he wants to see me, Ariadne?' she asked. 'Didn't he ask for Kyria Eleni?'

'Ohi, kyria. He asked for you.'

Lacey sighed. 'Well, you'd better bring him to me.'

When the maid had gone she reached out for the brief jacket that matched the bikini she was wearing and slipped it on, feeling rather foolish. After all, she had sunbathed in Evan's company on a number of occasions without feeling even slightly self-conscious, but she knew instinctively that everything had changed. She wondered why he had come, and again she experienced that faint uneasiness. He must know Troy had returned and it might have been better to postpone his visits until he knew they were welcome, she thought.

'Hello, Lacey.' He walked quietly across the terrace and

stood looking down at her with a smile. He was the old, friendly Evan, casually dressed in jeans and knitted sports shirt, and there was no reason in the world for Lacey to feel that he was a dark shadow hiding the sun from her.

'Hello, Evan,' she returned equally calmly. 'It's—it's nice to see you again, if a trifle unexpected. Helen will be pleased, I know. Have you seen her?'

'We've talked,' he said laconically. He hitched one of the garden chairs forward and sat down facing her. It gave the interview a feeling of intimacy she would have been glad to avoid, and she told herself she was being ridiculous. She had sat with Evan on the terrace before and felt perfectly at ease. Of course, Helen had always been there as well, but it was not as if they were really alone now. The windows into the *saloni* stood open and anyone from the house could walk out on to the terrace at any time.

She said rather hurriedly, trying to mask her growing feeling of disquiet, 'Actually, Evan, I'm a bit worried about Helen. It's as if she's brooding about something all the time.'

'Is she now?' he said, and there was a note of almost unholy amusement in his voice. 'Now, what could that be, I wonder?'

Lacey took off her sunglasses and laid them on the table that stood at her elbow. 'I think you know what it is,' she said slowly. 'Because I think you're involved in it. Evan, she's only a child. It's not fair to play with her emotions if you're not serious about her, and I don't believe you are.'

'Oh, she's no child,' he said lightly. 'But I can set your mind at rest about one thing. Helen and I are not emotionally involved and never have been. No, I'd say we had more of—a business relationship—with the emphasis on the past tense. My partner just ran out on me.'

Lacey stared at him. Nothing he was saying made very much sense, but at least she had the reassurance of knowing that Helen was still heartwhole.

'But why is she acting so strangely?' she asked. 'She seems so upset . . .'

'Helen's just learned her first grown-up lesson of her spoiled little life,' he said, and she was appalled at the venom in his tone. 'She's discovered it's easy to start something, but not quite so easy to finish it.'

'What are you talking about?' Lacey was really alarmed now.

'Oh, you'll know soon enough,' he said. 'Yes, ma'am, the balloon should go up any moment now, and the whole damned Andreakis family with it.'

'What have you done?' she demanded huskily.

He laughed. 'Nothing—yet. Oh, don't look so alarmed. Helen isn't hurt—except for having her pride dented, maybe. It must be really tough to set out to use someone, and then find they've been using you all along, but that's the way it goes.'

'But why should you want to use anyone? We've never done you any harm. I thought you liked us—liked me.' Anxiety made her stumble over her words.

He smiled slowly. 'Oh, I liked you, Lacey—a lot. You know how much, and I didn't act the way I did just to spit in your husband's eye either, although I was tempted.'

And so was I, she thought horrified. So was I.

'You see—Mrs Andreakis,' he emphasised the name as if mocking her, 'there are quite a few people in this world with a grudge against your lordly husband. I have buddies who've suffered at his hands—correction, at the hands of the strong-arm boys he and his pal Lindos employ to make sure everyone knows what they mean by privacy. Take this island, for example. Somewhere there's a list of people who won't be allowed on to it—ever, but I'm not on that list, and that's where Troy Andreakis made his first big mistake.' He smiled again. 'Well, his precious private life isn't going to be so damned private from now on—and anyone who's ever tried to get near him and been roughed up and had his film ruined in consequence is going to be cheering, believe me.'

Lacey was white. Evan knew! Somehow—and it had to be from Helen—he had found out about Troy and Michelle and he was going to sell the whole sordid story to the newspapers. There wasn't—couldn't be any other explanation. The thought of the repercussions—the blaring headlines, the scandal that would destroy any hope she might still cherish of being able to rebuild her relationship with Troy —made her feel physically sick.

'Evan!' She hated the imploring note in her voice, but she would grovel to him if necessary to stop him doing this thing. 'Please, you mustn't—publish anything. You've no idea of the harm you would do.'

'Wrong again.' His smile was charming, almost regretful. 'I've every idea. I didn't just dream this up overnight, you know. I put the idea in Helen's head while she was still in the States with her aunt and then let her sell it to me. Poor little Helen! I guess she really thought I was doing all this just to help her get back at Big Brother Troy, and to get her that one-way ticket back to California that she's been banking on. I'm afraid she's going to have to forget it.' He stood up and stretched lightly. 'Don't look so stricken, Lacey. If it's any consolation, Helen stopped wanting to go through with this some time ago. You see, she found she liked you too. But that's show business.'

He sighed. 'I think I'll go now—before the sailor gets home from sea. I don't really want to be around for that. I think Corfu is going to be definitely healthier for the next few days. By the way, while I was there I ran across a friend of yours—or should I say relation?' He paused. 'The staff at the Ithaca Hotel called her Lady Vernon, but she let me call her Michelle after a few drinks in the bar. She's a very friendly person—for a lady. She sent you her—love.'

Before she could move or resist, he had bent over the lounger and kissed her lingeringly on the mouth. He was smiling as he straightened up. 'Goodbye, Lacey. I'm sorry it had to be this way. You're very lovely—with or without your clothes.'

He flicked the material of the jacket she was wearing almost derisively and turned and went from her down the terrace steps and out of sight through the garden.

Lacey sat rigid, hardly able to take in the full implications of what he had said. Helen's involvement, the threatened scandal, all receded under the compulsion of the one overriding thought that beat and reverberated in her brain. Michelle was in Corfu.

She felt sick. Had Troy actually brought her with him

167

from England, discreetly ensconcing her in a suite at the Ithaca—out of sight, yet within reach? Lacey thought she had been hurt already, but it was nothing to the pain that gripped her now as she faced this new betrayal. Troy could never have had any serious intention of trying to make their marriage work, she thought, pressing her hand against her throat, trying to still the ache of unshed tears.

She closed her eyes and a picture of her stepmother as she had seen her last swam into her anguished mind. No wonder she had said 'au revoir' and not 'goodbye'. The implication that they would meet again, and soon, had been clear, but she had been blind to see it. Perhaps the visit to Corfu had already been planned then, she thought, recalling the amused malice with which Michelle had taunted her for Troy's apparent lack of ardour in sending her away alone.

And now she was on Corfu, so secure in her triumph that she could send her 'love' by a comparative stranger to torment Lacey.

Lacey shivered. What else had Michelle told Evan, apart from her name? she wondered frantically. Had she supplied wittingly, or unwittingly, the corroboration he needed for his story, or had her presence there supplied all the confirmation necessary?

She heard a slight sound and her eyes flew open, startled. Stephanos was standing framed in the *saloni* window. His usually friendly expression was censorious, hostile even.

'I beg your pardon, Mrs Andreakis.' His voice was like ice. 'Your guest's departure has obviously upset you. I did not mean to intrude, but I thought you were alone.'

He made her a slight formal bow and turned to go. With a sickening jolt, Lacey realised he must have been standing in the window for some time and had probably seen Evan take his leave with that last insult of a kiss.

She leapt up from the lounger, clutching the jacket more closely around her.

'No—Stephanos, wait. It isn't what you think. That man —he hates Troy. He knows he's having an affair with my stepmother and he's going to give the story to the newspapers. Helen's been helping him . . .'

Stephanos' frown was like thunder. 'What are you saying? What is this madness?'

Lacey was really crying now. 'That man—he's Evan Kent. He knows about Troy and Michelle. He's going to tell everyone about them and I can't bear it. I must see Troy—warn him.'

She made to push past Stephanos, but he caught her arm in a grip like iron.

'Kyria Lacey! You must calm yourself. If this man has threatened you in any way, he will be dealt with. But no newspaper would ever print such a story, rest assured. They would know at once it was a tissue of lies . . .' His voice broke off and he looked down almost wonderingly into her pale face, taking in her tear-brimming eyes and trembling mouth.

'Merciful God,' he said hoarsely. 'You believe these things?'

Lacey did not reply at once and he repeated his question in a sharper tone. 'You actually believe—this filth?'

She nodded mutely, unable to trust herself to speak.

'Mrs Andreakis.' He led her back to the lounger and seated her on it as if he was afraid she might break. 'Kyria Lacey, I knew all was not well between you and Troy, but I never dreamed it could be for such a reason. Who has told you this thing? Was it your stepmother—Lady Vernon?'

She shook her head dully. 'No, I found out for myself. Troy lost part of a cuff link one night when they were together. I found it later and realised what must have been going on. I taxed Troy with it, and he didn't deny it.'

Stephanos swore exasperatedly. 'You let him see that you believed this thing of him? You accused him? No wonder he did not bother to defend himself. Perhaps he hoped his bride might have more faith in him than to give credence to the idea. Troy is a proud man, Kyria Lacey. He would not take such a slur on his honour lightly.'

Lacey looked at him bewilderedly. 'It wasn't just the cuff link,' she said quietly. 'From the moment our engagement was announced, my stepmother was—odd. She made it so clear she resented my marrying Troy. She said—hinted things that would only make sense if she was Troy's mistress. And now she's come—she's here.'

'On Theros?' Stephanos was shocked.

'No—Corfu.' Lacey's lips twisted bitterly. 'I don't suppose even Troy would have the gall to make his wife accept his mistress in the same house.'

Stephanos took her hands in his. 'It hurts me to hear you speak of your husband with such bitterness. You wrong him when you say such things. I am not pretending he has been a saint, but all that is in the past.'

Lacey sighed. 'I'm not completely naïve,' she said in a low voice. 'I'm well aware that there have been other women in his life. It's just Michelle's part in his past that I can't accept.'

'Kyria Lacey, you are wrong. I swear this to you. Your stepmother is not and has never been Troy's mistress.'

Lacey stared at him, moved by his obvious sincerity.

'Then what is she doing on Corfu?' she asked.

Stephanos shrugged. 'Making mischief, perhaps—and succeeding beyond her wildest dreams, it seems.' He paused. 'There are things I see I must tell you, Kyria Lacey, although they may hurt you—things that Troy never intended you should know.' He hesitated again, choosing his words with care. 'I don't know how well you know your stepmother, but I believe she is a sick woman. I have had to be in her company a great deal in the past year and it seemed to me always she was obsessed—by herself, and by the money and possessions she seemed to think were her right.' He smiled faintly. 'You have a saying in England, Kyria Lacey—she felt the world owed her a living. That, it seemed to me, was Lady Vernon's attitude.'

Lacey thought sombrely back over the years and nodded.

'I always knew she had married Daddy because he could give her money and position,' she said. 'But I thought that it didn't matter as long as she made him happy.'

'Oh, she was probably content to do so at first,' Stephanos said quietly. 'But when things started to go wrong for Vernon–Carey, she grew alarmed. Her position, you see, was being threatened, and when your father became ill, she was desperate. Only one thing came to matter—the saving of Vernon–Carey—not for the sake of your father or the investors, but for the sake of Michelle Vernon.'

Lacey sighed a little. 'Perhaps we're doing her an injustice.'

'I don't think so,' Stephanos returned firmly. 'You were at your school, Kyria Lacey, but I was there. I saw her while the negotiations between your father's bank and the Andreakis corporation were going on. It was clear to Troy and myself that her sole motive was self-preservation—at any price. She was incredibly greedy—rapacious. She persuaded your father to ask for exorbitant terms. At one point negotiations had almost broken down altogether.' He paused again. 'We had stayed at Kings Winston and Lady Vernon had—forgive me—made it more than clear that she found Troy physically attractive.'

Lacey bent her head. 'I see—and Troy?'

Stephanos smiled slightly. 'What do you want me to say, Kyria Lacey? She is a beautiful woman and he is a normal man. He may have been—tempted, but it went no further than that. Troy liked your father and respected him too much to dishonour him in such a way, even though he knew that he would not be—the first.'

Lacey looked at him quickly. 'There were others?'

Stephanos nodded. 'She made frequent trips to Paris. Frankly, she was becoming notorious there. How much your late father knew and how much he closed his eyes to, it is impossible to say.'

Lacey was bewildered. 'But Troy was with Michelle in Paris,' she argued.

'Troy and I were in Paris,' Stephanos corrected her gently. 'He received a message one evening—apparently from your father. There were papers involved, essential to the negotiations, and he was told these were now ready for him to sign, on his own terms, so he went to the hotel at the time appointed. Instead, your stepmother was there, alone. Oh, she had the papers he wanted, or he would have left immediately,' he added, seeing her questioning look. 'But she had a private deal of her own for him—he was to make a substantial settlement for her abroad in return for her favours. I don't think it was the first time she had made

171

that kind of proposition, but it must certainly have been the first time she had been refused. She was—surprised, to say the least, and when Troy threatened to withdraw from the negotiations altogether, panic-stricken.'

'How do you know all this?'

'Because I was there.' Stephanos gave her a wry look. 'Your stepmother left Troy alone for a few minutes, presumably while she changed into "something more comfortable" and he was able to telephone me to join him.' He gave a reminiscent smile. 'Lady Vernon was not pleased to see me. I cannot altogether blame her. There were some angry words.' He sighed. 'Later Troy noticed he had lost part of his cuff link. He was annoyed because they held great sentimental value for him. They were one of the last gifts his father gave to him. He telephoned Michelle's hotel, but was told she had gone out of Paris for the day.'

Lacey nodded wretchedly. 'She'd gone to the convent to fetch me. Troy—rang again, didn't he?'

'I think so.' Stephanos studied her unhappy face with some compassion.

Lacey roused herself a little. 'But if Michelle wanted Troy for herself, why did she try and involve me?' She looked away, colour stealing into her pale cheeks. 'She did, you know.'

'I know.' Stephanos gave her hands a comforting squeeze before releasing them. 'Perhaps in some twisted way she hoped to make Troy—grateful to her. Or maybe she realised that in you she had a more—negotiable commodity. She had failed to sell herself, so she would sell you instead.' He paused. 'I think she would have done anything to make her future secure. As I said, she was totally obsessed.'

Lacey shivered. 'Well, she succeeded.'

'But not in the way she expected,' he said drily. 'Forgive me, Kyria Lacey, but I do not think she ever contemplated that Troy and yourself would marry. She could not accept his rejection of her and, I think, convinced herself that it had been prompted by a sense of misplaced chivalry. She was your father's wife, and therefore sacrosanct, but when she became your father's widow—ah, then things would be very different. When Troy announced that he was to marry you, she must have told herself that he was settling for second-best and that it was really herself he wanted. She hinted as much to him in my presence. That was why Troy came so little to Kings Winston while you were engaged. She was becoming an embarrassment—dangerously so.'

He looked down at his hands. 'There is one further thing you should know, Kyria Lacey. I do not wish to revive your sorrow, but your father and stepmother quarrelled not long before the attack which killed him.'

'You think it was about this?' Her voice trembled.

'Perhaps,' he said quietly. 'Troy was afraid it was so, and that was why he wished to get you away from Kings Winston so soon after the funeral. He wanted you away from her, before she could spread her poison any further, and cause you more grief. But, again, she has been more successful than she could have dreamed.'

Lacey shook her head. 'I—I don't know what to say.'

He smiled slightly. 'You don't have to say anything to me. It is Troy who needs to hear you, I think.'

Lacey swallowed convulsively, then got up from the lounger and walked across the terrace into the villa. The *saloni* felt cool and she shivered slightly as she stepped out into the tiled hall. The door of Troy's study was tightly shut. Another closed door between us, she thought, but perhaps it will be the last one. Her hand shook slightly as she knocked and waited for permission to enter.

There was no sound from inside the room, and, puzzled, she opened the door and looked in. Troy was at his desk, his head buried on his arms. For a moment she thought he was asleep, but as she hesitated in the doorway, he looked up. His face was like carved granite and there was a look in his eyes that brought her heart into her mouth. It was the wrong moment—she was horribly aware of that, although she didn't know why—but it had to be said, and she advanced towards the desk summoning a courage she was far from feeling.

'Troy, I've come to ask you to forgive me.'

He inclined his head courteously, but there was no softening of his expression as he looked at her. The palms of her hands felt damp and she wiped them unobtrusively on her jacket.

'I've—I've done you a terrible injustice. I know that now

173

and I'm truly sorry.' She paused nervously, but he said nothing. 'Troy, please help me. You're not making this very easy for me.'

'How unchivalrous of me.' His voice was quiet, but there was a note in it that made her shrink. 'What are you trying to tell me? That you've taken a more than adequate revenge for my supposed infidelity and are now prepared to call it quits?'

'No.' She stared at him. 'I—know that there is nothing between you and Michelle—that there never has been. I drew all the wrong conclusions.' She took a trembling breath. 'Perhaps I—wanted to draw them because I thought I hated you.'

'Only thought?'

She bent her head, her fair hair falling over her face.

'I was completely confused,' she said in a low voice. 'It didn't seem possible that what I felt for you—could be love. You were almost a stranger to me—the "groom I'd never seen".' Her lips twisted slightly. 'You don't know what I'm talking about, do you, but what I'm trying to say is that it just seemed easier to hate you.'

'I can appreciate that. Hating is often easier.' He reached out and picked up a large manilla envelope from the desk. Lacey stared at him, taken aback. Did his eternal business deals, papers, contracts and negotiations mean more to him than the fact she was there trying so hard to tell him what was in her heart? He was speaking again. 'And exactly when did love begin to seem a more appropriate emotion in all this—confusion?'

'Almost as soon as I got here.' She took a step closer to the desk, hoping that he would stand up and come round to her. 'I wasn't just angry about Michelle—I was jealous too.' She paused, but he made no move. 'And—oh, Troy, I've been so lonely.'

'Have you, *pethi mou*?' His voice was loaded with irony. 'I wasn't aware you had lacked for company.'

Of course he could have meant Helen and Aunt Sofia, but Lacey knew he didn't.

He went on smoothly, 'And what has prompted you to tell me all this—at this moment in time?'

174

'It was Stephanos. He told me . . .'

'How very obliging of him,' he drawled. 'What a pity he didn't embark on his doubtless comprehensive explanations a little earlier. Then you would not have been obliged to degrade yourself like this, *yineka mou.*'

They were beautiful photographs. Even in the first rush of shocked disbelief as they spilled out of the envelope, she could appreciate that. Against the harsh grittiness of sand and rock, the girl's naked body had the texture of silk, the line flawless from the small, proud breasts to the delicate curve of her hip. Her body.

His voice came to her remorselessly. 'I am sorry I was not here to receive your photographer friend when he called, but no doubt you have seen to it that he has been—adequately rewarded already. And of course the sale of the photographs to magazines and newspapers abroad will ensure that he has no need to fear a poor old age.'

'But how . . .?' Numbly she stared down at the prints which lay scattered across the desk top. 'We were alone, I swear we were.'

'Naturally.' He almost spat the word. 'Such an intimate scene demands solitude. Spare me any more details, I beg of you.'

Her eyes, wide with dismay, met the blazing anger in his.

'You think that I posed for these?' Her voice hardly rose above a whisper. 'You think that I did this deliberately to pay you back for Michelle?'

'Such innocence,' he approved ironically, his eyes raking her with an expression that brought the colour flaming to her cheeks. 'But like your sudden attack of modesty, Lacey *mou*, rather overdone.'

Two strides brought him round the desk to her and she heard the light material of the jacket tear under his contemptuous fingers as he dragged it from her shoulders. His breathing roughened as he looked down at her, his hand gripping her bare arm.

'Pose for me,' he invited with dangerous softness. 'I don't want to have to wait to see you on the centre-fold of some magazine, my dove. I've already waited too long . . .'

His hand went to the fastening of her bikini bra and she shrank from him.

'Troy—no! Please, not here, like this. You don't understand . . .'

'Try me,' he said roughly. 'You don't know how understanding I can be.'

It was not a kiss. It was a punishment, his mouth a bruising insult, his hands a brutality on her skin. Forcing herself to endure it, she tried to tell herself that he wasn't to blame—that she had misjudged him on much slighter evidence. While inside her, a smaller and more insistent voice warned that if he took her now, by force and in anger, they would both be dealt a wound from which they might never recover.

When he let her go, she was so near to collapse that she swayed and had to catch at the corner of the desk to steady herself. It was as if from a great distance that she saw the cause of the interruption—Aunt Sofia standing in the doorway crying and twisting her hands together. A flood of excited Greek poured from her lips and Lacey heard Troy curse softly as he turned reluctantly to face his aunt. Automatically, Lacey bent to pick up her jacket, to slip it on again covering the dark marks his anger had left on her flesh. She couldn't catch the drift of Aunt Sofia's complaint, but she was sure she heard Helen's name mentioned and she stiffened in sudden apprehension, her eyes going back to the photographs.

'What's happened?' she asked.

'My aunt claims Eleni has run away. Some of her clothes are missing from her room. Food has gone from the kitchen.' Troy's voice was impatient, but the savage note she feared had gone. He turned back to fire a series of questions at the distraught Aunt Sofia and Lacey took advantage of his preoccupation to slip away out of the room. Her own troubles had to wait. What mattered now was the guilty, unhappy child she had come to Theros to befriend. Helen had to be found, and quickly.

176

CHAPTER TEN

The search seemed to be well under way when Lacey came down from her room. She had hastily dragged a pair of levis and a cheesecloth shirt over her bikini, while she tried to figure out what Helen's most likely course of action would have been.

It was unlikely that she could have left the island, she decided. A message would soon have been sent to the villa if she had made any attempt to board the morning ferry to Corfu, so it seemed likely she was hiding in the vicinity. But why? It was unlikely that any of the local fishermen woud allow themselves to be bribed to take her off the island even under cover of nightfall, so what was left? One of the boats from the boathouse? Lacey almost groaned as she forced the buttons of her shirt into their holes. Surely not even Helen would be that foolhardy.

Aunt Sofia was seated in the *saloni*, rocking herself backward and forward and weeping. Lacey spoke to her gently, telling her that she was going to the boathouse, but she did not think the older woman had fully taken in what she was saying.

The roar of an engine greeted her as she went outside and she realised that Stephanos was taking off in the helicopter. She shaded her eyes and watched to see what direction he was taking, but he headed away towards the village, away from the shore below the villa.

But the boathouse was deserted when Lacey got there. Troy's sailing dinghy *Hera* rocked peacefully at her mooring, and the dinghy with the outboard did not appear to have been tampered with either. Lacey stood defeatedly for a moment. There was also a power launch, she knew, usually moored in the harbour at Theros village, but she told herself she was being ridiculous. That was utterly beyond Helen's capabilities. So what was left? A minute later she was clambering carefully over the rocks that led to the adjoining cave.

She jumped down on to the sand and looked grimly up towards the cave. There was no point in calling to Helen, if indeed she was there. She would either not reply, or she would run away again, which would solve nothing. She lifted her hand and wiped a trickle of sweat from her forehead. It was oppressively hot, the air like a great suffocating blanket laid on her lungs. She moved her shoulders restlessly under the thin shirt, telling herself that her sudden feeling of uneasiness had nothing to do with the weather.

She would have to climb again to reach the cave entrance, so she kicked off her espadrilles and moving as quietly as she could, began to traverse the slabs of rock and scattered boulders which helped mask the cave.

The opening itself was narrow, wider at the bottom than at the top, and Lacey had to bend nearly double to insinuate herself through the dark gap. It was not very inviting and she wished she had brought a torch with her. But the air inside the cave smelt dry and fresh enough, and the floor seemed firm if rough and pebble-strewn. She took a cautious step forward and heard a faint sound ahead of her in the darkness. Bats? Her skin crawled involuntarily at the thought. The sound came again and was followed by a faint grunt as if someone had jabbed themselves painfully against a rock.

'Helen?' Lacey spoke levelly. 'I know you're there. I've come to take you home.'

'Go away!' It was a desperate little appeal, couched with none of Helen's usual assurance.

'And leave you to what?' Lacey's eyes were becoming more accustomed to the darkness now. With what light was entering the cave, she thought she could make out her sister-in-law's figure crouching a few yards ahead of her. 'You can't stay here all your life.' A thought struck her. 'And you can't get to the boathouse no matter how long you wait. Troy has it watched.'

A gasp told her that her guess about Helen's plans had been an accurate one. She relaxed slightly. She had wondered if, in spite of everything, Helen had planned to leave Theros with Evan Kent. There was a pause, then Helen burst out, 'Lacey, I've got to get away. Help me, please!'

178

'Like you helped me?' Lacey asked drily. 'Out on the beach there with your friend with the candid camera in close attendance?'

'I guess I asked for that,' Helen muttered. 'I—I don't suppose it makes any difference—but I'm sorry.'

'Where was he—just as a matter of interest? On the cliff? I suppose that flash of light I saw was the sun reflecting off the lens.'

Helen sighed. 'I guess so. Honest, Lacey, I didn't really believe he'd be able to see *anything* from that distance. I —I didn't want him to do it anyway by then, but he said it was silly to draw back at that stage and that I'd never be able to lean on Troy to let me go back to California unless we did go ahead. But I was just going to tell Troy we had the pictures. I never meant Evan to use them.'

'I don't suppose you did,' Lacey said with a faint sigh. 'But he had other ideas.'

'That rat fink,' Helen observed sombrely. 'I thought he was on the level till he sent me that note saying there'd been a change of plan. I ran all the way to the village to stop him, but he'd hired Demetrios's boat and left already. I was really scared. I knew the whole thing had got away from me somehow.' She sighed. 'And it all seemed such a cinch when we set it up. In the beginning we meant Evan to get pictures of you and Troy—together, but then when you arrived alone Evan said pictures of you by yourself would be even better.' Her voice quivered. 'Is—is Troy very angry, Lacey?'

'Yes,' Lacey said quietly, trying not to remember the hurt and bitterness she had seen in his face as well. 'But— but not with you, Helen. You see, he doesn't know you're involved—not yet.'

'Gee!' Helen digested this for a moment. Her voice brightened. 'Then I'm in the clear.'

'You could say that—though you may find it awkward explaining why you ran away.'

'No problem. I'll say I wanted to go night-fishing with Yanni.' Helen sounded almost buoyant again, then a note of doubt entered her voice. 'You said he didn't know—yet. Does that mean you're going to tell him?'

'No. I was hoping you might feel like telling him yourself.'

'Oh, sure,' Helen said with heavy sarcasm. 'And other dumb things like cutting my own throat too.'

Lacey moistened her lips with her tongue. 'Is that your final word on the subject?' she asked carefully.

'I guess so. You don't know Troy when he gets mad,' Helen said, and there was a long silence. 'Lacey—Lacey, are you still there.'

'Yes, I'm here.' Lacey's voice broke. There were muffled scraping and thudding noises as Helen got up and came towards her, and presently two small cold hands reached up and touched her face.

'Lacey,' Helen said shakily, 'you're *crying*. Don't cry. It wasn't your fault Evan took those pictures. Troy won't blame you.'

Lacey spoke with an effort. 'I'm afraid he does, Helen. You see, for reasons which I won't go into, your brother and I—haven't been getting on too well, and he thinks I've done this—to hurt him. *Helen!* Where did you learn a word like that?'

'Sorry.' But Helen didn't sound particularly repentant. 'Well, if that's the way it is, you win. Home we go, and I'll face the music.' She brightened slightly. 'Perhaps Troy will be so sick of me, he'll be glad to let me go back to Aunt Dora.'

'I wouldn't bank on it,' Lacey said gently. 'Anyway, I have another idea. How would you like to go to school in France?'

'You mean that convent place you went to?' Helen demanded. 'You've got to be kidding. Can you see me in a setup like that?'

Lacey's lips twitched in spite of herself. 'Not entirely,' she admitted honestly. 'But perhaps Troy would be less angry if you agreed to try it at least. If it doesn't work out, we can think of something else. But I think you'll have to forget California.'

Helen sighed. 'I guess you're right,' she said without enthusiasm. 'Now let's get going before I change my mind.'

She scrambled out of the cave and stood looking round

as Lacey followed. 'Gee, it's hotter than ever, and so still. There isn't even a breath of wind.'

'No,' Lacey agreed, repressing a slight shiver. A strange brooding feeling seemed to hang in the air. The cave seemed suddenly to represent security instead of alien darkness when compared with the sullen, brazen light that now surrounded them.

'I don't like the look of the weather,' she began. 'Do you suppose there's going to be a storm ...'

At first, she thought the faint rumble she heard was thunder. Then she felt the ground beneath her feet stir and stretch as if waking from a deep sleep and she knew what was happening even before Helen's scream of warning. A shower of pebbles descended and looking up, Lacey, panic-stricken, saw that part of the massive overhang of rock above the cave had detached itself from the cliff and was beginning to slide towards them in an almost leisurely fashion.

'Back!' Frantically she seized Helen's shoulders and pushed her towards the cave opening. She heard Helen cry out in pain and felt the rock tear at her clothes and skin as they forced themselves back into the darkness and fell together panting on the stony floor. Almost in the same second the slab of rock came down behind them with a grinding roar that shook the cave like another earth tremor, cutting off the light and sealing them into the darkness.

Silence slowly returned, and she could hear her own tortured breathing as she fought for calmness. Helen said shakily, 'Are we still alive?'

'I think so.' Lacey eased herself off the floor, wincing. The fall seemed to have jarred every bone in her body. She remembered that Helen had cried out. 'Are you hurt anywhere?'

'My wrist,' Helen said in a small voice. 'I hit it on a rock. I—I think it's busted.'

Lacey smothered a groan. 'Oh, Helen, are you sure?'

'Pretty sure. I'm frightened to move it. It hurts like hell.'

Lacey looked round helplessly. She had thought the cave was dark before, but it was nothing to this stultifying blackness which had suddenly descended. She had no idea how to deal with an injury of this kind, or even to check if Helen was right.

'Well, keep it as still as you can,' she said, trying to sound reassuring. 'Someone will come soon and get us out of here.'

'Oh yeah?' Helen's tone was despondent. 'Who knows we're here? If Troy's that mad, he might just think we've both run away, and not bother to look for us.'

Lacey sat down rather limply and leaned her back against the side of the cave. This aspect had simply not occurred to her, but she was soon able to dismiss it. The far more disturbing probability was that by the time any rescue party found the cave it might be too late.

Already it seemed that the air in the cave was staler than it had been, or was it just this awful claustrophobic feeling of being shut in that made her think so?

She cleared her throat. 'Where's that food you took, Helen?'

Helen gave a little gasp. 'It's with my clothes. I left them on a ledge under the landing stage at the boathouse. Why? Do you think we're going to need it? Lacey, I didn't mean that just now. Someone will come for us, won't they?'

There was a hysterical note in her voice and Lacey guessed that pain and shock were taking their toll of her mentally as well as physically. She reached out in the darkness until she encountered Helen's ankle and let her fingers close comfortingly round it. 'Of course they will. They'll soon know we aren't at the village and then they'll start searching along the shore. We'll have to listen really hard and if we hear anything, shout our heads off.'

'O.K.,' Helen said dubiously. 'Lacey, am I imagining things, or is it getting awful stuffy in here?'

'It is a bit,' Lacey had to admit. 'But I think there is still some fresh air getting in.'

'Aunt Dora was stuck in a elevator once,' Helen said. 'Between the eleventh and twelfth floors. They were three hours getting them out. Aunt Dora said a woman in the elevator had a fit—foamed at the mouth and everything. Do you ever have fits, Lacey?'

'No,' Lacey said wearily. 'But if I did, this would probably be the day.'

'Me too.' Helen sighed. 'I think this is probably the worst day of my whole life. Before, it was the day Aunt Dora told me Troy had been appointed my legal guardian. He came to see me and told me where I was going to live and everything, and I really hated him. Then a while later he told me he was getting married and that you weren't a lot older than I was, and I hated you too. I figured anyone Troy was stuck on would have to be a pain.'

Lacey felt a pang. 'What made you think Troy was "stuck on" me?' she asked, trying to sound casual.

'Well, he was going to marry you, wasn't he?' Helen said reasonably. 'Besides, he used to talk about you all the time, and play records of piano music. He made me sick.' She sighed. 'Lacey, are you thirsty?'

'A bit,' Lacey admitted.

'Well, I am—very. And I'm hungry too. There was a bottle of fruit juice I took along with that food,' Helen said wistfully.

Lacey groaned. 'Try not to think about it.'

'What else is there to think about?'

Lacey bit her lip. 'Perhaps if you put your head on my lap, you could try to sleep for a while.'

'But if someone comes while we're asleep they'll think there's no one here and go again.' Helen sounded perilously near to hysteria again as she made her way slowly and painfully to Lacey's side, and Lacey gave her a comforting hug.

'I won't sleep. I'll sit here and listen for both of us.'

'O.K.' Helen settled herself. Her voice sounded muffled. 'Then I'll stay awake for you.'

Long after the younger girl's breathing had steadied to the quiet rhythm of slumber, Lacey sat stiff and cramped against the rock wall. Helen murmured restlessly and stirred at times, and Lacey guessed that this was caused by the pain from her wrist. She had lost count of time. In the darkness, seconds could seem like hours and her wristwatch with its luminous dial was in her bedroom at the villa.

She was finding it increasingly difficult to breathe. In

183

spite of her confident words to Helen, it did seem as if they were using up the available oxygen faster than it was able to penetrate the blocked entrance. Her mouth was agonisingly dry too, and she had to close her mind to thoughts of tall jugs of cool liquid, clinking with ice cubes.

She leaned her head back against the unyielding rock and closed her eyes. It couldn't do any harm—just for a while. She was feeling so drowsy, and the most disturbing pictures kept forcing themselves through the darkness, like a kaleidoscope of flickering images inside her weary eyelids.

She dreamed that she was dead and lying in the darkness while lumps of earth thudded down on the coffin. She tried to scream to them to stop, that she was still alive, but her throat was too parched and no words came out.

There was a baby in her arms, a boy with Troy's dark eyes who cried and cried and would not stop no matter how much she rocked him in her arms and tried to soothe him, and then it seemed that she herself was the baby, and it was her turn to be carried in someone's arms, high against their heart. It was safe in these arms. Some time—long ago—she had longed to be safe. Longed for high walls around her. Now all she wanted was to break down these walls that surrounded her, smothering her. She tried to cry out, to lash out and destroy them with her fists, but she did not have the strength and her limbs would not obey her, and somewhere the great golden ball of the sun was swinging in a wide, giddying arc that hurt her eyes and sent the helpless tears pouring down her face and over her dry, grateful lips.

It was not the sun that was shining in her eyes, she realised as she opened them wincingly. It was the pendant lamp in her bedroom at the villa. Wonderingly, she stared around, realising that she was lying on her own bed covered by a sheet. Her head throbbed and, glancing down, she could see there was an efficient-looking gauze dressing on her arm. Her eye caught a movement just outside the line of vision, and she moved her head rather gingerly on the pillow, bringing it into focus.

184

Troy was sitting in a chair at the side of the bed, his eyes fixed on her reflectively.

'Hello,' he said unsmilingly.

'Hello,' she returned, and somehow the beating of her heart was more painful than all her cuts and bruises put together. Memory began to return. The tremor, the flight into the cave, and then the stifling darkness. She tried to sit up. 'Where's Helen?'

'The doctor is fixing her broken wrist. She's just lucky it wasn't her neck,' he added savagely.

'Oh.' Lacey subsided back against the pillows. 'She—she told you, then?'

'Yes, she told me. If she'd told me days ago, none of this need have happened.'

She made a pathetic attempt at a smile. 'The earthquake would still have happened.'

'I didn't mean that,' he returned abruptly, and silence descended between them.

'How did you find us?' she said at last.

'You'd left your sandals on the beach. Then I remembered the cave. I used to play there when I was a boy. We saw there'd been a rock fall and we couldn't shift it ourselves. We sent to the village and men came with ropes and dragged it away enough for us to get in. It took—a long time.' He shut his eyes for a moment as if he was trying to block out a disturbing memory. 'We didn't know what had happened—if you were there, even. But it seemed the only answer. I just didn't know whether we were going to be in time—whether you'd been able to breathe.' He paused. 'Helen was asleep—a bit delirious but asleep, but you were unconscious.'

He looked at her, and there was agony in his eyes. '*Pethi mou*, I thought you were dead.'

'I thought so too for a while,' she told him candidly. 'Then I dreamed I was a child again, and someone was carrying me.'

'I was carrying you,' he said quietly, and there was another long silence. Then he said abruptly, 'Are you seriously suggesting that Helen should go away to this school of yours?'

'Yes,' she looked at him, tenderly noting the weariness in his face, the lines of strain around his eyes and mouth. 'The nuns are good women. They'll know how to handle her.'

'They'll need to be saints to do that,' he said, and smiled faintly for the first time. 'Do they have special classes for adolescent blackmailers. You know the details of the scheme she had hatched up with Kent?'

'Yes—but I do believe she tried to protect me from him at the end. He told me she'd grown to like me.' Her eyes sought his. 'Troy, what will happen about those pictures?'

'Ah,' he said meditatively. 'I'm afraid our photographer friend had a little ill fortune. He had chartered one of the fishing boats to take him to Corfu and he had an accident while he was transferring his equipment from the harbour wall to the deck.'

Lacey's lips quivered involuntarily. 'Did—did he lose anything of value?'

'I'm afraid he must have done. According to Stephanos, who saw the whole thing, it took two of the men to hold him from jumping in as well.'

Lacey sighed. 'So they're all at the bottom of the harbour?'

'Judging by his reaction, they are—all except for the set he gave me, and they are locked in my safe.'

She flushed a little. 'I thought you would have torn them up—burned them, even.'

'Why destroy a work of art? Besides, they will serve as a reminder.'

'Of what?' She looked at him shyly.

'Of the fact that I am as apt to jump to the wrong conclusions as other mortals,' he returned. 'Did you think I kept them to remind me how beautiful you are, Lacey *mou*? I need no photographs for that. I carry your image in my heart.'

There was another silence while she sought unavailingly for an adequate rejoinder, but there did not seem to be one and she said instead, 'What will happen to Evan now?'

'I haven't the least idea. Once the other prints and negatives were at the bottom of the harbour, he ceased to hold much interest for me. I imagine he has done what he in-tended and sailed for Corfu.' He paused and a note of irony entered his voice. 'Perhaps he and your stepmother will drown their sorrows together. They should have a great deal in common.'

Lacey stole a glance at her husband, but his expression was unreadable.

He said quietly, 'When Eleni goes away to school, Lacey, shall you go with her?'

'Is that what you want?' she asked. Her throat felt sud-denly constricted.

'What I want is no longer important. It is only your hap-piness that matters, and you have not been very happy up to now, I think. There have been—so many misunder-standings, so much bitterness. Our marriage has not had a good start.'

'But it's survived an earthquake,' she said, almost dreamily.

'Perhaps that's an omen,' he answered drily. 'So what are your plans?'

She hesitated for a moment. 'As I tried to say to you earlier, I think the trouble was that we were strangers when we got married.'

'You were never a stranger to me, my sweet one,' he said. 'I wanted you from the moment you stood in my room glaring at me over the top of those absurd flowers. I've wanted a lot of beautiful girls in my time, but I never wanted to take one of them in my arms and protect her for the rest of my life as I did you. That was when I knew I loved you—and I also knew I had to get you out of that house and away from that corrupt woman for ever. She was sick, Lacey *mou*, and your father was a dying man, as he and I both knew. You needed my protection.'

'Why didn't you tell me you loved me, Troy?' Lacey reached her hand to him and he caught it in his own and raised it to his lips, caressing her palm.

'Because I didn't think you would have believed me then,' he said wryly. 'But I was arrogant enough to think that I could make you fall in love with me, once I became your husband and your lover.'

'I think I did,' she said slowly. 'But I was fighting my feelings for you all the time. I thought it was—wrong somehow to want someone I hardly knew as desperately as I did you. That we ought to have time to get to know each other.'

'And now?' His dark eyes were fixed on her face with an expression in them that sent a sweet sensuous languor sweeping through her body.

'Now we have the rest of our lives,' she told him shyly.

'Hmm.' He got out of his chair and stood looking down at her, his hands on his hips. 'Do you feel well enough to travel?'

'Travel where?' She stared up at him.

'To Corfu in the helicopter tonight, away from any further tremors, and later on to Nassau to pick up the *Artemis*. I think we deserve our real honeymoon.'

'Yes.' Lacey lay back against the pillows and watched him under the veil of her lashes. 'But couldn't we start tomorrow instead?'

'Why?' he raised his brows interrogatively.

'Because I want to spend the night here with you, and I don't want to have to waste any of it in travelling,' she told him simply.

'The beginning of the rest of our lives?' The smile in his eyes reflected her own. He began to unbutton his shirt. 'So be it, my darling.'

Lacey crossed her arms behind her head and watched him.

'*Andras mou*,' she murmured as he slid into bed beside her.

'I approve of the sentiment.' He drew her into his arms, his hands gentle. 'But your pronunciation needs correction.'

'But not now.'

'Certainly not now,' he whispered as his mouth came down on hers.

Mills & Boon Romances Go Historical

Available Now:
Four Superb Novels in the
Mills & Boon Masquerade Series

Now we'll not only continue to explore the modern world of
Romance, but we'll also be travelling back through the pages
of history to bring the Romances of bygone ages.

A ROSE FOR DANGER *by Marguerite Bell*
A smoothly-spoken highwayman is terrorizing the lonely
roads around Canterbury when Juliet Ware and her aunt
visit friends there for the summer. Torn between her host, the
darkly fascinating Sir Nicholas Childe, and the mysterious,
but equally attractive Stephen Thorne, Juliet finds herself
deeply involved with the intrigue and in danger of becoming
one of the highwayman's victims.

THE RUNAWAYS *by Julia Herbert*
In England of 1760, Georgina is abducted by the evil Duke of
Quinton. As his magnificent coach sweeps across the West
Country to his Wiltshire estates, his pretty prisoner is
glimpsed by young Richard Barr. He daringly succeeds in
rescuing her from the Duke's clutches, but Georgina's
abductor soon picks up the trail of the runaways and a hair-
raising chase ensues.

THE SECRET OF VAL VERDE *by Judith Polley*
Antoinette Dubec arrives from France to the war-torn
Mexico of 1866 in time to learn of her soldier father's death.
The Mexican, Major Chavez, who breaks the news, behaves
strangely towards her, but Antoinette is determined to
discover how her father died and avenge him. Her
investigations lead her into danger, passion and high
adventure.

ELEANOR AND THE MARQUIS *by Jane Wilby*
Two cousins, Eleanor and Beatrix, leave their Yorkshire
homes to enter fashionable society in London at the time of
the Regency. Eleanor is the daughter of a country parson
with no prospects, while Beatrix comes from a wealthy
family background. Their chaperone in London is an ageing
Dowager Duchess who enlists her aristocratic nephew's help
in making the poor country girl the toast of the town.

Only 50p each

Available 6th May 1977

June Paperbacks

A GIFT FOR A LION *by Sara Craven*
Arriving uninvited on the mysterious Mediterranean island of
Saracina had seemed like a game to Joanna – but its overlord,
Leo Vargas, didn't see it like that!

SIX WHITE HORSES *by Janet Dailey*
Why should Morgan Kincaid care that Patty was still
hopelessly in love with Lije Masters after all these years?

AVENGING ANGEL *by Helen Bianchin*
Could Terese marry Manuel Delgado – a man she hardly
knew – even to save her beloved stepfather from disaster?

BRIDE OF BONAMOUR *by Gwen Westwood*
Falling in love with Jerome de Villiers was a big enough
problem for Sara. But then another problem confronted her,
even more serious . . .

VOYAGE OF ENCHANTMENT by *Elizabeth Ashton*
Audrey's godfather might have treated her to a
Mediterranean cruise, but she soon found there were strings
attached – involving Damon Grivas!

THE HASTY MARRIAGE *by Betty Neels*
Laura was resigned when the man she loved decided to marry
her pretty sister Joyce. Then, without warning, Joyce walked
out on him . . .

MASTER OF BEN ROSS *by Lucy Gillen*
Melodie was fascinated by the man she met on her Highland
holiday – Neil McDowell, the enigmatic local laird. But Neil
loved another woman . . .

THE THISTLE AND THE ROSE *by Margaret Rome*
When Helen set out to gain revenge on the Marquis of
Sanquhar for his cruelty, she had no idea how it would all
end.

DARK VENTURER *by Mary Wibberley*
To Mia, Cory Galen was a means of escape from the life she
hated; when she found out that he had his own plans for her,
it was rather too late!

STOLEN HEART *by Mary Burchell*
It was madness for Joanna to be burgling Simon Gray's flat,
but she had promised to help her sister. And then –

35p net each
Available June 1977

Your Mills & Boon Selection

- [ ] 005
  SECRET HEIRESS
  Eleanor Farnes
- [ ] 130
  THE AFFAIR IN TANGIER
  Kathryn Blair
- [ ] 179
  THE PATH OF THE
  MOONFISH
  Betty Beaty
- [ ] 228
  JOURNEY TO AN ISLAND
  Hilary Wilde
- [ ] 287
  THE PRIDE YOU TRAMPLED
  Juliet Armstrong
- [ ] 302
  BELOVED SPARROW
  Henrietta Reid
- [ ] 310
  ROSALIND COMES HOME
  Essie Summers
- [ ] 338
  A MIST IN GLEN TORRAN
  Amanda Doyle
- [ ] 919
  THE IRON MAN
  Kay Thorpe
- [ ] 931
  HEART OF THE
  WHIRLWIND
  Dorothy Cork
- [ ] 938
  PALACE OF THE HAWK
  Margaret Rome
- [ ] 948
  THE FLIGHT OF THE HAWK
  Rebecca Stratton
- [ ] 955
  LORD OF THE SIERRAS
  Anne Weale

- [ ] 960
  HIGH-COUNTRY WIFE
  Gloria Bevan
- [ ] 965
  THE SWALLOWS OF SAN
  FEDORA
  Betty Beaty
- [ ] 970
  GATE OF THE GOLDEN
  GAZELLE
  Dorothy Cork
- [ ] 975
  HEART OF THE LION
  Roberta Leigh
- [ ] 980
  DESERT DOORWAY
  Pamela Kent
- [ ] 985
  STRANGER IN THE GLEN
  Flora Kidd
- [ ] 991
  COVE OF PROMISES
  Margaret Rome
- [ ] 996
  A SMALL SLICE OF SUMMER
  Betty Neels
- [ ] 1001
  REEDS OF HONEY
  Margaret Way
- [ ] 1010
  AFFAIR IN VENICE
  Rachel Lindsay
- [ ] 1011
  HENRIETTA'S OWN CASTLE
  Betty Neels
- [ ] 1048
  ANNA OF STRATHALLAN
  Essie Summers
- [ ] 1054
  SO DEAR TO MY HEART
  Susan Barrie

All priced at 25p. Please tick your selection and use the handy
order form overleaf.

Classic Token